T0013289

ALSO BY NICOLA MASTERS

Happy Happy Happy

READY FOR IT

nicola masters

LAKE UNION
PUBLISHING

Text copyright © 2023 by Nicola Masters
All rights reserved.

Published by Lake Union Publishing, Seattle

www.apub.com

Amazon, the Amazon logo, and Lake Union Publishing are trademarks of Amazon.com, Inc., or its affiliates.

ISBN-13: 9781662503948
eISBN: 9781542039185

Cover design by Emma Rogers

Cover image: ©Anna Kutukova / Shutterstock

Printed in the United States of America

*For the friends I've known for years
and the ones I met along the way*

CHAPTER ONE

Natalie

I wish I could be more like Fiona. That's the main thing that goes through my head as I read the text that just popped up on my phone. For one thing, Fiona's never even had to *look* at a dating app. Except for when we've had a wine and I let her loose on my Tinder profile. What must that be like? I should have stayed with my childhood boyfriend like she did, even though I'm pretty sure he's in prison now. That would actually work for me. Nobody thinking there's something wrong with you *and* getting to enjoy your own company in the evenings? Sign me up.

So, it's not like Nigel's message has *upset* me, per se. And, honestly, who is even called *Nigel* anymore? I was doing a gracious thing by looking past that and agreeing to drinks. And then the cinema. And then dinner. But if he doesn't want to go out with *me* anymore, that's fine. It's not like we were the romance of the century or anything. We never even kissed. We only started seeing each other because of a lack of alternatives. Because why not? Because it's nice to have a fallback for Meerkat Mondays when Fiona's busy being an Adult with a capital A – furniture shopping or whatever with Matt.

And, let's be real, Nigel's name is *Nigel*, and that's more than enough reason for someone to end up slogging their way through Tinder too. Hence us ending up in each other's orbits for a minute.

NIGEL: Hope you can understand x

I look at his last message again. The *cheek*. Of *course* I can understand! I think the tone is what annoys me. Because, what? He's *sorry*? For *me*? He should be just as sorry for himself since we are *both* at the bottom of the pile. But I bet that hasn't occurred to him. Honestly, god grant me the self-confidence of any man on any dating app ever.

I pause on the high street and take a shaky breath. It sticks in my chest. I wince. A couple of cars race past. They literally race, oversized exhaust pipes screaming as they go. Absolute twats. The teenagers driving those cars are much more deserving of my annoyance, so I direct it their way, cursing them in my head for a while. And these boys will grow up to be the Nigels of the world, and what hope is there for any of us?

The kids racing around in those cars would probably look at me and see an old woman. *I* would have looked at me and seen that when I was their age. When Fiona and I were young we promised ourselves we'd never be like every other adult in the world. We were going to be cool. We weren't going to get ourselves stuck in the same traps everybody else seemed to. Jobs, marriages, a tedious obsession with interest rates. None of it meant anything to us. We'd lie under the climbing frame in her garden, long after we got too big to actually *climb* the climbing frame in her garden, and we'd plan all of our adventures.

'I'm going to live in America,' Fiona might say, eyes shining. 'In New York. I'll have a huge apartment like they do on *Friends*. And I'll travel all the time. And you go somewhere different, and then we can visit each other.'

'I want to go someplace sunny,' I'd tell her.

'Go to LA! It's always sunny. And when I come and stay we'll go to the beach and just hang out.' We never let the fact that we were two of the palest people in the world, who would both burn if we so much as thought about the sun, get in the way of a good daydream.

And, after we went to uni, it really seemed like we might get to travel the world. At least for a while. I mean, Fiona still did. Because things work out differently than you plan sometimes. And I was behind her every step of the way, because what's the point in being anything else? The decision's already been made.

A screech of tyres from one of the boy racers brings me back to the present. Honestly. One day they're going to kill someone. I can feel my anger creeping back. It's mostly still directed at them, because they are dicks. But it's Nigel as well. Or it's me. I don't know.

I shove my hands into my coat pockets and turn up one of my favourite side streets. Everyone who lives along here has amazing taste in interior design and seemingly no concern about ever closing the curtains. There's always something to look at. Is it creepy? Definitely. Will I stop? Never.

Now that I've put some distance between myself and the dangerous driving, I can hear more of my thoughts. Not necessarily a good thing. At the moment, anyway. There's that 'I wish I could be more like Fiona' thing again. Which would be all very well if I had a time machine. But, since I don't, it's really not very productive.

I just . . . I love her like my own sister. I imagine I love her like my own sister, anyway. I don't actually have a sister to compare her to. But there's no denying she's, well . . . she's had some better luck than me. That's all it is, and there's no point having hard feelings about it, but still. I can't help wondering how my life would look now if we'd both travelled together like we intended, if Matt's dad hadn't died when he did, left Matt all that money, and Fiona hadn't gone off with him instead.

'I'm sorry,' she said at the time. And, to be fair, she really did seem it. 'I just . . . You know I've always wanted this, and we'll never have a chance like it again. Matt and I, I mean.'

And I nodded along, because what else are you going to do? Tell your best friend she *can't* ditch you to travel with her boyfriend? And now I can't even convince just about the only not-obviously-murdery man within a fifteen-kilometre radius to go on one more date with me. Whose name is *Nigel*. At *our* age. Come on.

I kick a stone that's escaped from somebody's gravel driveway. It clips a garden wall and skitters into the road. He's not even worth this. I know he's not. I might feel equally negative if I *did* have to go out with him again. He's not exactly a sparkling conversationalist. That's why I'm pacing out my annoyance before I go back. He does not get to be a part of the memories of my and Fiona's last night. No way. I don't want to look back when I'm writing my maid of honour speech or something and remember how mad I was at a near stranger called Nigel who just happened to pick a bad time to text me.

In the next window I pass, a man and a woman who must be in their forties are sitting down watching TV. They have shelves stacked with books, and I wonder if they ever actually read any of them. There's an elaborate cat climbing frame as well. I feel like my rightful next move would be to get a cat. Except I can't even do that because, hello, renting.

I shake my head, then glance at the next window. The key is never to *look* like you're looking. I mean, obviously that's the key or else you'd terrify the neighbourhood. In this house, a man and a woman sit with their backs to the window, also watching TV. A child plays on the floor.

Fiona's probably going to have kids one day. That's what you do. It's definitely what you do when you've been with a man since you were seventeen years old. If you supported him through the death of his father, and then travelled the world together on his inheritance.

Who honestly expects to end up marrying their first ever boyfriend? It's mad. Again, though, mine is serving time for possession with intent to supply, so . . . I might not be a qualified judge. But moving in together is a big step. And I'm happy for her. Of course I'm happy for her. I'd be a monster not to be happy for her.

I just sometimes wonder if I might look a bit tragic in comparison. Like, 'Poor Natalie, we had such high hopes. But not only is she still in her first job out of uni, but she might also die alone. Isn't that sad? Isn't she *sad*?'

I'm not ready for this. I don't want everything to change. Not again.

I turn left down an alleyway that brings me out into a field. I stick to the edge, scaring a couple of birds as I go. They flap into the sky, squawking. I hold my hand out and brush my fingertips against the purple flowers growing here. I'm definitely getting my shoes muddy, but at least I can do whatever I like with them from tomorrow onwards. Rub them all over the sofa if I so choose . . . Why not? Just kidding, I would never. Fiona's trained me too well. But still. I could.

I stop to get my breath back. I am not a natural athlete and I've been walking for upwards of fifteen minutes. When I turn around, I can see the whole of Crostdam laid out in front of me like a boardgame I am not winning. The high street winds through the middle and rows of neat little houses give way to sand dunes on the opposite side. The beach is beyond that, but I hardly ever go. The sun's going down and the sky is a wash of pink.

Fucking Nigel, though. I huff. My phone vibrates in my pocket.

FIONA: How long does it take to buy wine??? x

FIONA

Sometimes I wish I was more like Natalie. I slip my phone back into my pocket. At least she doesn't have to wear a bright pink and white striped blouse and clean up at least one puddle of ice-cream sick a day. If you think there's a risk that your child will throw up after being given a giant ice cream, probably don't buy it for them. It seems like a no-brainer to me. I can spot a puker before they even get over the threshold. It's a fine art. And a fat lot of good it ever does me.

The very thought of the pink puddle I cleaned up today makes me shudder and I feel an overwhelming urge to wash my hands for the hundredth time. I stub my toe on a box as I walk to the kitchen. Of course I do, they're literally everywhere and I'm still not finished. Don't get me wrong, I am *supposed* to be finished. But I am who I am.

I run the tap for ages until the water heats up. I will not miss trying to coax any semblance of warmth out of our ancient boiler. I'm sure it's playing havoc with our bills. Still, not my concern anymore, I guess. When the water finally runs hot, I wash my hands. I wonder if I should put the soap in one of my boxes. I think I was the one who paid for it so it's *technically* mine? I can't decide. I don't want Natalie to think I'm an arsehole for taking something she needs, but I also don't want her to think I'm an arsehole because I've left her with my rubbish. But soap isn't rubbish, is it? I'm still running my hands under the tap. Maybe it's actually just me who's playing havoc with the water bills.

I lean against the sink as I dry my hands. Is this my tea towel? Maybe a joint purchase? Honestly, *the politics*. But I've been trying so hard not to be the dick in this situation. And it's difficult anyway when you're the one leaving someone else in the lurch. But when you've notoriously left her in the lurch in a big way before? Nightmare. Treading on eggshells all the time.

I survey the boxes in front of me. Most of them are still open. A couple of them have things sticking out of them that Natalie has already pointed out won't fit, but I'm not willing to accept the obvious truth yet. If they don't go in the existing boxes I'll have to build *more* boxes and, honestly, I'd rather die. I just want to skip to the good bit: Matt and I living together, without having to do any of the heavy lifting that entails.

I switch the kettle on since I'm standing right next to it. I should get changed. I'm still in a blouse that's been uncomfortably close to today's pool of vomit. And, see, this is the thing. This is why I wish I could be more like Natalie. She *never* has to think like that.

I pour hot water on a tea bag. I go to the fridge for the milk, but when I reach to lift the bottle out of the door, an image of today's . . . um . . . puddle flashes in front of my eyes, and I suddenly find I'd prefer to drink it black. I wait for my stomach to stop flipping over.

It's not even like I want Natalie's job, necessarily. She certainly doesn't think it's anything special. But she has her own desk, her own space, which feels like a luxury to me. She has drawers she can lock. She keeps a pair of shoes in her bottom one for when she walks to work in trainers. She has a plant. She has a box of paracetamol, some cereal bars. She has her own mug that nobody else touches. I got it printed specially when she started. It has a photo of us on it. She gets to be her own person at work, with her

7

own stuff. I dress like a Flump and I don't even get to lean on the counter when my feet hurt. I'm just ready for something to change.

And I know it's kind of my own choice. And it's not like I *regret* travelling, because Matt and I saw some amazing stuff. It's just that, when you come home, no employers seem to care that you've seen the sun rise over Koh Samui, or thought you were going to die after getting bitten by what turned out to be a perfectly benign spider in Australia. That kind of thing just joins the drama degree (that you didn't really want but you got because your school basically forced you to go to university) on the pile of life experiences people go 'oh, cool!' about in conversation before they move on to the next person.

But when we came back for good, Matt had an offer that was too good to pass up (thank you, Matt's mother and your many unexpected connections in the accountancy world), so I had to take what I could get. And I know Scoopz isn't forever. Everybody in an entry-level job in the whole of Crostdam's just waiting for somebody to die or retire so the rest of us can shuffle around a bit. And, in the meantime, it seems Matt's mother's connections do not extend to anybody who could help someone with a drama degree and no major ambition beyond having a fun life and seeing as much of the world as possible.

Anyway. I pick up my cup and take it back to the living room. I bash my shin on one of the boxes and slop tea into it. Shit. I peer inside, but it's kitchen stuff, so it'll be fine. I'm not about to take anything *out* of boxes – I've got enough putting *in* to do tonight without doing extra because I'm clumsy.

NATALIE

My key clicks in the lock and I try to ignore the stab in my chest as I remember that this is the last time I'll open this door and find Fiona behind it.

My glance falls to the boxes as the door opens. It's hard not to, honestly. They are literally everywhere. Who knew she had so much stuff? It's just all melded together over the past eighteen months since she's been back, our two lives growing over and through each other like brambles.

'Alright?' Fiona looks up at me from where she's sitting with her feet up on a box. She's clasping a mug and looking considerably more relaxed than she has any right to. She's not even nearly ready for tomorrow. 'I wondered where you got to.'

'I . . . um . . . wanted to choose the perfect bottle. Did you know Kylie Minogue makes wine now?' I wipe my feet extra-thoroughly.

'Well, the kettle's not long boiled if you want one.'

'I'm OK, thanks. Don't you have stuff to be . . .'

Fiona groans and lets her head loll back onto the sofa cushions. Drama queen. I press my lips together so she can't see me smile.

'You're not going to tell me off again, are you? I've *just* got in.'

'I've *just* got in more recently than you,' I counter, losing the fight with my grin.

'Yeah, but I've just got in from something worse, I bet.'

She probably has, to be fair.

'I'm not telling you off, anyway,' I say, changing tack. 'I just want you to get everything done so that we can have a nice last night together.'

FIONA

Once we've got changed out of our work clothes, and I've wrapped mine in a plastic bag just to be on the safe side, we make a start on the last bits of packing.

'I'll take the kitchen, you do your bedroom,' Natalie tells me. I do as instructed. Or, well. I stand in the room and wonder if I could just burn the place down instead of putting anything else in boxes.

My phone pings, and I pick it up, eager for any distraction. Whatever it is, I'll take it. Scam? Bring it on. Marketing? Love it. Wrong number? Prepare yourself for an unexpected conversation with a stranger who desperately cannot be arsed to do any more packing.

As it is, it's a message from the 'I Really Really Really Wanna Zig Ah Zig Ah' WhatsApp group Natalie set up when we went to see the Spice Girls. There's at least four groups that I know of with a different combination of the same people in each. I kind of like that they're using this one. I'm not invited tomorrow. I know it's nothing personal, and I think I'm doing a very good job of hiding my envy. Would I rather go with them and get a pedicure instead of hauling boxes around all day? Of course. Is that an option for me? Very much not. Which is fine. Natalie arranged the whole thing so that she could be out of the house in a, and I quote, 'non-depressing way'. Apparently, staying out of the way at a spa is nicer than loitering around the shops until the pub opens or sitting on the beach in the drizzle. She did actually offer to help with the move at first, but I couldn't ask her to do that. So, basically, the day doesn't include me, but it's still nice to feel involved in my own little way.

ALICE: What's the plan for tomorrow, ladies?

I tap out a reply.

FIONA: Matt's coming to help at 10am so you could come and get Natalie at the same time?

'Stop texting and get packing!' Natalie shouts from the living room.

'I'm helping plan *your* day!' I laugh.

But she is right. I pick up a couple of candlesticks that have never actually seen candles and lay them carefully in the middle of a sweatshirt. I take my time smoothing it over them, wrapping the fabric in between them both so they don't break each other. Then I place the bundle in the box and sit back on my heels.

The photo collage I've diligently added to ever since I first moved in spreads across one wall. Lots of pictures of Natalie and me as toddlers in nursery, proudly showing off our first school uniforms, grudgingly modelling our secondary school ones. Then there are photos of us at sleepovers, at the beach, selfies once camera phones became a thing . . . There's a lot.

And then Matt starts creeping in as well. In the background of photos from school trips. In smaller groups at bowling parties and school discos. Right next to me at the prom. With Natalie on the other side of me, obviously. I always think it looks like he asked us both, like we're in some weird sister-wife situation.

There are pictures of me visiting him at uni, sitting around tables of boardgames with his accounting-course mates. Then there are the ones of him looking *extremely* uncomfortable at burlesque nights and immersive theatre experiences with my rather more . . . bohemian drama friends. Who, despite our promises to stay in touch at graduation, I now only hear from or contact via our annual 'happy birthday! xxx' Facebook posts.

Then there are photos taken from dates, from our first holiday together, and then when he started becoming my plus-one for things instead of Natalie. Which she was very gracious about. I'm not sure I would have been.

And then Natalie disappears altogether and there are the travel photos. Matt and I stand in front of sunsets, on beaches, and with people who appeared in our life out of nowhere and disappeared just as quickly, but for a moment we really believed we'd be friends forever.

'How's it going?' Natalie shouts from across the landing.

'Nearly done!'

'Are you actually nearly done' – the door opens – 'or . . . Oh. Wow. Genuinely nearly done.'

'I did say that.'

'Yes, but you also said you wouldn't leave this all until the last night.'

'I didn't. I left it 'til the last *evening*. Big difference.'

Natalie laughs. 'If you say so. Anyway, I've finished in the kitchen. I can help in here now.' She steps gingerly between a box and the bed and heads for the wall with the photos. She reaches up to peel the first one down.

'Don't!' I bark. She snatches her hand away and raises her eyebrows.

I shrug. 'I'm doing that last.'

NATALIE

'I was going to suggest we get a takeaway, anyway,' I say as I step away from Fiona's photo display. It's always been her pride and joy – I shouldn't have been so blasé about taking it down.

Her face lights up. 'What are you thinking?'

'Leaver's choice, surely. You decide.'

'Chinese? No, pizza.'

I nod, but she's not finished, which I definitely should have been ready for. I smile as she continues, 'No, Indian? Thai.'

'Right, well, I'll leave it with you. Keep me posted.'

I pick my way out of the room and lean against the landing wall for a second. It looks so empty in there. The magnolia walls, something I've barely noticed for years, are suddenly so aggressively . . . magnolia.

12

I return to the kitchen and look around at the now-sealed boxes. I wrote everything that was inside each one next to the tape at the top. I'm not sure Fiona will notice but it's a little gesture for Matt, at least.

Messages keep buzzing into the group chat. Once the time is sorted (I do also reply to confirm that ten a.m. suits me, but that's because I am a giant hypocrite), it all devolves into excited, definitely inappropriate chatter about male massage therapists. I put the phone down on the side and keep packing for a while.

When I pick it up, one of the other group chats has started up as well. 'Ice Cream Is Shit' this time:

AMY: Hey ladies! Hope the last night's going OK. Try not to be too sad!

And then ten minutes later:

AMY: That good eh?

I don't answer. I'm never quite sure how much Amy wants to hear from me. She's Fiona's friend, really. They work together. Amy and I only ever message a couple of times a year, and only ever in chats with other people. And, anyway, I'm a very busy lady.

I give the cupboards one last check, but there's nothing in there now that isn't mine. I'm going to have to get some new plates. Or add 'owns plates' as a requirement when I do get around to advertising for a flatmate.

My phone buzzes against the work surface again. I pick it up – I have never been so popular, I swear to god. But this time it's *Nigel?* Way-too-young-to-have-that-name, Sorry-I-just-don't-feel-a-connection Nigel. Honestly, the audacity of the man.

NIGEL: So you're just not going to reply to me? I see how it is. Rude.

I make a sound of protest. Out loud. Alone in the kitchen. Literally *what* does the man want me to say? Like I don't have bigger things going on right now than not going on a fourth date with a guy I'm not interested in with an old man's name? It's not like we have some deep and meaningful history that needs hashing out before we can move on. It's not like we need to divide our assets. I don't even know if he knows my surname. *I'm* rude? A new wave of anger at Nigel bubbles up inside me, followed by another one at myself for paying him any attention tonight of all nights. I laugh bitterly, shaking my head in the silent kitchen.

'What's wrong?' Fiona asks.

FIONA

Natalie jumps when I speak. She whips her head up, slams her phone down on the side. She does it so hard that it'll be a miracle if she hasn't cracked the screen. Again.

'What's the matter?' I repeat. She's acting like I've caught her doing something illegal. Her eyes seem to search the wall behind my head for something to say before she opens her mouth. This is weird. It's not her.

'It's nothing. I don't even know.' She shakes her head. 'It's nothing.'

She pulls her face into a smile I don't believe.

I raise an eyebrow. 'I'm not an idiot.'

'I don't want it to ruin our last night.'

'I will ruin it myself by giving you the third degree if you don't just tell me.'

She gives a heavy sigh and shuffles her feet, shifting her body into a more comfortable position against the worktop.

'Nigel.' She shrugs.

'Who's Nigel?' She brandishes her phone at me and I twig. 'Wait. *Tinder* Nigel?'

'Tinder Nigel.'

'I see.' I offer a silent prayer of thanks to the god I don't believe in that I'm still with the man I met at school. 'I'll order the pizzas, you open the wine.'

'I'm paying for the food,' Natalie reminds me.

I try to protest, but she narrows her eyes. She goes to her bag, takes out her purse and holds it out. I stare at it, but I don't take it straight away. She can't afford it. She's about to have to pay double rent and double bills for god knows how long. I know she hasn't even started looking for someone to replace me. She waves it, glaring at me, until I give in and take it off her.

Natalie uncorks a bottle of champagne (!?) while I'm on the phone with the pizza place. I widen my eyes and she does a tiny curtsy.

'Cheers.' She hands me a glass after forcing me to order twice as much food as we can actually eat.

'So, what did he do, then?' I ask, taking a sip from my glass. It's a tumbler, not a champagne flute. I think I own the champagne flutes. In fact, I spot the words 'champagne flutes' printed on the box closest to me in neat black sharpie. Aren't I fancy?

Natalie clambers over a couple of boxes and sits on the sofa. I follow her. Where she manages it smoothly, I trip over, because of course I do. She curls her feet under her and leans against the arm nearest the radiator.

15

'You've done a box of all the things you'll need first, right? Ow!' She rubs her ankle where I just kicked her.

'We're not doing admin, we're doing Nigel.'

'Oh, I'm absolutely certain that *nobody* is doing Nigel,' she mutters into her glass.

I laugh. 'What happened?' I press.

She lets out a frustrated noise. Kind of a growl. '*Nothing* happened. That's actually what's *so* annoying. He texted me.'

'The bastard.'

She pulls a face. 'Just wait. He texted me to say that he doesn't think it's going to work out. And, like, fine. I don't even think I like the guy. Whatever.'

'Well, that's still shit, I'm really sor—'

'Oh, no.' She cuts me off, holding up a finger.

I have to suppress a smile. I don't like that she's upset but I do kind of love it when she goes off on one. She makes me laugh. And I suspect she loves making me laugh as well.

'That wasn't even the annoying thing. I didn't answer that because, like I said, whatever. We had nothing in common, *and* I didn't want to spend the rest of my life explaining that, yes, my partner's name is Nigel, but, no, really, he actually is the same age as me, and, no, I don't know what his parents were thinking either, you know?'

I let a little giggle slip out as I nod and Natalie smiles too. Then she makes another frustrated noise.

'So, I haven't replied to this text – because I don't owe the man anything. I'm at work when he texts me, and I'm, I mean, normal. And then he texts *again* just now to be all "Oh, I see how it is", all arsey. Like, do you not *know* how all of this works by now, or . . . ?'

She leans back into the chair and gulps her champagne as if it's something much cheaper than champagne.

The buzzer goes and I jump up to meet the pizza man. I run down the stairs two at a time because muscle memory means that I'm an expert at this point. I dodge the pile of junk mail on one side of the bottom step without even needing to think about it and open the door.

'Starr?' the man asks, peering over pizza boxes.

'That's me.'

I smile as I easily assume Natalie's surname. We always do that. Food orders, reservations, hotel check-ins. I wonder, with a little squirm in my stomach, if I'll still do it when I live with Matt. When I'm claiming to be Fiona Hayden it'll *mean things*. Plenty of time for all that.

NATALIE

I've had a word with myself by the time Fiona gets back with the pizzas. No man is worth ruining our last night for.

While I was packing up the kitchen I found an old box of confetti left over from some wedding or other. Whoever's it was, I'm sure Fiona and I sat off to the side and joked-but-not-really about how scary it was to see people *we* know growing up so fast, how weird it was to see all the other guests in Ted Baker instead of their normal clothes. Mad to think Fiona might be next, really.

Anyway, when she materialises at the door again, I sprinkle confetti over her. She squawks as unexpected shapes flutter in front of her face, until she realises what they are and laughs.

'I nearly dropped the food!' she scolds, picking pink love hearts out of her hair. She lets them fall to the floor in front of her.

'You'd never drop the food. You're better than that.'

'That is extremely true.'

She takes the pizzas over to the living room, putting them on top of a couple of boxes. They smell *incredible*. All of my annoyance at Nigel and I think I was mostly just hungry. He's still a twat, though.

My phone beeps.

'If that's Tinder Nigel again tell him he'll have me to answer to if he doesn't leave you alone tonight of all nights.' Fiona gestures towards the boxes.

I look at my screen. 'Just Sophie. I can text her back tomorrow.'

'Mmhmm.' Fiona rolls her eyes.

'She's *nice*,' I scold.

Fiona sighs. 'I just don't approve of you having friends who aren't me.'

'You were on the other side of the world, what was I supposed to do?'

'You were *supposed* to sit at home in mourning attire and wait for me to come back, I honestly can't believe we're still having this discussion.' Fiona holds my gaze for a moment and then we both collapse into laughter. She flips the lids on the pizza boxes.

'Anyway,' I say, 'I might need Sophie now that you're ditching me. You'll be off at the gym with Matt in the evenings or drinking out of two straws in the same protein shake or something.'

'OK, I love the man, but I draw the line at that.' Fiona takes a slice of pizza out of the box, pulling it high into the air because the cheese is too stretchy. 'Promise me you'll never replace me as your pizza buddy. I'll have no reason to live.'

I produce another hidden bottle (prosecco this time, I'm not made of money) and pop the cork while Fiona finds whatever cutlery is left in the drawer. We will obviously leave the cutlery untouched, but it's nice to pretend.

We play episodes of *Friends* as we eat. We barely pay attention to the food or the TV, we're so busy talking about all the things

Fiona will miss, all of the exciting new things she'll get to do and, perhaps most importantly, how she can convince Matt that what their new place really needs is a pink velvet sofa.

'This has been the best,' Fiona sighs, wiping her mouth with a napkin and then dabbing a tear of mirth away.

'I know. I'm glad you told Matt he couldn't interrupt you.'

'No.' Fiona puts her napkin down and lays a hand on my arm. She points between us with the other one. '*This* has been the best.'

CHAPTER TWO

FIONA

The next morning, Natalie and I crawl out of our rooms about an hour before Matt's due to arrive and make a beeline for the few slices of cold pizza still sitting out in the living room. It's probably a bit dicey, but at least we won't be sharing a bathroom anymore by the time any horrible food poisoning sets in. My head aches. I'd quite like to go back to bed.

'Ready for the off?' Matt asks when he arrives. He's far too chirpy. He carries a cardboard tray of coffees in one hand. He knows Natalie's order as well as he knows mine. She takes the tray and puts it in the recycling.

When her back is turned, I squeeze Matt's hand. He brings it to his lips and brushes them against the back of it. When Natalie turns around again, he drops it like it's burned him.

NATALIE

I like Matt. Always have. To be fair, I've known him basically as long as I've known Fiona. I'm glad she's with him and not some total arsehole. But things like that have always annoyed me.

Because, I mean, there's no need to hide your PDAs like I'm Miss Havisham and I might lose my mind and burn the place to the ground if I so much as sense somebody else's happiness? I'm not self-conscious about being the third wheel until somebody makes me feel like maybe I should be. And, really? You're worried about me seeing you give my friend a quick kiss, but you'll openly help her steal the trip I dreamed about us going on? It makes no sense. But *no*. Stop it. I shake my head. I'm just being oversensitive. I know I am. Although knowing it doesn't make it easy to stop.

Matt leaves to put the seats down in his car while Fiona disappears to her bedroom. I wonder if she's taken the collage down yet. Maybe that's what she's doing now. The final sign that she was ever here.

'Hey.' She makes me jump as I carry the jar of tulips over to the windowsill. I nearly drop them. 'I wanted you to have this.'

She hands me what looks like a piece of paper. She casts a furtive eye towards the door. We left it on the latch and Matt might be back any minute. I don't know why that matters, but it seems to. I put the flowers down and take what she's holding out.

It's a photo. Me during my pixie cut phase (do not advise if you're not willing to spend a lot of time and money on your hair) and her with the fringe she cut with her mum's kitchen scissors when she'd just got back from travelling. We're holding up a bottle of cheap wine. You can tell it's cheap because the brand name on the label is literally just 'Fruity Red'. It was all we could afford that day, when she officially became my flatmate. I swallow a lump in my throat.

When I look at her, she's welling up. I really thought we weren't going to do this. We've handled the actual move like bosses so far.

I sniff, and she pulls me into a hug. It's probably weird to know what your friend smells like, but I *do* live with her. And as she hugs me I catch a whiff of her perfume mixed with her shampoo. The front door opens quietly and I see Matt appearing over her shoulder. But he turns around at the sight of us and closes it again, easing it shut silently. He really is a good egg.

FIONA

I wanted Natalie to have the photo as something to remember me by. Which is *dumb* because she doesn't need to remember me. We'll still live in the same town. We already have brunch plans for next weekend. But still. A whole week. That's basically the longest we've gone without seeing each other, aside from when I was off travelling. I feel further away than that now.

And she seemed to like it, and that's the main thing. When she breaks away from me she brushes her eyes with the heels of her hands and leans the photo against the jar of flowers on the windowsill.

'Hey.' Matt comes back in from sorting out the car at just the right time. 'Where do you want to start?'

NATALIE

The doorbell rings before Fiona has a chance to answer.

'That's my cue.' I grimace. It feels weird. I'm suddenly very aware that I'll go out for the day and, when I come back, Fiona will be gone. Which, like, yes. That was obvious. But denial is a powerful thing. And now it's here and I don't know if I'm ready.

I glance back at Fiona as I go to answer the door. There's a puppy-dog quality to the look she gives me back. But what am I supposed to do? I can't sit around all day and watch her and Matt slowly remove any evidence that she was ever here, can I? That would be extremely bleak.

'Spa day!' Sophie shrieks as soon as I open the door. I haven't even pulled it wide enough to see her face.

I laugh. 'Not that you're excited or anything.'

'Do you *understand* how long it's been since I saw a hot tub?' She pushes past me into the living room. Alice follows her in, giving me a quick one-armed hug as she enters. I glance over at Fiona and catch her staring pointedly at their unremoved shoes. Well, my house, my rules now.

'We had one at Jasmine's hen do, didn't we? That was only last month.'

'That was an inflatable hot tub, which doesn't even count. Basically a warm paddling pool. Or, like, a dinghy or something. Anyway, can we not split hairs? I've been waiting for this, is all I'm saying. Hi, Fi! Matt.'

Sophie strides over to Fiona and pulls her into a hug. Fiona pulls a face over her shoulder, like Sophie's squeezing the air out of her. Sophie releases her and nods at Matt.

'How's things?' Matt asks, leaning on the kitchen counter and taking a sip of coffee. Fiona slips an arm around his waist, resting her head on his shoulder, like she's trying to remind us what she has.

'Yeah, good.' Sophie grins. 'You?'

'Yeah, good, thanks.'

'Good. Fiona, you all ready to become a boring grown-up?'

'I'm not going to be *boring*,' Fiona protests. She's laughing, but her cheeks are going pink.

'I don't know, I think moving shit around all day is pretty boring when you could be getting a facial and being pampered.'

Fiona opens her mouth. Then closes it again. Then she seems to decide what to say back.

She nuzzles a bit further into Matt's neck. 'I'm OK with my plans, thanks.'

And then we all stand around in excruciating silence for a couple of seconds until Alice releases us from the awkwardness.

'We should be heading off, shouldn't we? Don't we have to check in soon?'

Sophie glances at her phone. 'Christ. Yes.' She turns her attention to Fiona and Matt. 'Listen, guys, I hope it all goes well today. Try not to kill each other when you can't find the salad servers or something.'

Fiona laughs. 'We'll manage. Thank you. And I want to have everybody round once we've unpacked a bit. I'll let you all know.'

'Definitely. Congratulations.' Alice walks over to Fiona and hugs her while Sophie moves to stand behind me, places her hands firmly on my shoulders, and steers me towards the door.

'Bye, guys! Have a good move!' Sophie calls as she pushes me out into the hallway.

I twist my head around at the last moment and catch Fiona's eye. I give her a rueful smile. She raises the hand that isn't resting on Matt's hip and gives me the tiniest wave in return. Sophie pulls the door shut.

FIONA

The door closes on the whirlwind of Sophie, Alice, and Natalie, leaving Matt and me in silence. Matt puffs his cheeks out.

'Right, shall we get on? Bedroom first, I think.'

I nod, letting him walk ahead of me. I glance back at the door while I wait for my stomach to stop feeling a tiny bit weird. Look. Would I have liked to go on the spa day too? Of course, I am only human. Was that *ever* an option? Obviously not, I have shit to do.

That was the whole point of them taking Natalie away on the spa day in the first place. I shake my head.

'Are you coming?' Matt calls down the hallway. 'Taking this bed apart is a two-person job.'

NATALIE

'You're not going to be sad when you get back, are you?' Sophie asks as women in matching tunics smooth oil onto our faces. I can feel my lips being squashed together and then stretched apart as my cheeks are massaged. This cannot be a good look.

'What? No.'

'Alright.' I didn't realise I sounded defensive until Sophie reacts to my tone. 'I'm only asking.'

'Yeah, no. I know. I'll be fine.'

'Well, you weren't fine last time, were you?'

'I was.' I sound defensive again, but I stand by it. It's important that the people doing our facials don't think I'm a *total* simp. 'And that was different. She was on the other side of the world. And she took Matt. And I thought I was going to go. And I didn't have you guys.'

'Well, you could have had us, you just thought you were too good for us.'

'I did not th— You know what? I'm not getting into this again. You're destroying my chi. Or my zen. Or whatever. We're supposed to be relaxing.'

When we've finished our treatment, we admire our shiny faces in the mirror, and then return to Alice, who's stretched her arms along the sides of the Jacuzzi and is allowing herself to float into the middle. A couple of women in brightly coloured swimming hats bob up and down in the next-door swimming pool, their hair never touching the water.

'Alice,' Sophie demands. Alice opens one eye and then allows her body to sink back onto the seat. 'Will you please confirm that Natalie used to think she was too good to hang out with us.'

Alice catches my eye and pulls a face. 'You're never going to live this down, pal.'

I pantomime an eye roll. 'Don't I know it.'

Sophie is like a dog with a bone. 'I'm just saying, if I hadn't called you over to come and sit with us in the pub that night, your life might be very different now.'

'She made you who you are,' Alice laughs, parroting the words we've heard a hundred times before.

'I *did* make her who she is, though,' Sophie insists.

'I mean, I was already . . .' I try, but I don't get far.

'God knows I love Fiona, I think she's great. Super-brave. Amazing Instagram. But what kind of friend just drops everything and leaves out of the blue?'

'It wasn't out of the blue, we were planning it for ages,' I remind Sophie. 'And she had an amazing chance. Couldn't pass it up, obviously.'

I allow my mind to drift back to the postcards I used to get weekly from seemingly every part of the world. Of course they stung sometimes. But if *my* boyfriend's dad had left him a ton of money and he'd wanted to travel with me, I'd probably have dropped Fiona too. Carpe diem, right? She carpe-d the hell out of that diem. And I still got a guided tour around Florence when I joined them for one weekend away.

Sophie looks like she's going to keep going but Alice cuts her off.

'Anyway. We're not here to rehash this, are we? Can you two keep an eye on my stuff while I get this massage?'

Sophie and I hang out in the Jacuzzi for as long as humanly possible because when you have a Groupon you make the most of it. I try not to think too hard about what Sophie was saying, try to ignore the revived sting of Fiona flaking on our plans to travel together in favour of going with Matt instead. Because it doesn't help anyone, does it? What was I going to say? 'No, you have to stay behind and wait for me, even though your boyfriend's come into this money and he's suddenly decided he wants to go *and* is ready.' It was happening anyway, the only person I would have hurt by being hurt was myself. And I really didn't think I was *too good* for these guys, I just didn't know them. Yes, we went to school together, but it's not like you hang out with every single person in your year. That would be madness. If they are good at PE and you are good at English, your social circles are not about to overlap.

'Hey, I meant to ask. How's Tinder Nigel?' Alice asks when she joins us again. Sophie leans over to top up her glass, and does mine too while she's at it.

'Oh, dead to me.' I wave a hand and sip my topped-up drink.

'Really? That's a shame.'

I scoff but don't say anything.

'Ooh, I know a guy I can set you up with, if you want!' Sophie chimes in.

I shake my head. 'That's fine. I think I'm going to give it a break for a bit. Get the taste of Nigel out of my mouth.'

Sophie's mouth drops open. 'You *didn't*.'

I frown for a second and then the penny drops. I kick water at her. 'Ew, no!'

'Mind my drink!' she squeals, lifting it into the air.

FIONA

FIONA: Hope you're having a good time :) x

I don't really expect Natalie to text me back. After all, if she's having any kind of spa day she'll be poolside, and she's far too sensible to have her phone anywhere near a body of water. Especially if there's alcohol on the go. And if she's *any* friend of mine there will be a bottle of prosecco open somewhere.

But I definitely hope she's having a good time. Because, fuck me sideways, moving is tedious. One of us should be.

NATALIE

The flat's empty when I get home. It's dark, and quiet, and I feel a little flutter of panic. It threatens to undo all of the zen I built up while I was out. Well, it technically wasn't so much zen as a light prosecco buzz. But either way. It is in jeopardy, and I don't want to lose it. I try to shake the tingling out of my fingers.

There's no point berating myself for not advertising Fiona's room earlier. She was still in it. I wasn't ready. And I can't change it now, anyway. Why beat myself up?

I take a picture of the now box-free living room. I will use it on the advert for the room when I put it together, which I think is something that is best not done mildly tipsy, so it will have to wait until tomorrow. So, for now, I just add it to a message to Fiona.

NATALIE: So weird! X

My thumb hovers over the 'send' button but, in the end, I can't do it. She's barely been gone six hours and . . . What? I can't go even that tiny amount of time without being in contact? No. I have my dignity. Or, well. I have it sometimes.

CHAPTER THREE

FIONA

'Did you get flowers?' I shout when Matt gets home. I'm busy getting the flat ready. And by 'busy getting the flat ready' I mean 'running around the place like a blue-arsed fly because there's so much to be done I can't actually commit to one thing'. I do not know what I was thinking, having people over so soon. I wanted Matt and I to officially be up and running as a co-habiting couple as soon as possible after the move. And because I am that much of an idiot, I arranged dinner with his friends, and mine, one calendar week after moving day. And *this* dinner is a practice run for the dinner we're hosting next weekend for our parents. If I could go back in time and slap myself, I would.

'I did.' Matt appears in the kitchen doorway with a rustle of plastic wrappers and carrier bags. 'I didn't know which ones to get, because, well . . .' He gestures towards me in my Nice Top and apron. I know he means 'because you've gone a bit mad'. And I accept it. 'So I got options. Tulips, and something called als – alsto' – he picks them up to read the label – 'Alstroemeria.'

'Alright, Monty Don.' I smile and kiss him on the cheek. 'Thank you.'

He pulls me into him and kisses me properly. For a second, I forget about the lasagne on the side that still needs the cheese sprinkled on top, or the flowers, or the red wine I have to open so it can breathe, even though I'm not clear why it needs to. If it's our first Grown-Up Dinner we're hosting as Adults Who Live Together, and the internet says that the red wine needs to breathe, then the red wine will breathe. *I* have not breathed all afternoon. But this bottle of wine will, goddammit.

'OK.' I put both hands on his chest and push him away from me. 'I need to get on.'

'There's nothing left to do.'

'There is, I need to do the wine.'

'You mean . . . this?' He picks up the bottle that's right next to him on the side and twists the cap off. 'Done. Breathing.' He tries to pull me back into him.

'Nope,' I say, bumping him away with my hip and heading for the living room.

'You know, if it's a twisty cap I don't even think it needs to breathe.'

'Well, a little breath won't hurt it,' I shoot back, now lining up coasters on the coffee table and making sure the stack of books is perpendicular to the edge.

'You're overthinking this.' Matt appears in the doorway, leaning on the frame. 'Nobody's going to notice if a bowl of crisps is out of place.'

'Oh my god, crisps!'

I push past him and head back to the kitchen. I can't believe I nearly forgot. I do know Matt's right but also . . . Well, I just need all of this to be perfect. I need people to know . . . What? I guess that I'm just as good as Matt, even though he landed on his feet when we got back and I do what I used to do as a teenager. I want them to know that I'm not inferior. That, if anything, I'm the admirable one. I'm doing what I have to for work so that he can have his career, and I still host a banging dinner party. But, like, in a selfless, heroic way, rather than in a 1950s housewife way.

The buzzer goes.

'Jesus, get that,' I bark. Matt gives me a long look. I look right back at him. Then he puffs out his cheeks and heads for the door.

I stuff the open bag of crisps into the empty bread bin because who actually uses a bread bin? Then I scurry through to the living room with the bowl.

NATALIE

'Natalie.' Matt opens the door with a solemn voice and one hand behind his back like a butler. I take in his outfit. Oh god, he's actually dressed up. He's wearing a shirt I only ever see when we're evening guests at weddings. He's got non-jeans trousers on as well. They look a tiny bit ridiculous with his socked feet. I meet his eyes again. I have no choice but to style out my jeans and jumper now.

'Matthew.' I adopt the same sombre tone and present the bottle of wine I brought with a little curtsy. Matt takes it with another bow, like we're performing some sacred ceremony. The Matt I can take the piss with is my favourite kind of Matt.

'May I take your coat?' he asks, keeping his act up.

'I did not bring a coat,' I point out, keeping mine up too.

'Fair point. Come in.' He lets his act drop and so do I.

He closes the door behind me, and I stand in the hall, suddenly awkward. Matt looks at me. He holds his arms out a tiny bit. We've never really been huggers. We weren't even huggers when I waved him and Natalie off for an unspecified period of time. But maybe we're huggers now? I step into him and put one hand on his back while he pats mine. It's weird. It's new. I'm sure we'll get used to

31

it. We release each other as quick as you can without seeming rude and then I shift from foot to foot.

'Fiona's just—'

'Hey!' She appears in the doorway as if she's been summoned. Christ. She's dressed up as well. I tug down the sleeves of my sweatshirt and hope nobody else got the memo about this being fancy.

Fiona steps towards me and air kisses me. We have never air kissed in our lives. But it would seem we're air kissers now. Whatever. I am the guest, I follow the host's lead, so I air kiss her right back.

When we release each other I hesitate in the hallway. Matt and Fiona look at each other. They're probably wondering what the hell is wrong with me but, I mean, I haven't been here before. It's like I'm a vampire waiting to be invited in.

'Shoes off, right?' I ask to break the silence, and Fiona jumps as if she'd forgotten that I'm a guest and there are rules she has to explain.

'Yes, please,' she says.

I push my shoes off without untying the laces. And then we all just stand in the hallway again. Which is getting weirder by the minute, but I also don't think I can just *assume* and invite myself through to the living room. I don't even know which door *is* the living room.

'Come through!' Matt suddenly barks. Fiona jumps. But then she looks relieved, like she was trying to think what came next and Matt's just reminded her. It's not like we've ever had to invite each other in before. We've always just . . . been in already.

'Yes, oh my god, sorry, I didn't even think. Come through.' The buzzer goes again as I follow her down the hallway. 'Matt, could you—'

'On it.'

He does a little salute behind Fiona's back and heads for the door again. Fiona leads me into the living room and stands awkwardly in the centre, arms outstretched, as if to say 'this is a living room'.

'It looks great.'

I can hear people arriving at the other end of the hall. There's a fair amount of shrieking and laughter, so . . . I think it's the rest of Fiona's side of things. Matt's friends are far too grown-up, from what I remember.

'Natalie's here!' Amy shouts when she gets through the door. I don't turn around immediately. I give myself a second to perfect my 'I don't feel weird around you for no discernible reason and I definitely believe that you like me and never talk about me behind my back' facial expression.

'Hey!' I grin. Immediately too loud. Bring it down a notch.

I hug Amy, then Alice, and then Jasmine. No Sophie, but Sophie is basically Fiona's version of Amy, so that's to be expected. All three of them are dressed super-casual too. In fact, Jasmine is wearing a t-shirt I have definitely seen her sleep in before now. I'm so relieved I want to hug them all again. Even Amy.

'Have a seat!' Fiona says. I do as I'm told, so do Alice and Jasmine. Amy steps towards the bookshelf and starts picking up framed photos for a closer look.

'Can I get anyone a drink?'

I peer at Fiona. 'Why are you talking like that?'

'Like what?'

'I don't know, like a waiter at a posh restaurant.'

'You've never been to a posh restaurant.'

'I know, I'm assuming.'

'I'm not doing that, anyway.'

'You are. You're doing your phone voice.'

'Well, how would I usually sound?'

'I don't know. You'd just say "Drink?", wouldn't you?'

'OK, well, drink?'

'Yeah, go on, thank you.'

'What would you like?'

'Have you got vodka?' Alice asks.

'Yep,' Fiona says, sounding a bit terse, maybe?

'I'll have a vodka and coke then, please.'

'Ooh, yeah, me too.' Amy puts a photo frame down, interested in the conversation now that vodka's had a mention.

'I'll just have the coke. Driving,' Jasmine says.

Fiona looks at me. I'm getting the vibe that she'd like us to be fancier than we're being at the moment, but I am who I am. 'Could I have a spritzer, please?'

'You don't fancy a red? I got a really nice one specially.'

'No thanks. Too wine-y for me.' I grimace. 'Is that OK? I don't want to be—'

'It's fine!' Fiona gives me the *fakest* smile I've ever seen, but I'm not about to call her out in polite company. Or company, anyway.

FIONA

I smile and head back to the kitchen. Matt's in there making garlic bread in accordance with the schedule I compiled ahead of tonight. *Not* that I have been overthinking anything. It's just that if I plan this stuff now, I know what I need to tweak for the Big Event next week. It just makes sense. And, yes, fine. I also want everybody to be impressed with the leaps I've taken since Natalie and I used to host the occasional beige buffet of Iceland spring rolls, with a 'cock-tail bar' that was just a bottle of Bacardi and some cans of coke.

I open the fridge and pull out whatever white wine is in there. Some supermarket own-brand pinot grigio or whatever.

'Are we not having the . . . ?' Matt points a butter-smeared knife at the bottle of red that might even have over-breathed by now. If that's a thing.

'Not just yet.' I open the lemonade with a hiss.

NATALIE

Fiona brings the drinks through on an actual tray. I can't believe she owns a tray now.

'So, how's it all going?' I ask as she hands them out and sits down.

It's a weak question, and one I've asked every time I've seen her, spoken to her, or texted her since she moved. But I can't think what else to say anymore. When you move out you should be required to provide paperwork to your old flatmate detailing everything you'll be eating, listening to, watching on TV. That way, you could both slip back into the old easy chatter next time you see each other. In the *absence* of that very useful paperwork, 'how's it going?' is the best I've got.

'Yeah, it's good.' She nods, maybe for slightly too long. 'It's different.'

'It had better not be good different,' I joke. Although I'm not sure it lands.

The buzzer goes again and Fiona gives us an apologetic smile and disappears.

'Do we know who's coming from Matt's side?' Jasmine whispers, watching her go.

'I think Tiffany and Michael,' I say, sipping my spritzer.

Jasmine mimes being sick. 'The married ones? From his work?'

'You literally got married three weeks ago,' Amy says, coming to sit with us. I shift up so far on the sofa to make sure she has room that I basically end up in Alice's lap. I can hear Fiona answering the door, the muffled chatter as shoes are removed.

'Yeah, but I don't feel the need to bring Jason *everywhere*, you know? I can have a night with my friends unsupervised. Those two are *married*. They're so married they're married to the idea of being married.'

'That'll be Fiona next,' Alice says. 'Just watch.'

Beside me, Amy scoffs.

'Don't you th—' I start.

But I don't get to finish before Alice jumps to her feet. 'Hi, guys!'

She loses her confidence once she's up on her feet, clearly having no idea what to do next. So, she just stands there. Tiffany and Michael stand in the doorway, eyeing Team Fiona warily. Or maybe not 'warily', but certainly with looks that say 'why have you brought us here to hang out with these children?' Tiffany is actually younger than all of us. Fiona told me once, in an incredulous 'I can't believe how boring and grown-up she is' kind of way. But I guess she has her sights set on being like her now.

'Feel free to sit down,' Amy says. 'Here, we can shove up.'

She squishes up to me, and I move along too. Eventually, the four of us representing Fiona end up basically sitting on top of one another, leaving half a sofa.

Michael frowns at the space we've made. 'Matt not around?'

'Just doing some stuff in the kitchen. Here, let me give you a tour.'

FIONA

'Can *we* have a tour?' Jasmine asks as I direct Tiffany and Michael out of the room. '*We* never got offered a tour.'

'No, well, you got offered a drink.' I smile sweetly and will her to shut up. Whoever thought it would be a good idea to have these two worlds collide?

'Why can't we have both?' Amy asks. And she knows how badly I want this evening to go well. I've barely talked about anything else all week. Why can't anybody just have my back and be normal?

'Guys, come on,' Natalie says, and, I swear to god, if she doesn't help me I'm going to have a tantrum and leave. Right now. 'You know you can't take vodka and coke in the bedroom. We'll do a tour later.'

I shoot her a grateful look and she nods her acknowledgement.

'This way.' I point Tiffany and Michael back up the hallway.

NATALIE

When the food is ready Fiona asks us to sit at the table while she sorts things out in the kitchen. Matt is also in the kitchen. So, for a while, it's just all of the guests. Which . . . well, it's not *not* awkward. Alice, Jasmine, Amy and I marvel about how Fiona has room for a *table* in this new place, and how grown-up it is to own a proper table. Whenever we had people around when Fiona still lived with me, we would *always* do pizza because there was nowhere to sit and pizza doesn't need that. And now she's preparing a meal to bring to a table.

'I don't . . . How do you eat dinner if you don't have tables?' Tiffany asks, a little frown creasing her forehead.

'Just with . . . like . . . trays?' I offer.

'I just stick my head straight in the bag from the takeaway,' Alice says, and *I* can tell she's joking, because I know her, but Michael looks appalled. I kick her under the table. Jasmine raises a hand to her mouth to stifle a giggle.

The food is taking ages. I listen out for any clues as to what's going on in the kitchen. Which is easy to do because, after a few half-hearted attempts at conversation, the random selection of people at the table have kind of given up. Not acrimoniously or anything. Just, like, 'I don't know what else I can say to you so I'll just smile if I catch your eye and fiddle with my cutlery for the rest of the time.' Except, of course, Tiffany and Michael would not dream of fiddling with their cutlery.

I wonder if I should get up, go and help. If we were still living together I'd just go and see what was happening, grab some stuff to bring out, get things moving along. Not out of impatience, just so we could all focus on enjoying ourselves. But I can't work out what to do here. Or, I guess I can. I was told to sit at the table, and I am a guest, so I will do as instructed. I can't just start wandering around willy-nilly. My stomach rumbles.

'Sorry about that!' Fiona calls eventually, her voice sounding too cheery. I can just about see her behind Matt, who's carrying a huge, bubbling dish of lasagne very gingerly, wearing blue stripy oven gloves. 'Had a bit of an error with the garlic bread, won't be a minute!'

I follow the progress of the lasagne until it's safely on the table, and by the time I look up Fiona's disappeared again. Matt sits down on the other side of the table, opposite Michael. He's actually sweating.

'Where's she gone now?' I ask.

'Seeing if she can salvage the bread.'

I nod. We sit there in silence for a second. Matt gulps half a glass of wine in one go. He's on red. 'Actually, don't tell her I told you about salvaging the bread. That's meant to be a secret.'

Jasmine giggles into her glass and I widen my eyes at her. She turns it into a cough. I smile at Tiffany, who's been watching this exchange. She returns it with maybe half the enthusiasm.

'Course. Do you think we should . . .' I hover out of my seat but Matt shakes his head.

'I'd just leave her to it, I reckon.' There's a warning in his look.

'Really?'

'Really.'

I nod again. And everybody sits in silence again. This time, Matt and I both lift up our glasses and sip simultaneously. We catch each other's eye. Smile. Take another sip. We speak at the same time.

'So, are you—'

'So, how's—'

'Sorry, you go. You're a guest,' Matt says. And honestly, at this point, I have to say that being a guest is terrible.

'I was just going to ask if you're enjoying it here.' I shrug.

'Do you know what? It's awesome. It's so nice to just . . .' He's smiling, and then he looks at me, and his face falls.

Oh my god, have I become a *mood killer*? Someone who turns happiness into pity by simply being in the room? I open my mouth, I want to tell him to carry on, to tell me he's enjoying himself, to promise him that I won't *die* of jealousy, because I'm not some maiden aunt who's . . .

'Sorry about that!' Fiona trills, *way* too cheerily. She's holding a plate of chunks of garlic bread. There aren't many, and they all seem to be the middle bits. Some of them have had the crusts peeled away.

FIONA

The man can't work an oven. I can't believe the man can't work an oven. Guess what? If the dial is pointing to a number higher than the number in the recipe, your food gets burned. It's not hard.

Natalie's giving me a funny look, everybody else is determinedly avoiding eye contact. Matt is gulping his wine, and I need to calm down. Hostess with the mostest, hostess with the mostest, hostess with the mostest. What would Nigella do? If it's coming apart at the seams now, what's it going to be like in a week?

I reach across the table to serve the lasagne, which is when I realise that we don't have a spoon or anything. I start to get up, but Matt shoots up quicker.

'I'll go,' he says. 'Spoon, right?'

I nod. He leaves the room and then it's just me and our guests. I smile at Michael as he takes a sip of red wine. At least *someone* appreciates it.

'Here we are.' Matt brandishes a fish slice like it's some kind of trophy.

'How's it all going in the flat?' Matt asks as people eat. Everybody's already made polite yummy noises and pretended not to notice the state of the garlic bread. Or what's left of it. Conversation has touched on Scoopz, and I redirected it quickly, which made Amy narrow her eyes at me. Matt tried to start a chat about politics, but Jasmine *literally booed* him. Tiffany and Michael told us all about the process of getting a mortgage, which left my end of the table looking horrified.

'But what if you break up?' Amy asked.

'Sorry? We're married,' Tiffany said with a frown.

'Don't we know it,' Jasmine sighed. I narrowed my eyes at her.

'Being married doesn't mean you won't break up,' Alice chimed in. 'Look at my parents. Look at Amy's. Look at Matt's.'

Natalie has been wonderful in that she hasn't said very much. She's laughed in all the right places and agreed with things (almost exclusively things that Tiffany and Michael have said) that she definitely doesn't actually agree with, just to keep the peace. I should have just invited her. Much more low-pressure for my first ever

Proper Grown-Up Dinner Party. She even smiled and giggled along when Matt told stories about funny things that happened while we were travelling and, well . . . She doesn't ever say anything, but I know that must be a sore point. Anyway. What I mean to say is, my best friend is a legend, and a dream dinner party guest, and I love her, and, yes, I have had one more wine than I should have.

'How's the flatmate hunt going?' Matt asks in the end, looking at her. Tiffany and Michael look at her with a bit of a sneer, and even I hate them for a second.

Natalie's face falls infinitesimally, but she's back in control of it before most people would even notice.

'Yeah, it's . . .' She shrugs.

'That bad, eh?' Matt smiles wryly, and my god, man, would you let her save a tiny bit of face here? I open my mouth to interject, to steer us back to safer ground, but Natalie speaks before I can.

'Well, it's not ideal, let's just say that.'

'Can you not find anybody who's interested?'

OH MY GOD, MATTHEW, DID YOU NOT HEAR HER SAY 'LET'S JUST SAY THAT'? IS ASKING MORE QUESTIONS ABOUT SOMETHING THAT CLEARLY MAKES HER UNCOMFORTABLE 'JUST SAYING THAT'??? I dig my fingernails into my palms. I'm not about to intervene anymore, she can take care of herself, but really. I clear my throat loudly, in the hope that Matt might take the hint. All that happens is that Tiffany refills my water glass with a smile and pats my arm. Matt *still* doesn't take the hint.

'I don't know.' Natalie shrugs. 'There's been a couple, but then they go silent on you, or they're very obviously going to kill you in your sleep, that kind of thing.'

'That's so weird. We have friends in London and they always seem to be able to find new flatmates,' Michael says, frowning.

'Yes, well, people actually want to live there, I think that's probably the difference,' Natalie replies sweetly.

'Well, people actually want to live here too. Look at Tiffany and me, we're not going anywhere. Or Matt and Fiona. Anymore, anyway.'

I glance at Matt, and he grins at me from the other end of the table. I smile back, forgetting, for a second, that there's anybody else here.

'Well, that's really nice for everybody,' Natalie says, bringing me back to the present. She takes her time with her words. 'Because if I *don't* end up finding anybody I can move in with one of you. Good to have a backup plan.'

Tiffany looks genuinely horrified, like she doesn't realise that Natalie is joking. I put a hand on her arm. She looks at me and I shake my head the tiniest bit.

'Oh!' she says, and bursts out laughing. 'That's funny!'

When she's gathered herself we all sit in awkward silence for a minute. Tiffany and Michael don't seem to know what to say, and somewhere along the way most of *my* friends seem to have lost any interest they had in helping me out.

'I've got a friend, actually!' Matt suddenly breaks the silence.

'That's nice, I knew you could do it if you put your mind to it.' Natalie's eyes shine as she finds herself back on safe ground. Alice giggles too. Natalie can playfully abuse Matt until the cows come home and he'll take it because he knows that's her love language.

'No, I mean I have a friend who was looking for a new place to live. It's a guy I know from work, actually, but he seems OK. He hasn't murdered anyone.'

'That you know of,' Amy clarifies.

'Well, yes, that I know of. But I don't think he would.'

'They did say that about Harold Shipman, though,' Amy points out, her eyes shining with amusement.

'Oh my god! Look. I'm just saying I could put you both in contact if you think that would be helpful?'

'I mean, hey, send him my way,' Natalie says, graciously, picking up her drink.

'I definitely will. And I guess that guy you've been seeing has no interest in moving in? Probably a bit early, I guess. What's his name? Neil? No, Nigel, right?'

I am too far away, but luckily Jasmine's quick with her elbows. I nod my thanks.

'Ow! What?' he demands, rubbing his arm.

'We're actually not seeing each other anymore,' Natalie says lightly. There's a flush creeping up her neck.

'*Another* one that's not good enough?' Matt laughs. Tiffany and Michael give each other a glowing look, clearly congratulating themselves on being well out of the dating game. Natalie smiles too, but it's tight. It doesn't go all the way to her eyes.

'What can I say? I guess I'm picky.'

We eat in silence for a while. Amy scrapes her plate with her fork, and I can tell Matt's grinding his teeth.

'Oh, have you thought any more about that guy I was telling you about?' Alice asks. I feel a prickle of jealousy that I don't know what guy she's talking about. Or when they were talking about him. Which I know is mad. *I'm* the one who moved out, I can't expect to have every little thing reported to me. But still.

'No, I have not,' Natalie says, shaking her head and eating a forkful of salad.

'Would you just go out with him once? Please? I think you'll like him.'

'I don't know anything about him.' Her voice is muffled through lettuce. I happen to glance at Tiffany. She purses her lips as Natalie talks with her mouth full.

'He's great!'

43

'*You* barely know anything about him!'

'Natalie.' Alice reaches across the table and takes Natalie's hand. Natalie returns her gaze defiantly for a couple of moments until she seems to relent.

'Oh god, fine. Set it up.'

NATALIE

The meal was . . . well, weird. There's no other way to describe it. Like, the food was great. You really can't go wrong with a lasagne, can you? But the vibes? The vibes were way off.

Fiona gave off some manic energy I did not understand at all, and Matt seemed just as confused as I was. Mine and Fiona's friends would clearly rather have been out at the pub on a Saturday night, and Tiffany and Michael would clearly rather have been at home with a chicken Kiev watching *Pointless Celebrities*. And I'm not saying that anybody was more fun than anybody else, I am simply stating facts. And, while I'm giving feedback, I could definitely have lived without the entire 'Matchmaking Natalie' portion of the evening.

As she says goodbye to everybody at the door we hear the crash of breaking china from the direction of the kitchen and I swear to god Fiona's eye actually twitches. Luckily, Tiffany and Michael have gone already. Probably had a nine p.m. bedtime to stick to. So, at least it's only the cool half of the dinner party who'll suspect that she and Matt are human after all.

As we queue up to leave, she reaches towards Jasmine and tries to air kiss her.

'What are you doing?' I sigh.

'Saying goodbye.'

'So do it like a normal person,' I say. I step towards her and pull her into a hug. Alice joins in, and so does Jasmine. Amy stays on the opposite side to me, but she's there too. We all squeeze each other until someone squawks because we're about to fall over. When we break apart, Fiona's hair is in disarray, her cheeks are pink, but she's laughing. I haven't seen her laugh all evening.

'Text me when you get home,' she says.

FIONA

Matt's washing up when I've seen everybody out. I don't say anything, just grab a tea towel and start doing the drying. We carry on like that for a minute or so.

CHAPTER FOUR

Natalie

I plump the cushions on the sofa again while I'm waiting for this guy, Nick, to ring the bell. Or text me. Confirm that even if he isn't actually coming, he is not dead, basically.

I don't always mind lateness. Myself, or Fiona, or both of us are usually a few minutes late whenever we meet up. That is if we weren't literally leaving from the same house at the same time. There's always traffic, or you forget to factor in part of the journey, or you might even just leave late. I understand it. I honestly do. But, like, text me and tell me? I sort of expected this 'Nick' person would definitely do that, because if *I* was the one who'd been put in touch by my colleague, I would assume that the colleague would be getting a thorough report on the meeting after it happened. And, I mean, this is not a good start. Strong black mark on this guy's record. I check my phone again, and then check the clock on the wall in case my phone is somehow wrong. But, no. He is actually twenty minutes late.

I sit on the sofa, but I don't want to lean back because I just plumped the new cushions for the third time, so I stand up again. I walk to what will certainly *not* be this guy's room at this point but hey, I guess we're carrying on with this charade for a while longer. I'm just wondering when it's acceptable to give up when my phone rings.

'Hi, it's Nick. Um, Matthew's friend? I'm here to see the room? I'm downstairs.'

I wait for a couple of seconds. I'm not even trying to throw shade, I just really thought he might want to apologise.

'Hello?' he prompts. So I guess not.

'Sorry. Hi. Yes. I'll be right down.'

I take a quick scan of the living room before I leave. The place is tidy, the plants look healthy, and the space looks full enough to seem like somebody actually lives here. I wonder about putting a pot of coffee on, because that's a thing, isn't it? A thing I should have thought about earlier, though. And it's probably not a thing at nearly nine p.m. That would say a lot about me and I don't think any of it would be good. The buzzer goes off twice (so nice that he's found that), and I have the strong feeling that this guy won't be worth wasting a scoop of coffee on anyway.

'Hi, sorry, come in,' I say, stretching my face into a smile as I open the door to the road. It actually doesn't lock anyway, but he doesn't need to know that.

'It's nice to meet you,' Nick says as he follows me up the stairs. 'Matt's told me loads about you.'

'Has he?'

'Yeah. Well, enough to sell me on living here anyway.' He laughs. And, oh my god, I am not even exaggerating when I say it echoes around the entire stairwell as we walk. Why is it ten times louder than his voice? How is that a *thing*? 'It's shit, isn't it? When everybody around you starts shacking up and we're the losers who get left behind? Believe me, I get it. I do. I promise that won't be me.'

I've met the man for forty-seven seconds at this point and, even without his reassurances, I'm already confident that he will

47

never successfully 'shack up' with anybody. Fucking hell, Matt. I don't even want to know what he's been telling this guy about me. I unlock the door when we get to the top of the stairs, and he tries to stick his head in before I've even removed the key. His shoulder collides with mine, he's so keen. He's like a dog trying to reach its bowl before it's been put on the floor. It suddenly strikes me as funny that *I've* been picky about people who seem murdery up until now, because I am about to *become* the murdery one. I elbow him back, but in a nice way, so I can get the door open.

'Oh,' he says when we untangle ourselves and he's got past me into the living room. It is not a good 'Oh'. I know this because, unlike him, I have the ability to read another person.

'Oh?' I repeat.

'Yeah, it's just . . . Do you know what? It's lovely. Cute.'

'OK.' I frown.

I haven't given him any invitation to do so, but I watch him walk around the perimeter of the living space. He does the kitchen first, opening drawers and taking out a garlic press, and then a potato peeler, holding them up to the light. He puts them down on the side and moves on. He stands at the sink and turns on the tap. He opens the fridge, takes out a jar of pesto (?), opens it (??), sniffs it (???), and then closes it and puts it back. It's like he's running a drugs bust, not doing a viewing. I'm so surprised I basically just let him do his thing. I occasionally wonder if I should be giving him information, but I don't have any details to impart about the contents of the bin or the cupboards so I just stand there, mystified.

He moves on to the living room, where he peers at the shelves, taking down a couple of books and flicking through them. He touches the soil in the plant pots and then rubs his fingers together. He plumps the cushions I ALREADY PLUMPED THREE TIMES and I wonder if it's possible to expire with rage.

'Would you like to see the room?' I ask, through gritted teeth. I honestly just need him to stop inspecting my belongings before I pick up my paperweight and bludgeon him with it. 'If you were to take it' – LOL, not in a *million years* – 'we could obviously move some of my stuff out of here so that yours could fit too.'

Nick makes a non-committal 'uh huh' noise that I know means he has no intention of moving any of his stuff in at all. And while I am relieved, I'm also annoyed. I mean, I know why *I* do not want to live with *him*, but he should consider himself *lucky* to get this close to living with me.

'And this would be your room,' I tell him, stepping inside.

'Oh, cool. I always wondered what it would be like to live in a cupboard,' he jokes. I mean, I *think* it's a joke because he does that godawful booming laugh again. It's all I can do to keep from wincing, it's *so* loud. There's a tap on the wall from Sheila next door and rightly so.

'It's a pretty decent-sized room,' I say. 'I mean, it fits everything. I don't know what else you'd need.'

'Well, I have some bodybuilding equipment I'd be bringing.'

I take in his skinny arms, his almost concave chest. 'Do you?'

'Yeah. I mean, it's new, obviously.' He flexes the spaces where muscles would usually go, and then laughs absurdly loudly again. There's another tap on the wall. 'Wow, sensitive neighbours, huh?'

I'm not sure how to say 'they've never done that before, but no human being has ever produced a sound that loud before either', so I just shrug.

'So, bathroom?' he asks, standing to one side and holding out an arm to indicate that I should lead the way. I close my eyes, just for a moment, and take a deep breath.

'Come on, chop chop.' He CLAPS HIS HANDS behind me to chivvy me along and laughs that ludicrous laugh again.

Fiona

'Ask her how it's going,' Matt says for the third time this evening. We're watching TV. Allegedly. But neither of us is doing a good job of it. Matt is wondering if he's miraculously fixed things for Natalie so he can stop feeling bad yet. And I'm hoping that the one time I actually met Nick, he was the way he was because he was drunk. Because if not, what we've just done to Natalie is unforgivable.

'*You* ask her. You have her number too.'

'I can't ask her! He's my friend, she won't be able to tell the truth.'

'Why would she not want to tell you the . . . Oh my god, tell me he's not always the way he was when we met him at that wedding.'

There's a long pause. He just looks at me.

'Matt!'

'*What?* She needed help. I'm helping her.'

'Trying to get the dullest, most inappropriate man on the planet to live with someone isn't helping them!'

'Oh, come on, he's not that bad.' He sounds confident, but he doesn't look sure. 'I just thought . . . She needs to find someone, doesn't she?'

'Matt, he told me a fifteen-minute story about home brewing when I first met him. I don't even drink beer. And then he asked me what birth control I was on!'

'Look, this is all just . . . Would you just ask her how it's going?'

'Well, I think we both know how it'll be going, don't you?' I huff loudly and take my phone out. I write out a text, and it takes everything in my power not to end it with 'please forgive me'.

'What were you thinking?' I ask when that's done. Matt just shrugs, which isn't good enough. 'No, seriously. I want to know.'

'I don't know, we both feel bad about leaving her in the lurch. I wanted her to be sorted so we could just get on with being happy. And we wouldn't need to feel guilty anymore. I wanted to skip to the good bit – is that so wrong?'

He looks at me with these puppy-dog eyes and I feel a kind of lurching in my ribcage. Did he do a good thing? One hundred per cent not. No question. It's indefensible. But it's still *kind of* nice in its own weird way. I shift along and curl up next to him on the sofa, my phone forgotten in between the cushions.

'What's all this in aid of?'

'I've decided to forgive you.'

NATALIE

FIONA: Hope everything's going OK over there! Let us know x

Her text was sent a good half an hour ago, because *that* is how long it took to get Nick out of my flat. And yes, definitely *my* flat. Never *ours*.

I mean, my god. After he chivvied me to the bathroom he made a very close inspection of the contents of the cabinet, even though I asked him not to ('Oh? But I thought I'd be able to put some of my stuff in here as well?' Well, you probably can, but you won't be keeping your stuff *inside* the Imodium box, will you?). He also told me how I could better prevent mould on the shower sealant, and that I wasn't storing my toothbrush correctly. On the way down the hallway, he stuck his head into my bedroom. Then he asked if we could discuss swapping rooms.

'Unfortunately not,' I told him, putting a hand on his back to try and physically push him out.

'So, you're saying this flat wouldn't be run as a democracy?'

'What? That's not what I-I'm . . .' I didn't know what to say, so in the end I just pushed harder and he seemed to get the hint.

'Well, I'll let you know,' he told me at the door.

'OK, thank you,' I said in a tone that I hope made it very clear I never wanted to hear from him again.

And now I stare incredulously at Fiona's text. I just . . . I don't understand how . . . Maybe Fiona's never met that guy but Matt has, right? If they work together, Matt's probably sat in meetings with him. He probably bumps into him on their way in and out of the office. They've probably stood together next to the kettle and made awkward small talk as they made cups of tea. What I'm getting at is that it seems reasonable to assume that Matt has *met* Nick before tonight. And Matt has known me for almost our entire lives. And he *still* thought Nick was someone I should spend an extended period of time with? I truly can't get my head around it. I feel *depleted* by this evening. I don't even mean tired, just . . . like there is less of me now than there was before Nick walked into my life. Like he's sucked away part of my very essence. I know I'm being dramatic, but honestly. I puff out my cheeks and flop back on the sofa.

I stare at Fiona's text again and then dial her number. I would like to know what someone in that brand-new household was thinking. Do they think I'm so desperate for any human being to fill the Fiona-shaped hole that I don't want to find someone with . . . oooh, maybe basic social skills and some awareness of boundaries? What, like suddenly Fiona and Matt are moving on with their lives and because I'm the one who's left behind I don't get to find someone good? Like a 'beggars can't be choosers' kind of thing? I want to be a chooser. I should still *get* to be a chooser. Have they forgotten that they *put* me in this position?

The phone rings out.

I dial again and wait for Fiona to pick up. I know I'm talking myself into being annoyed here, but I *did* just lose a full ninety minutes of my life. Who takes ninety minutes to look around a small, two-bed flat? But I'm sure it's all been a misunderstanding. Chalk it up to that. It's fine. The phone rings out.

I dial one more time. I wouldn't always, but she texted *me*. She wanted my report. And I am more than ready to give it. I listen to a couple more rings on the other end of the line before the rest of my brain starts working again. And then, I mean . . . What the hell am I doing? Things have changed now. I can't just keep ringing until she picks up because I do not have her undivided attention anymore. Matt has that now. I look at the time. Nearly ten p.m.

I hang up and throw my phone away from me in horror. They could be doing anything. Her message was sent a while ago. But she won't have sat around just waiting on tenterhooks to hear from me. They're probably all over each other on the sofa, while her phone keeps ringing, and Matt tells her to ignore me, and she does, but I just *keep* ringing apparently, because I have no respect for the new boundaries they've built, and . . . I cringe.

Oh my god, I'm as bad as Nick. I *might be* their Nick.

CHAPTER FIVE

Fiona

'I'll get it!' I call when the doorbell goes.

I cast a frantic eye around the flat, which, honestly, I think we've done a *very* good job on. It was getting there last weekend anyway, but I got up unpleasantly early this morning to do the finishing touches, and now it's really starting to feel like a home. I stick my head into the kitchen to check the wine is breathing, because I do not care if my philistine friends didn't even *drink* the wine in the practice run, I know Elizabeth Hayden is a different beast. Maybe just a beast? *No*, Fiona. That's not very nice. I smooth down my dress. And as I put a hand on the doorknob, I offer a quick prayer to any and all available gods that it will be *my* parents waiting on the other side and not Matt's mother.

No such luck. Obviously. I must have summoned her with my bitchy thoughts.

'Fiona, wonderful to see you,' Elizabeth says as she plants a kiss about three inches into the air above each of my cheeks. And I am ready, because I practised this.

'You too,' I squeak. All the preparedness in the world apparently couldn't make me sound normal in front of her. I don't know how she manages to do this to me. I clear my throat. Try again. 'You too.'

She looks at me for a second, and I wonder why, until I remember that she can't come in until I get out of the way. I hop to one side and she strides past me. I open my mouth as she walks past the shoe rack but, ultimately, I decide I'd rather die than tell her we're a shoes-off household. She could rub her shoes on my pillow if it'd make her happy. And I suspect it probably would.

'Can I get you . . .' I begin, but she's already disappeared. I stick my head into the living room. Matt is being held in a death grip. She is literally a foot and a half shorter than him, and he's bent at the waist so that his head rests on her shoulder. It's like I kidnapped him and took him to the moon. Except we live in the same town and she hasn't seen him for, what? Two weeks? Has texted every day, though. Video called too. I think they went for coffee. Matt pulls a face and I shrug back.

'Can I get you a drink, Elizabeth?' I try again. I really just want her to release her son because, honestly, her vicelike hug has gone on more than long enough and it's verging on weird. The doorbell goes again before she can answer.

'Oh, hold that thought,' I say and scurry back down the hall.

I open the door to my own parents. My dad holds a bottle of wine in one hand and a bouquet of carnations in the other. My mum thrusts a loaf of bread towards me.

'Tradition,' she says, pulling me into a quick hug before sitting down on the bench in the hallway to take off her shoes.

'Alright, love?' my dad says, handing me the wine, patting my shoulder with his now-free hand, and then handing me the flowers too.

'Yeah, good, thanks,' I reply, even though what I want to say is 'FOR THE LOVE OF GOD TAKE ME AWAY AND LET'S GO AND GET FISH AND CHIPS.'

NATALIE

'Hi, how can I help?' a waitress in a black shirt and pinny asks as I get to the counter.

'I'm here to meet someone. His name's Ryan. I'm not sure if he's here yet.'

I'm sure her lip curls, but I must be imagining it. 'Oh, yeah. He's here. Follow me, I'll take you over.'

She walks me through the mostly empty tables and deeper into the restaurant. The only other people here are easily twenty years older than me. When Ryan wanted to meet early, I didn't really question it. After all, if this turns out to be terrible (and I have a one hundred per cent record for these things being terrible) then I'll still get a bit of an evening to myself. And yes, I will definitely spend it trying to find a new flatmate and wondering why no other human wants to hitch their wagon to mine in any context. But it is, at least, nice to be able to have that kind of crisis in the comfort of your own home, with your own PJs and a face mask on. It's called self-care.

I spot Ryan before he sees me. It's not difficult. He's literally the only person amongst a group of empty tables. He's staring at his phone. He keeps staring as we get closer, even when I stub my toe incredibly hard against a chair. I yelp, the chair scrapes across the floor, and Ryan keeps his eyes on his phone. He doesn't even look up when I pull out the chair opposite him. The waitress turns to leave and I'm sure I hear her mutter 'Good luck'. I *must* have imagined it.

I don't really . . . know what to do if he just won't look at me? Like, do I announce my arrival? I guess so, but should I *need* to? I would look up from my phone if anybody sat down opposite me when I was having dinner, even if they weren't someone I had specifically arranged to meet. I feel a flare of annoyance, wonder if

I should just get up and leave again, and then scold myself because what if he has some kind of . . . something. He could be deaf, or blind, it's not like I ever *asked*. Whatever happened to being kind? He could have any number of challenges that . . .

'Sorry,' he says, holding up a finger and continuing to scroll, 'be right with you, just dealing with a fucking secretary's fucking fuckup.'

OK, or he *might* just be a twat.

FIONA

I take the gifts my parents brought through to the kitchen, and they follow me. I sort them both out with drinks before we join the others in the living room. I feel bolstered now that I'm no longer outnumbered by Haydens. But also, if that hug is still going on when I get back, I will call social services. Or someone. I don't even know.

'Oh, nothing for me, then?' Elizabeth asks sweetly, looking up as my parents enter the room. She's scrutinising the shelves like I knew she would. I deliberately filled them with cookbooks and classic novels.

'You know you don't have to do that?' Matt said earlier as I pushed past him with an armful of #girlboss books and travel guides to hide under the bed.

'I want to,' I said, aiming a quick kiss at him as I passed. 'I want her to like me one day.'

'Aw, Fi. You're cute.' He caught my arm and pulled me towards him, planting a kiss on my forehead. 'You know she'll never do that.'

His mother greets my parents now, clutching each of their hands in turn. She doesn't shake them so much as try to squeeze the life out of them for a couple of seconds.

'Linda. David. So nice to see you again.'

My parents smile benignly. Maybe a little bit strained. We all know this evening is an endurance event, not a jolly. I catch Matt's eye and he grins at me, which makes my stomach flip. So it's worth it, really.

'Was there any chance of a drink at all?' Elizabeth asks, looking pointedly at my parents' glasses.

'Yes. Of course,' I say. 'What would you like? Let me—'

'I'll go,' Matt says.

He walks towards the door, caressing my hand as he passes. I see Elizabeth see. Not that it's a secret gesture. My parents see too, and my mum smiles in an 'oh, aren't they cute?' way. Elizabeth's face, however, is inscrutable. And I'd honestly rather it stay that way because her relationship with Matt makes me *extremely* uncomfortable sometimes.

Matt returns with the drinks and everybody sits in an awkward row on the sofa. So far, so like last week. We're all on track. I stand by the window and watch them make small talk.

'Do you want to sit down, love?' my dad asks, threatening to get up.

'No. No, you stay there. I have to go and sort the food anyway.' I dismiss him with a wave of the hand.

'I would help,' Matt clarifies to my parents, 'but I've been banned. Had a mishap with the garlic bread when we did our prac—'

'Well, you're in charge of the drinks and chitchat portion of the evening,' I interrupt quickly. I don't want you-know-who to know I did a practice run. I want her to think I'm an innately-gifted-lasagne-chef-slash-hostessing-genius. I try to convey this to Matt using just my eyes. He does the tiniest nod. There's a strong chance he's just humouring me.

There's not that much to check on in the kitchen since it's mainly just doing its thing in the oven. I unwrap the garlic bread (shop-bought this time because there is clearly not a single benefit to making it from scratch) and stick it in the oven. I give the salad a toss. Then I drink half a glass of the as-yet-untouched red wine.

NATALIE

Ryan finally deigns to look at me when the waitress comes to the table to take our drinks order. I get a white wine and lemonade on account of it being six p.m. He orders neat whiskey. The waitress looks pointedly at his car keys on the table, but he doesn't take the hint, so she sighs and writes down his order. My face starts heating up. I want her to know that I came here without prior knowledge in case she thinks less of me. I try to catch her eye, but she bustles off before I have the chance.

'So, tell me about yourself.' Ryan leans back in his seat and crosses his arms as he looks at me.

'I'm sorry?' I say, caught off guard. Y'know, because he sounds like he's interviewing a candidate for a job, not chatting to a stranger on a blind date.

'You,' he says, like *I'm* the one who's being really weird. 'Tell me about you.'

There is absolutely nothing in his tone to suggest that he actually wants to hear anything about me but we already have drinks on the way, so I do need to fill at least twenty minutes. Ten if I drink fast. Which this guy *does* make me want to do, in fairness.

'I don't know, I was born and raised in Crostdam, I've lived here my whole life. I work at St James' School, I do admin. How about you?'

Our drinks arrive just as he replies. 'Estate agent.'

The waitress gives a derisive laugh, which she covers with a cough straight away. She puts the drinks down and disappears quickly.

'Oh, cool,' I say, trying to make that convincing. 'Do you . . . like that?'

'Oh, love it,' he says. He sips his drink and winces. 'It's satisfying, you know? It's so nice to be able to go home every day knowing that you're really making a difference in people's lives. Really helping them.'

I feel a rush of relief and laugh. But then I realise that he is not, in fact, being sarcastic.

'So, what's your deal?' he asks, engaging Job Interview Mode again.

'My . . . ?'

'Your deal. You know, relationship? Living situation? What you're looking for?'

'Oh. Right. Well, not in a relationship, obviously' – although, does *he* think that would be obvious??? – 'I guess I'm just looking to meet people, see what's around. I don't, like, want to get married tomorrow or anything.' I laugh nervously. He does not react. 'And I was living with my best friend, but she actually moved out recently, so I guess now I'm in between flatmates for the time being.'

Ryan bangs a hand down on the table, jangling the cutlery in its holder. '*Yes*.'

'Sorry?'

'That's why we're here.'

'What's why we're here? I thought—'

'Look.' He leans back and cocks an eyebrow. Somehow I can already tell I'm about to get very annoyed. 'We both know we're not a good match. I'm more into girls who are . . .' He *waves a hand* in front of my face. 'You know?'

'I can't say I do, no,' I say through gritted teeth. Because I think I might have an idea.

'Just, like, someone who takes care of themself a bit more. Nothing personal, obviously. *But.* Maybe I can help you on the flatmate thing. Let me just . . .'

He ducks under the table for a second and when he re-emerges he's genuinely holding a laptop.

'Oh, listen, this has been fun,' I begin. If he's about to open a PowerPoint, I want to go home. I want to go home when that happens at my actual job, and I'm being *paid* to sit through it then. 'But I think I'm going to—'

'No, just wait a minute.'

He taps a couple of keys and the screen lights up. He puts it down on the table and starts typing in his password. I take the opportunity while he's distracted, gulp down my spritzer, and scarper.

FIONA

Matt carries the food to the table when we've all sat down.

'Oh, you've done such a wonderful job, Matthew, thank you,' Elizabeth says, positively glowing with pride.

'Well, this is my only contribution. I told you, Fiona did everything. You should thank her.'

He sits down next to me. His mother makes a little 'mmhmm' sound in my direction. I press my leg up against Matt's under the table and he squeezes my knee.

'It really does look great, Fi. Good job,' my mum says.

'Well, everybody dig in.' I feel a little thrill as I say it. It feels weirdly grown-up to be the one giving everybody permission to start.

For a while, nobody talks. My dad even comments on it.

'Nobody's saying anything, that's when you know the food's good.'

We all make noises of agreement and keep eating. Except Elizabeth. Elizabeth prods at the mince with her fork. I try very hard to focus on my own plate and ignore her. Once we've finished eating, Matt sits back and sighs.

'That was amazing, Fi, thank you.'

'Yes, honestly, so good, love,' my mum adds. 'I have to say, you two have put together a proper little home here. It's so lovely. I think you'll both be very happy.'

'Thank you.' I reach over and squeeze her hand, touched. I glance at Matt and he grins at me. My cheeks feel warm.

'Yes, it's amazing what you can do once you finally decide to be sensible,' Elizabeth says quietly, holding her glass close to her face so you can't see her lips move. My dad chokes on his wine. I can't tell if she meant that to be audible to everybody or just to Matt.

'Sorry, Elizabeth, I didn't catch that,' my mother says, her tone all sweetness with just an edge of danger.

'Nothing. Nothing. I was just saying, I'm glad these two are finally in a position to settle down.'

'Me too,' I agree. Matt squeezes my knee again.

'So, Fiona, what are your plans now, if you don't mind me asking?' Elizabeth continues, and I think longingly about being anywhere else than here. If I'd just kept living with Natalie I wouldn't be getting the third degree now. Yes, I might occasionally get it in a restaurant over lunch, but not in my home, in front of my parents.

'How do you mean?' Matt asks. He's frowning, as if this is a new development on his mother's part.

'Well, I mean, is she going to keep working at the ice cream shop? Now that she's got a more stable living situation, will she be looking for something better? I'm just making conversation, darling.'

'No, you're making this into a careers—'

I laugh. 'It's fine.' I hope I sound breezy and not creepy. My parents stare at their empty plates. 'I would love to find something better, Elizabeth. I would. But obviously, we have to stay here for Matt's work' – cue her cold stare becoming a proud, shining gaze as she turns her attention back to Matt – 'and the options are . . . limited . . .' Elizabeth opens her mouth and I cut her off before she can say anything. 'Anyway. Dessert, anyone?'

Dad nods. 'Love some.'

Matt starts collecting up plates, but Dad takes them off his hands, gesturing that he should sit back down.

I think I've aged a hundred years by the time we've waved everybody off at the door. My parents left to walk home twenty minutes ago, and when Elizabeth's cab turns up I am so grateful I'd happily kiss the driver. And after doing so I'd warn him that she is *on one* tonight.

We revisited my career ambitions over slabs of Viennetta. We picked at my not immediately wanting to move in with Matt upon our return from travelling while we had coffee and after-dinner mints. Which is very confusing because she doesn't exactly seem thrilled that I've moved in with him now, so why would she have wanted it to happen eighteen months earlier? And then we moved back to the sofa for a round of everybody's favourite game, 'Yes, well, I'm sure the travelling was a wonderful experience, but it's nice to see you both finally decide to settle down. It's what your father would have wanted, Matthew.'

'You're a rock star,' Matt says when he gets back to the living room and finds me in a state of collapse on the sofa. 'I know she's a lot.'

I give him A Look. 'She's not a lot. She'll just never forgive me for being allowed to marry you when legally she can't.'

'OK, that's the worst thing I've ever heard.'

'Not wrong, though.'

'*Very* wrong.'

'OK, fine. Not *incorrect*, then.'

'Anyway, you'd marry me?'

I pick my head up and look at him. 'I mean, I might do one day, is that OK?'

'Yeah. Just interesting, is all.'

'That's also not what I said. I said I'm *allowed* to marry you. But so's my dad, to be fair.'

Matt gives a melodramatic sigh. 'Yeah, if only Linda would take the hint, our great love story could begin.'

I laugh and cuddle into his side. 'Your mother's head would explode.'

'All the more reason. Sorry, woman. When that day comes, you'll be out on your arse.'

I laugh and take out my phone. I do the rounds of the usual apps, and I'm just swiping through some memes when I remember that Natalie had her date tonight.

FIONA: How did it go???? xx

NATALIE

When Fiona's text buzzes through I am eating oven pizza with my feet up, watching back-to-back episodes of *Friends*. I actually intended to order a pizza in as a reward for being a trouper and spending literally any amount of time with or near Ryan. But by the time I got home I'd talked myself out of it because I couldn't afford it, so Chicago Town it is. Ryan has already texted me twice to outline what he can do for me and how much it will cost, and also to remind me that there's 'no hard feelings your just not my type ;)'. My eye twitches when another message comes through, but I'm relieved it's Fiona.

FIONA: How did it go???? xx

The thing is, I don't really know what to say to her. I should just tell her it was shit, but if I do that I'll have to relive it every time we meet up for a while, and I really don't want to. Fiona will find it funny, which she should because it *is*. And I'll have to retell it for her amusement whenever she sees me until something else funnier comes up. And it was fine to do that when we literally lived together and had all the time in the world to chat shit to each other. But now that that's not the case, I'm not sure I want to feel like she's bought tickets to a show every time I see her. Plus, the whole thing is a bit tragic and I don't feel like I come across well in comparison to her, with her nice flat, and her live-in boyfriend, and her sophisticated night entertaining the new family unit.

NATALIE: Was fine. Not sure it'll go anywhere but still nice :) xx
NATALIE: How was dinner?

I haven't even managed to put the phone down when another text comes through:

ARSEHOLE RYAN DO NOT ANSWER: My commission's usually 10% but I'm willing to 9.5% mates rates for you ;)

I throw my phone across the sofa.

FIONA

I smile when Natalie's text comes through. I'm glad she had a nice time. I'm not super-sure how to answer the question about dinner, though. She knows how anxious I was about it. She was so great at the trial run. I just . . . I don't want to admit to her that after all of that, I still came out of it feeling kind of like shit.

And also, I left her in the lurch to move in with Matt, having famously left her in the lurch once before as well. I glance at Matt, who's texting too, keeping his screen very carefully angled away from me. I would bet thousands that his mother's trying to convince him to come home right now. I don't want Natalie to know that I left her in a tricky situation for anything less than perfection. We have to be blissfully happy with completely-on-board families or it's just rude. All of which to say, I lie:

FIONA: Dinner was sooooooooo good thanks!! xx

CHAPTER SIX

NATALIE

My job is not exactly interesting at the best of times. I know some people find a lot of value and fulfilment in working in education, and that's fantastic for them, but, oh my god, admin is not the one. I mean, it's fine, and it's not like there are a ton of options in Crostdam, but I can normally do everything I have to get through in a couple of hours and then I spend the rest of the day reading on the internet or texting under my desk. The weather isn't helping. It's disgusting outside today, the sky looks heavy, trees bend in the wind, and rain is actually slapping against the window. Slapping. Gross.

At the moment, I desperately want to text Fiona. I don't even have anything to say, it's just muscle memory. We'd text each other all the time, normally. Just things like 'remember to send me £50 for the gas', 'could you get some eggs on the way home?', '*Love Island* tonight?' So by the time it hits two p.m. my thumbs are twitching. I could text someone else, sure. I could probably still text Fiona. But I just feel like maybe this is my time to be a grown-up and consider . . . not texting anyone. I can make it through one afternoon, surely?

I have, however, taken to logging on to SpareRoom on the hour, every hour, and all through the night as well. I've come into work today with an honest-to-god poster, which I stick on the noticeboard. I hope somebody good notices it, and not the creepy lab technician who's always boiling the kettle but never seems to make any tea. A couple of colleagues who knew about Fiona's move ask me how it's all going, and I smile and nod and say that yes, yes, she's all moved out now, and yes it *is* very different, and no, not yet, but if you know of anybody feel free to let me know! And it's exhausting. I just want to skip to the part where this is all sorted and I'm looking back and remembering how stressed I got and thinking, with a smile, about how it was all worth it in the end.

Because I *am* starting to get stressed. On the day she left, my flatmate panic was just one of a ton of different feelings. It was too difficult to parse it out from any of the others. Now, though? I've had time – more time than I really want to have had – to get used to the place being empty. Time, and almost no interest. And I haven't told Fiona that I'm panicking. I can't.

At lunchtime, I sit at my desk with my sad sandwich and a bag of Hula Hoops and refresh my messages even though I checked twenty minutes ago and there was nothing there. This isn't productive. I should go for a walk or something. But it's still pissing down with rain and I'd honestly rather die than get completely soaked and then have to have wet socks all afternoon while my coat drips onto the carpet from the back of my chair.

When my phone rings I go out into the corridor to answer it. I usually hate the corridors because they do tend to be full of kids when you work in a school. It gets kind of depressing to see them wandering around, arms linked, chatting away just like I did not even that long ago. Or, it *feels* like it wasn't that long ago, anyway. I'm sure they look at me and think I'm ancient. But I even used to wear the same uniform. And every single one of those kids probably thinks they'll do something amazing with their lives. And some of them might, to be fair. But some of them might also end up working in the office and trying to avoid answering the group line every time it rings.

Anyway, the corridor is quiet today because the school is a bunch of separate buildings. The kids will be hiding out in the computer block, or the library, or the canteen, and nobody in their right mind would run all the way over to the office in a downpour. Works for me.

'I've got the best idea ever,' Sophie says when I answer the phone. I haven't even had a chance to say hello.

'Sorry?'

'I know how to solve the whole flatmate thing.'

'Really? How?' I will happily take suggestions at this juncture.

'Just don't bother getting one.'

'I don't think that's reall—'

'Hear me out. If you had a job that paid more, would you still need to get one?'

'I mean, I guess not? But it's not like there's loads of—'

'And if that job was also *amazing*, that would help too, right?'

'Yeah? But, again—'

'Because we're hiring at CLC. I could recommend you. You'd probably have a better shot and I'd get a little bonus if they hired you too. Not that it's about that.'

The thing about Sophie's company is that . . . well, it's insane. I don't even know all of the ins and outs, but they basically create libraries for fancy hotels in glamorous places. If it sounds mad, it's because it is. Sometimes it blows my mind that there's even a company doing something like that here in Crostdam. Like, it's so jarringly glamorous considering where we are. That there's a company like that operating out of a grey concrete building on the industrial estate in between Screwfix and a bathroom warehouse always tickles me. But what would it be like if I actually got to work there? Am I even remotely qualified to . . .

'Are you still there?' Sophie interrupts my train of thought.

'Yeah.' I clear my throat. 'Sorry, I just . . . I don't know.'

'Wouldn't you want to do it?'

'No, yeah, I would.' I answer so fast it even surprises me. 'I just . . . Would they want me? Like, would I even be qualified?'

'You have an English degree. They want someone with admin experience, good organisational skills. You have those. You'd be an account manager, so just helping people out with things. You could totally do it. Plus, you'll come with the Sophie Lawler guarantee.'

I nod, which Sophie definitely can't see. My brain whirrs, cycling through all of the things that could go wrong. And maybe it's just the living nightmare that is trying to find a flatmate, but there don't seem to be *that* many things. They could say no, which would mean I'd wasted my time doing the application. That's all I can think of. And I could use all of that time flatmate hunting instead and still end up with someone like Nick in my house again, so . . .

'Would I need to know about, like, travel and stuff?'

'You do know about travel and stuff.'

'Yeah, I mean, I *know* about it. But . . . well, I never got to go, did I?'

I swallow. I remind myself that it's fine. It's not Fiona's fault. She had an opportunity she couldn't pass up. I would have done the same if I was her and I had the same chance, which I'm not, and I didn't, and there's just no point in making a whole drama out of it, right?

'Nat? You still there?'

'Yes. Sorry.'

'Look. You know your shit, even if you never put it into prac-tice. If you're passionate, that'll be enough. And I've met you. I know you are. This is a great idea, right? Shall I send over the details?'

I try to keep my voice casual. I don't want her to get her hopes up. Or me to get mine up, for that matter. 'Yeah, I'll have a look through.'

I spend the afternoon writing an email to myself with bullet points of things that I need to say when I definitely do my application. Because there's no doubt that I'm going to do it. Sophie was as good as her word and sent the details. And it sounds Ah-Mazing. I update my CV, which I've barely even *looked* at for like, five years. I'm surprised to find that I actually sound quite good now.

On the rare occasion that this kind of thing has come up in the past (by which I mean a job I would be interested in. This *specific* kind of job has *never* come up before and I imagine it never will again), I've always managed to talk myself out of it after a couple of hours. I become convinced that the one area where I lack experience will overwhelm the ten areas where I have it, and I can't shake the feeling that time spent putting together an application will be time wasted. Now, though? The more time I spend thinking about it, the more I feel myself getting excited. And having Sophie in my corner will surely be a plus point too. And it won't matter that I'm going to live alone forever and die an old maid, because that just means I'm more suited to flying around the world at the drop of a hat in the meantime.

Fiona

The first Monday back to work after the parental housewarming dinner is miserable. Literally. It pisses down with rain so much that I don't even bother wearing my uniform on the way into the shop because it doesn't stand a chance. Matt did offer me a lift, but it would have made him late for work, and his mother's comments about me are still ringing in my ears – I don't want to give her more ammunition. By the time I get home I've been soaked to the skin twice.

'Hey.' I force my face into a smile when I see Matt in the living room. He's sitting with his feet up on the coffee table, frowning at his laptop. At least nobody expects me to be able to serve ice cream at home, I suppose. I've learned quickly that people often expect him to 'just take a quick look' at a financial statement or a report after hours.

'Hey,' he says, without looking up. I sit down next to him and he *still* doesn't look up straight away.

'So, someone tried to get *all* the flavours put on one cone today,' I begin, determined to share this stuff. People talk about their days when they live together, right?

'Sorry. Sorry.' He finally looks up at me. 'I just have to do this *one* thing. Sorry. Jamie just asked if I could quickly. And then I will be right back with you, and we can talk about ice cream.' He flashes me a grin and *oooh* I'm immediately annoyed. What, so my job isn't as valid as his? A tiny voice in my brain suggests that maybe I shouldn't blow this out of proportion, but my socks are wet, and my back hurts because I think I pulled something getting changed in the tiny staff toilet. So, unfortunately, that tiny voice does not get the consideration it probably deserves.

'Talk about *ice cream*?' I demand.

He looks up again, startled by my tone.

'Yeah? If you want to. Look, sorry, I literally just have to send out one report that someone forgot to do and then I am right back in the room with you.'

I sit and stew while he types whatever he's typing. Sure, he can type stuff out, but does *he* get complimented on how great he is at the lettering on the specials board? No, he does not. God, I'm a child.

'Is it safe to "talk about ice cream" now?' I ask as he closes the computer. I am obviously being sarcastic.

'Of course.' He grins. He does not seem to realise that I'm being sarcastic.

'Well, I don't even want to now. It doesn't even matter.'

'Suit yourself.' He shrugs, his ears turning pink.

He unmutes the TV and laughter fills the room. He stares at the screen far too intently, and I do too. I can't speak for him, but I just . . . I don't want to have our first proper argument as a live-in couple in the same month as we *became* a live-in couple. What would that say about us? What if it means that we weren't ready for any of this after all? What if it means we're – not that I want to sound like I'm being too pessimistic here – doomed? I would never live it down. The washing machine starts spinning, adding to the noise in the room.

'We should think about dinner,' Matt says. He's right. *We* should. It's so weird having to do every little thing together. 'I could do Bolognese?' he adds, and I know that's him wanting to clear the air, so I give him a grateful smile.

'I can help.'

'No, you stay there. Put your feet up.'

Matt hands me the remote and goes to the kitchen. After a moment I can hear him chopping an onion. I head off to our (still so weird to say 'our') bedroom to change out of the questionable t-shirt. Then I do as I'm told and put my feet up.

My phone buzzes. It's Amy.

AMY: Have you seen this???

She's sent me a link. The laughter on the TV show carries on, the washing machine is still rumbling in the kitchen, and I can

73

hear the extractor fan now too. All completely ordinary things. Mundane, even.

And yet this link is to my actual dream. It's an Instagram post. The image says 'Wanted' in bright yellow text on a pink background.

'Do you love books? Do you love travel? Do you want to help set up bespoke libraries at luxury hotels in far-flung locations around the world? Then we want you at the Creative Library Company! If you're an excellent administrator with a flair for organisation, an interest in adventure, and a love of books then you might be just what we're looking for. Hit the link in our bio and apply today!'

My whole body tenses as I read. I'm frozen to the spot. Like, if I so much as move, that bright pink and yellow square will disappear.

The further I read down the job advert Amy's sent me, the more I become convinced that I'm reading about my future. Except the sounds in the flat are still the same old ones. I kind of expect them to be drowned out by choirs of angels or something.

FIONA: OMG!

AMY: They're only on the industrial estate. Isn't it where Sophie works?? DO ITTTTTT

I read the link again. It's too perfect. I must have missed something crucial, like you have to have a PhD, or it's actually an unpaid internship, or both. But there's nothing. The salary looks . . . well. It really doesn't take a lot to beat an ice cream shop salary, so it's not like it's *hard* to be better.

The weird thing is, I can actually picture myself in this job. I've never had that. When we used to think about careers at school, I always got overwhelmed quickly. It never seemed fair that I had to pick something at the age of sixteen, and that was the thing I'd do for the rest of my life until I was too old to do anything anymore. It just seemed mad to me. How could anyone make such a huge decision? But now – only, what? Eleven years behind schedule – I know what I want to do and it's this. And if that sounds dramatic, then good. Because my heart is pounding dramatically at the thought.

I want to go and show Natalie, but then I remember she doesn't live here anymore. Should I text her? No. She'll be busy. And I don't want to jinx it. And I've already got a new flat recently, isn't it showing off to start talking about a new job as well? I can tell her next time I see her, when I'll probably already have done the application. Because I'm ready to do the application *now*. I get up and go to the kitchen.

Whatever Matt's doing, it smells amazing. He stirs a pan and I creep up behind him, wrapping my arms around his waist. He jumps and then turns around and laughs.

'Sorry. Not used to it yet.'

He turns the flame down on the hob and folds me into a hug, and for once in my life I feel a leap of excitement. Because this *isn't* it. This is one thing that's happening in my life, but there's going to be other things too. One day, I'll be getting back from a long-haul trip somewhere exotic and Matt will be cooking, just like this. I'll regale him with stories about my latest trip, and he'll be hanging on to my every word. We'll see other people our age in the street with their buggies and their shopping bags, and they'll comment on my tan and my expensive clothes, and I'll wave away their compliments because I'll hear them all the time.

NATALIE

I send my application to Sophie to look at, and she gives me loads of feedback. I do it again, and she does it again. We get there between us. I squeeze my eyes shut as I hit 'send'.

FIONA

'Have you thought any more about that job?' Amy asks while the shop's still quiet. I'm wiping out the freezer, taking out two tubs at a time and cleaning underneath. She's *supposed* to be cleaning the tables. But I guess we're doing career counselling now instead.

I shrug. 'I don't know.'

And I really don't, either. I've always thought that imposter syndrome is just something that talented people made up so they could get more attention, but maybe it's real after all. I was so excited when I first read the job ad, but then I saw all of the other excited people commenting on it, and I had a look at the state of my CV, and the voice in my head started up as well. By the time Matt and I went to bed, my mood had dipped, possibly lower than it was when I got home and started picking fights with him. I was a real treat to be around. Amy slaps her cloth down on the table and, a couple of seconds later, looms over me as I kneel next to the freezer.

'Why?' she demands, arms crossed.

I rearrange my face to look casual, like this isn't something I even care about. 'I just . . . It'll be loads of work to do the application, and I won't even get it, anyway. I did a cost/benefit analysis. It's not worth it.'

'Why won't you get it? You just said "cost/benefit analysis" and sounded legit. You might. You won't know if you don't try.'

I groan. 'But if I do try, and I don't get it, then I'll know I wasted all that time.'

'Why don't you talk to Sophie about it? I bet she'd help you.'

I scoff. 'I want as few people as possible to know that I failed when I fail, thank you. If I even take it that far.'

Amy huffs and stomps off. I stick my head back into the freezer to wipe out a hard-to-reach corner. And then I nearly jump out of my skin when she hammers on the cabinet.

'Hey!' I yell. She looks at me through the glass. I feel like a turtle in an aquarium, so I back out and stand up.

'Why do you think you'll fail? You like books, you know *loads* about travel, you've probably been to half the countries they operate in and have ten restaurant recommendations for every one!'

'I know, I just—'

'Just what?'

'None of that's on the job description, is it? They want Excel skills, experience.'

'Yeah, but you have all of the *desired* stuff. They *desire* what you have. *Desire.*'

I throw my cloth at her and laugh. 'Stop saying "desire". I'll think about it.'

'You will bloody well *do* it, or I'll start saying "desire" again.' She prepares herself to do it but a family walks in just before she can, so she scuttles back to our side of the counter instead.

I still don't think she's right. But I do stop in to the library at lunch to use the computer. And I go back every day that week. I chip away at my application, telling myself that if it's still shit by the closing day, I don't actually have to send it. I could probably do it more quickly from home but I sort of don't want Matt to know. He'll ask if I've heard anything, and when I do inevitably hear that they aren't interested, he'll be so nice, and so sorry for me, and it's really not what I want.

On Friday, five minutes before I need to be back at the shop (the shop is definitely more than five minutes away so I've written some stuff about timekeeping which is not strictly true), I hit 'send' because, well, I've written the thing now. I might as well.

CHAPTER SEVEN

NATALIE

I'm already sitting at the table at Reggie's when Fiona arrives for our customary Sunday Morning Brunch. This was customary before she moved out as well, by the way. We did it every week for almost eighteen months. Sunday Morning Brunch is sacrosanct. The world could fall into ruin, and Sunday Morning Brunch would still happen somehow. Apart from the past couple of weeks while The Split took place and Fiona got used to her new life. But there really does have to be a life-changing event afoot to get it cancelled. And we are back in business now.

It's not super-busy in here today, but there are a few people around, sitting on bright red leather seats and tucking into stacks of all-day pancakes. My stomach rumbles. I lift up my phone to check the clock. I don't begrudge her being late. She has a new route, it would throw anybody off. And the eggs Benedict I've been eyeing up will taste twice as good when I'm twice as hungry.

'Oh my god, I'm so sorry,' Fiona says when she finally arrives. She looks flustered, wild-eyed, wilder-haired. She scrapes her chair on the floor as she pulls it back and drops into it gratefully. A waiter comes over to fill her water glass.

'It's fine.' I take a sip of my coffee as she gets her breath back. Her face is red, a sheen of sweat on her forehead.

'I thought I'd walk through the park because it's a nice day, but . . .' She stops, puffing out her cheeks. 'Bad idea.'

'Honestly, it's fine.' I smile. My phone pings on the table. I point at it. 'Sorry, do you mind if . . . ?'

Fiona waves a hand and picks up her glass again. I look at the message. For a second this week I thought I might actually have managed to find someone to live with. Connie seemed cool, she was gainfully employed, appeared to have good personal hygiene, and actually sounded quite keen (?) to watch my *Friends* box set together with a takeaway sometimes. But now:

CONNIE (ROOMIE???): Hey Natalie. Really sorry, but something's come up and I won't be taking the room after all. You seem great, though. I'm sure you'll find someone soon. Best of luck with it!

My heart sinks and, for a moment, all I can hear is a high-pitched sound in my ears. I can see other people chattering in the restaurant, I just can't hear what they're saying. It's like I'm in a bubble. All of the relief I was starting to let myself feel. The hope. The tentative excitement. Gone, just like that.

FIONA

A shadow crosses Natalie's face as she reads whatever just came through on her phone.

I've *just* about got my breath back after my epic trek here. It didn't even need to be epic. I can't believe how long it took. One wrong turn in the park and I came out of the wrong exit. My phone suddenly couldn't find it on a map because why *would* it when I actually needed it? And I was convinced that Natalie was

79

going to be fuming with me. First I uproot both of our lives, and then I nearly miss our most sacred tradition the first week back. Unacceptable. She seems miraculously fine, though. Or she did. Until whatever just came through on her phone.

'What's up?' I ask as she puts it face down on the table again.

'Nothing.' She gives me a tight smile and I don't believe her. I narrow my eyes. 'It's *fine*,' she insists. I don't stop glaring at her, so she waves a hand and adds, 'Flatmate hunting. Count yourself lucky that you've got Matt.'

'You haven't found anyone yet, then?' I ask. I'm not sure how interested I'm allowed to be. Like, I *am* interested in who's going to replace me. I'll probably run into them a lot, they need to be cool. I also desperately want Natalie to have everything sorted, purely because I want my friend to never ever be stressed. But I can't gauge how much I'm allowed to ask considering I'm the person who put her in this situation in the first place. Will I sound sympathetic? Or will I sound like I'm rubbing it in?

'Not yet.' She grimaces. 'Thought I had there for a second, but . . .' She lifts her phone.

'Oh. Shit. Look, if you need help with the rent or anything . . .'

She laughs and I frown. 'Sorry. That's really nice. I'd never ask you to do that, though.'

'But I'm just saying, you *could*.'

'No, I couldn't. I never would.'

NATALIE

The waiter comes over, and I'm grateful to him for breaking up the awkward moment. Fiona orders a giant stack of pancakes, and I get my eggs Benedict with a side of sausage. We each order a coffee too – her first one, my second. Oat milk for her, cow for me.

'I thought you might have gone all healthy now you live with Matt. Like, protein powder and stuff.'

'Are you kidding? Even more reason that this is necessary. I'd end up with a maple syrup deficiency if I was around him all the time.' She laughs and takes a sip of her water. The waiter brings our coffees over and she takes a sip of that too.

'So, actually' – she clears her throat – 'I did want to tell you something.'

Is her face going red? She looks down at the table, picks the skin at her cuticles. 'You're not pregnant, are you? You've lived with a man for three w—'

'No! Christ, no. Imagine. No. I've . . . Well, I've applied for a new job.' She looks sheepish, which is insane because this is excellent.

I can't help grinning. 'That's amazing, good for you.'

'Thank you.' She looks genuinely pleased at the praise. Her cheeks go a bit pinker. 'Yeah, I just figured, even if I don't get it, because I probably won't get it, it's worth a try, you know? I don't know what they'd see in someone who dishes out ice cream for a living, but you have to have a go, don't you?'

'Totally! Honestly. This is now officially a celebration brunch.' I hold up my coffee cup and she clinks hers against it. My own job news can wait. I'm not in the business of overshadowing my friends. 'What's the job?'

'Oh my god, it sounds *mad*. It's for this company that's apparently down on the industrial estate that creates, like, bespoke libraries for super-posh hotels all over the world. Loads of travel, loads of— What?'

I don't notice that my face has fallen until she stops, but it makes sense because my stomach also seems to have dropped into my legs and I feel sick.

'You don't think it's a bad idea, do you?' Her face falls. I hate that her face has fallen. I try to rearrange my face. Of *course* it's not a bad idea. It makes perfect sense, I can't believe I didn't see it before. 'I just thought . . . because, you know, I love books, and I've travelled loads, it just felt like a really great fit, don't you think? You *don't* think, do you? Have I made an arse of myself?'

FIONA

In some way I haven't predicted, I've definitely made an arse of myself. I can't see how, though? Like, I thought it all through. I imagined myself *having* the job. It felt right. It made so much sense.

'No.' Natalie clears her throat.

'Then what?'

'No, it's really nothing. It's fine. It's just . . . I applied for that too. Sophie told me about it. She helped me with the application.'

I fight to keep my face looking simply interested instead of . . . well, like my very fragile hopes have been shattered. Because that is melodramatic. I *knew* I wasn't going to get it. Who was ever going to want someone with an unused drama degree and zero ambition to work for them anyway? This is just that coming true in an unexpected way.

'Oh, right. Of course she did.' I keep my voice determinedly neutral. Which it would be anyway, obviously. Because I do feel neutral. So neutral.

'Which,' Natalie continues, 'I mean, her working there could be good for you too. She can be your ally just as much as she can be mine. If she refers people and they get in she gets a bonus, so I'm sure it'd work for her. She probably just didn't realise you'd be interested.'

'Sure.' I nod, but I don't really believe it and I think Natalie can tell. We both know I'm not going to ask for help.

'I really think she just told me because she knew I could do with the money. But I don't know, I could withdraw my application if it's a problem. In fact, no. No "could" about it. I'll do that. I just – with the rent and everything. But—'

I hold up a hand to stop her talking. She chews her lip as she waits for my response.

'If you get it, can you take me with you to one of the hotels one day?' I ask, not really sure what else to say. That might be nearly as good, right? Not a *huge* break from the norm, but a little one, at least.

'Oh my god, and if you get it, same question.' She looks relieved. 'Listen, I don't think this needs to be weird if you don't? It's such a ridiculous job, it's like applying to be on *The X Factor* or something. Right? What are the chances that either of us will get it, really?'

'True.'

She picks at her thumbnail for a second, while I dig around in the foam of my coffee with my teaspoon.

'It's fine,' I say eventually, shaking my head. 'It'll be fine.'

'It's *so* fine,' she agrees, staring off to one side as she nods.

CHAPTER EIGHT

NATALIE

I'm still thinking about that awkward brunch on Monday morning. Not that you would necessarily even call it *awkward*, it was just . . . No. It was awkward. Because I know I have a better shot than her, is the thing. I have Sophie on my side, and they want an administrator. And now, instead of being excited that I'm probably going to get this job, I'm worried that when I do Fiona will get hurt. I just wanted it to be a fun 'Yay! Exciting! Girl power! Business Bitches!' brunch moment and it turned into a minefield. I shiver as I think about it. Fiona obviously didn't want to seem like she was trying to take something from me, I *desperately* didn't want to seem like I was taking something from her, and the whole meal from that point on was like treading on eggshells. I don't know. It's so difficult. Because also, if I'd known, would I have done anything different? We can't live our entire lives in deference to each other, can we? But if we *were* doing that, it's surely my turn for a bit of deference from her. And it's not a competition, but she *is* the one who made the first move and forced us into more separate lives which, by the way, I cannot afford, and I just . . . It's just really difficult.

My phone buzzes against my leg when it's getting close to lunchtime. My heart jumps into my throat and I force myself to exhale slowly. I've been doing this thing lately where I assume every notification is somebody getting in touch about the room, and it almost always leads to disappointment. It's probably Instagram, I tell myself. Or my horoscope. Or one of the software updates I keep putting off because I truly cannot be arsed.

When I've wrestled my hopes back to a normal level I glance down at it and see the little email icon.

> FROM: Mara Hamilton
> TO: Natalie Starr
>
> Dear Ms Starr,
>
> Thank you very much for your recent application for the role of Library Creation Co-ordinator. We were very impressed by it and would like to invite you to an interview on Thursday 17th at 3:00pm. Please could you let me know if this time works for you?
>
> Kind regards,
>
> Mara Hamilton

FIONA

I lean against the dumpster at the back of the shop for a surreptitious look at my phone. Sometimes, if a day is feeling especially long, it's the only treat I can give myself. Just a *quick* little something on TikTok and then I'll go back inside where a small child is currently having a screaming tantrum because he wasn't allowed banoffee ice cream because he's deathly allergic to bananas.

I watch a video of someone's puppy being cute. Maybe Matt and I should get a puppy? Maybe if I get this job that I definitely will not get, but if I *did*, then we could get a puppy. I think we'd make a cute little family with a puppy.

I can still hear the kid screaming, but it's chilly out here in just a stripy blouse. One more minute and I'm going in. I check my email quickly. I'm still on the mailing lists for all of the travel companies we used a few years ago, and I still like to see what they have on offer. It's just to remember that other places exist. I feel a raindrop on my bare arm.

It's not all marketing emails in my inbox, though:

FROM: Mara Hamilton
TO: Fiona Maitliss

Dear Ms Maitliss,

Thank you very much for your recent application for the role of Library Creation Co-ordinator. We were very impressed by it and would like to invite you to an interview on Thursday 17th at 3:45pm. Please could you let me know if this time works for you?

Kind regards,

Mara Hamilton

NATALIE

I'm hiding in the toilets, looking at my phone. I can't decide whether I should say anything to Fiona, or whether I'll just make it weird again, or if she'll be upset if she *hasn't* heard anything. It's so hard to know how to behave. We were not ready for something like this to come in between us. I've already claimed that I have a dentist appointment on Thursday and confirmed that I'll be at the interview. *That* stuff is fine. It's all the rest that's difficult, the balance between being excited and not wanting to hurt Fiona's feelings.

As I think about her, her name flashes up on my phone. It's like I've summoned her.

'Hello?' I answer her call in a whisper, aware that a cubicle with a six-inch gap at the bottom and top of the door isn't exactly soundproof.

'Hey. Did you hear anything?' she asks in an equally low voice. She's next to the bins, I can tell. That was the first place she showed me when I worked there in the summer holidays as a teenager and she was tasked with giving me 'the tour'.

'This is the only place you can get any peace and quiet,' she told me at the time.

Now I can hear a breeze whistling past her. I also think I can just make out the sound of distant screaming in the background. I hope for Fiona's sake that it's not another pukey child. God, she needs this job. I feel a stab in my chest.

'Did you . . . hear something?'

'Yeah! I' – she accidently shouts, then lowers her voice again – 'they want me to come in for an interview.'

'That's amazing!'

'Yeah, it's really . . . No, do you know what? It's terrifying. I haven't had an interview in . . . well, not since before we went away.

Since then it's been "Can you pick bananas? Great." "Can you clean a toilet cash in hand? Fab." And then, like, "Can you remember how to scoop ice cream? Yeah? Here you go, then, crack on." I don't know how to do proper questions.'

'Come to ours – I mean, mine – on Wednesday night. We can prepare together.'

'You got one too.' Her voice sounds a tiny bit less excited than it did a moment ago. But I'm not in a position to judge, am I?

'I did, but it's fine' – it all comes out in a rush – 'like I said, come to ours – mine – on Wednesday, we can prep together.'

'O-OK.'

There's silence down the phone for a second. I can hear a car going past and, once that's gone, I can still make out the sounds of a child screaming.

'Sounds like it's all kicking off over there,' I say. So lame, but anything to fill the silence.

'Yeah, it's . . . Right. Well, I'll see you on Wednesday, then! Let me know if you want me to bring anything.'

'Just yourself.'

'Done.'

FIONA

'How was your day?' Matt's face appears around the living room door when I get home. I smell like ice-cream sick, and I've changed out of my usual shirt and into one of the old, branded t-shirts we usually give the summer staff. That should really be his answer. But this is the first true disaster I've had since we started living together. Quite a good run, actually. I was so busy watching Banana Allergy Boy like a hawk, and trying to arrange time off on Thursday, that

I didn't clock the kid who came in looking green around the gills. Rookie mistake.

I drop a carrier bag – tied at the top and containing my normal blouse – onto the floor. When Natalie occasionally used to see me come through the door in a different top to the one I'd been wearing when I left, she just knew to get the wine out of the fridge and not ask any questions. Matt hasn't had a chance to learn this yet. He comes to the door and kisses me, which is lovely in its own way, but also not part of the drill.

He's still holding on to me when I bend down and pick up the plastic bag.

'Sorry, I just really need to . . .' I wave it and he must catch a whiff because a look of revulsion crosses his face, as well it should. He releases me.

'God, yeah.'

I carry the bag into the kitchen at arm's length, then empty it into the washing machine without looking at it or breathing through my nose. Do I dare put other things in there? I suppose that's the good thing to do. I pull the loaner t-shirt off and sling that in because it's tainted by the memory of today's incident.

I dash down the hallway to our bedroom and tip the washing basket upside down on the carpet. There's not much in here. I yank open Matt's drawer. He has a (I think) very odd little habit of putting t-shirts he's worn once in there, laying them flat on top of the neatly folded, unworn clothes, so that he can wear them again. Men are weirdos. There are a couple of tops in there so I grab them because they might as well go in and, when I do, something falls to the floor.

It's a little box. I pause. I stare at it just lying there on the threadbare grey carpet, like if I take my eyes off it, it might scuttle away as if it were a cockroach. But, well, it's a little box. And I have *seen* TV, I know what little boxes generally mean.

I stoop to pick it up, and I open it. Inside, nestled into some velvet, is a gold band with a little row of diamonds, some scrollwork along the sides. I stand in my bra, all thoughts of grabbing another top forgotten, and widen my eyes. I can hear ringing in my ears. Not wedding bells, or anything insane like that, because that would be *mad*. Just regular, garden variety panic ringing.

'Are you OK?' Matt calls.

'Yeah,' I shout back. It comes out hoarse the first time and I have to repeat myself. I stand up, snap the box shut, and shove it back into his drawer. I lay the worn t-shirts back over the top of everything. Not worth it. I don't want him to know that I know.

I bustle back through to the kitchen with the few items of clothing I managed to scare up and shove them into the machine. I scrabble around in the cupboard under the sink, looking for the detergent. Where is it? Why can't anything be in a normal place, just for once?

'You sure you're OK?' Matt is suddenly framed in the doorway, frowning.

'Yes! Why wouldn't I be?'

'Well, you're crawling around on your hands and knees, in your bra, muttering to yourself, so . . .'

'I didn't realise I was muttering.' I stand up, put my hands on my hips and stretch out my back. 'Where's the washing stuff?'

'I put it in the cupboard in the hall, it was taking up too much space.'

'Why would you put it somewhere *not* next to the washing machine, though? That's insane. You can't just make decisions like that.' I storm past him, grab the detergent, pour it into the machine.

I'm about to storm past him again to put the bottle back when he catches my arm and forces me to look at him. 'You're sure everything's OK.'

I sigh. 'Yes. Why?'

'Well, like I said, you just seem . . .' He waves a hand in front of the bra-wearing lunatic having a tantrum over laundry detergent and, I mean, he kind of has a point. I let him pull me into a hug. My arms hang limply by my sides for a moment, but then I rest them on his shoulders. I don't know how to move anymore, how to act with him. I don't . . . I guess I just need a minute to adjust to this new information. I don't think that's too much to ask. The person currently rubbing my back has a *diamond* in the drawer with his t-shirts and I just . . . It's a lot.

'I should go and have a shower,' I say eventually.

I leave early for work the next morning. I just . . . I have to. I need some time to think, and I don't . . . I just have to leave early.

'Why?' Matt groans when I get up just after six a.m. and start getting dressed. He opens one eye and looks at me.

'Go back to sleep, it's fine. We have a . . . delivery.'

I pull on my jacket, grab my bag, and am out the door a full two hours earlier than I normally am. But I didn't sleep. And, compared to lying awake all night freaking out about something I'm not supposed to know about that I am in no way ready for, being able to move is a relief.

My mind races as I follow the route Natalie showed me. The high street is dead quiet at this time, just a couple of lorries on their way through town. But, otherwise, I can just hear birds squabbling in the hedges and my own steps. When I reach the top of the field that looks over Crostdam, I stop. I don't . . . I can't . . .

Look, I know I was keen to be a grown-up, to settle down with Matt, to prove that we weren't less than everybody else because we disappeared for a couple of years. I wanted us to catch up with everybody else, overtake them if we could. But, I mean, there are *limits* surely? We're getting *married* now? I stare out over the whole of Crostdam and think about how this might end up being my home forever. And, like, academically I knew that, but it hasn't really hit me until now and I'm just not *ready* for something like that. I love Matt. So much. I think we're great together. I want to be with him forever. But I'm not ready to be a wife. I'm not ready to be a mother. And that's not far behind, is it? I'm not ready to have people making plans for me that they don't even tell me about first. I know we've taken some steps recently but that is a fucking big step not to discuss with someone first. And I *know* I bought up the M-word first, but come on. That was just banter, right? I also talked about marrying a cute old man from a video on Twitter and a pot of really nice hummus this month alone. You don't see *them* going out and acquiring rings, do you?

I shake my head. I thought maybe I'd find an answer up here, figure out a way that everything would be OK. But I don't know if there is one and I have to get to work.

CHAPTER NINE

Natalie

I straighten up some cut figs on the charcuterie board. I don't even know how you eat figs, but that's not the point. The point is, they're all over Instagram, and now they're all over the food I'm preparing, because I want Fiona to know that all of this is definitely fine.

Fiona

It's *so weird* to now be standing on the wrong side of what used to be my own front door. I clutch the neck of a bottle of pinot grigio in one hand and rap on the door. I wipe my feet on the doormat while I wait for someone to answer.

'What are you knocking for?' Natalie demands as she pulls it open. 'I left it on the latch for you.'

'I just didn't know . . .' I hitch my bag further up my shoulder.

'Well, now you do. No knocking. Not for you.'

I hold out the wine bottle. She frowns at it. 'And no more bringing gifts, it's not right.'

'To be clear, this isn't so much a gift as something I would like to open now, please.' Lord knows I need it. I haven't been able to stop thinking about that ring, and I'm no closer to knowing what the hell I'm supposed to do. So until I come up with a better idea I'm just going to drown the memory of even seeing it.

'OK. Then I forgive you.' She takes the bottle from me and bustles away from the door. 'But definitely don't start knocking, and don't start acting like a guest,' she calls back from the kitchen.

'Got it. You know, your new flatmate might not feel the same way about any of that.' I remove my shoes, hang my bag on the hook I always used to favour.

'We'll cross the flatmate bridge when we come to it. And we might never come to it.' Natalie looks genuinely worried for a split second, but she has her face back under control a moment later, and I'm not even sure I saw anything. She puts two glasses of wine down on the coffee table.

'No luck yet, then?' I don't want to rub it in, but what else are we supposed to talk about? Me? At this moment? I think not.

'Come and see the charcuterie board I've put together, it's absolutely mad. I couldn't fit anything else on if I tried. I figured that's a good dinner, though, right? So, we can just pick as we go, we don't have to stop. Go and sit down, I'll bring it over.'

NATALIE

'So, tell me about yourself.' Fiona sits on the sofa on the other side of the coffee table, trying her best to look stern. I fidget in my folding chair.

'Well, my name is Natalie, I live locally, and I currently work at St James' School, where I provide administrative support to a busy senior management team. I'm a conscientious worker and a self-starter with excellent . . . excellent . . . Shit, what was it?'

'Excellent organisational skills,' Fiona prompts, reading off a sheet.

'Yes.' I wave a finger in the air. 'Excellent organisational skills and a positive attitude. I'm a strong team player and equally good at working independently. I've worked my way up from my original role as receptionist, which is an achievement I'm very proud of, but I think now is the time to look for a new challenge, and working for the Creative Library Company really appeals to me. I love reading, I've always wanted the opportunity to travel, and I think the combination of my experience and my enthusiasm means I can bring a lot to the table.'

It's such bullshit really, but I do expect something for remembering it all. I couldn't say what. Applause? Praise? An Oscar for Best Actress? But Fiona just stares down at the piece of paper in her hand and frowns.

'What's up? Did I get something wrong?'

'No. Nothing.' She shakes her head. 'Now do me.'

We walk clockwise around the table so that I end up on the sofa and she ends up in the much-less-comfortable interviewee seat. I take a moment to get into character.

'So, Fiona, tell me about yourself.'

'Um . . .' Fiona begins, and I widen my eyes at her. We talked about this. Not that I'm the world expert on interviews, but she doesn't sound confident when she starts things with 'um'. 'I mean, not "um". Just, nothing? I didn't say anything. Ignore that bit.' She puffs out her cheeks. 'Hi. My name's Fiona. I'm an avid reader and an experienced traveller. My partner and I spent a couple of years travelling a while back. I came home eighteen months ago. I've seen most of Europe, a lot of Asia, and Australia. Oh, and South America. And some bits of Africa too. There's nothing like it. I obviously didn't see the world from luxury hotels' – she pauses for a laugh and I oblige, even though I've heard that joke three times already this evening – 'but I discovered that I love it more than anything, and the idea of having a role that might incorporate it is really exciting. Even just working with people in other parts of the world remotely would be so inspiring. And I think I could put together an excellent library if I was given the chance.'

I look down at the piece of paper and back up at her. She's eyeing me, waiting for the verdict.

'Perfect.'

Her whole body seems to relax. I lean over the coffee table to hand her the paper. 'Honestly. Now you just sleep with it under your pillow so that it soaks into your brain, and you're golden.'

'That seems scientific.'

'You know me, all science all the time. Hey, what does Matt think about this, by the way? Is he excited for you? You'd be a proper little power couple if you got it.'

FIONA

'Oh. Yeah. He's . . .' I pause. I didn't bother telling him about the application, because why would you tell someone about something that's ninety-nine per cent guaranteed not to come to anything? And I *was* going to tell him about the interview, but then there were rings, and then I was panicking, and then I spent hours trying to figure out how to broach *that* subject with him, but then I realised I couldn't. But if he's not telling me about that, then why would I tell him about this? And I also don't want to *ruin* his plans, even though I'm not ready for a single thing he's apparently planning, and, all in all, it just seemed better if maybe I didn't say anything and we just sat in silence and watched a lot of *Taskmaster*.

'Are you OK?' Natalie peers at me.

'Yes! Sorry. Yes. And yes, Matt thinks it's great. Just, don't mention it if you see him? I, um, don't want to get his hopes up or anything.'

'Sure.' Natalie frowns, but if she has follow-up questions (and who could blame her?) she doesn't ask them. 'So, OK, test me on something else now. Just something random.'

We get up. She walks around to the interviewee seat, and I take her place on the sofa again. I pick up the book of job interview questions Natalie found somewhere, flick the pages, and open it randomly. 'Describe a time when you showed good teamwork skills.'

Natalie's phone beeps at that moment and she holds up a finger. 'Sorry, can I just . . . ?'

She reads the message, looks around the room, and then looks at me.

'It's a guy who says he wants to come for a viewing.'

'Well, that's good, isn't it?'

She frowns. 'I guess. I don't know. Sometimes I just wonder. Is it a really dumb thing to advertise the fact that I'm a woman who lives alone to strangers on the internet? What if he's, like, a serial killer or something?'

'Can you ask him?'

'He wouldn't tell me if he was, would he? And if he's *not*, why would you want to live with someone who thought you could be?'

'No, true.' I think for a moment. It's just a relief to have something to think about that isn't a terrifying interview or terrifying life moves. And to be able to avoid Matt without *looking* like I'm avoiding Matt, of course. And maybe that's it. 'I know! I'll be here as well. Like backup. If he tries anything.'

It would be my honour to defend my friend in her hour of need. More importantly, it would be great to spend the bulk of another evening here instead of spending it staring at Matt from the other end of the sofa, wondering how he could be ready to make such a big decision so much faster than me.

'Are you sure you wouldn't mind?' Natalie asks.

'Not at all.'

'OK. Maybe we'll do that, then.'

She taps out a message on her phone and then launches into a tale of some parents' evening she organised where she had to cover for someone or something? I'm not even really paying attention, just nodding on autopilot as she speaks. What would *I* say? I've been covering Amy's shifts this week because she's on holiday? I've stepped in when customers have been fuming that we ran out of their favourite flavour after they queued for ages? I've been nice and haven't said anything to my boyfriend even when I found out he was planning something completely insane? I feel like that's not the kind of teamwork anybody actually cares about. They want to hear about clean, corporate teamwork. The kind with spreadsheets and emails.

'You sure you're OK?' Natalie stops my train of thought.

'Yeah. Why?'

'Well, you're still nodding and I already stopped talking.'

'Oh. Sorry.'

'No, it's good, I can only hope they're that enthusiastic.'

NATALIE

I'm sitting on a hard, blue armchair by the reception desk when the door to the office opens. I jump and straighten my spine, pull my shoulders back, and plaster a smile across my face. But it's Sophie. She has her brown hair up in a bun, which I don't think I've ever seen before. She's wearing the whitest trainers ever, and has a blouse tucked into her black skinny jeans. God, I want to work here. She looks so cool. I could look that cool.

'Hey,' she says, glancing at the receptionist before looking back at me. 'I just wanted to come and wish you good luck.'

'Thanks.' I smile, trying not to let the nerves show.

'You're nervous, huh?' she says, so . . . not my best effort.

I shrug. 'Maybe a bit.'

'Honestly, you'll be fine. It's my colleague, Jenny, who's interviewing you. She's . . . Well, she's a bit of an oddball. Keeps herself to herself mostly. I don't know much about her, but she's never had anyone working for her before so I don't think she'll be a mean interviewer. And then Mara from HR will take notes.'

'Oh yeah, she emailed me about the time.'

'Yeah, her. Honestly, you'll be so fine. I don't think they'll try to catch you out or anything. And you'll be in the meeting room so you'll see me when they take you through too. I'll send you good vibes through the window.'

'Thanks.'

Sophie pulls me into a bear hug and I do find myself relaxing a tiny bit.

'Look, I should go. I don't want them to think I'm helping you.'

Sophie heads back into the office. I actually do feel a bit calmer now. I can breathe, anyway, which makes a lovely change to the past ten minutes of getting more and more light-headed. I am going to do my best, and Fiona is going to do her best, and what happens happens, and that's all there is to it.

'Natalie Starr?' someone calls from the door. I smile and stand up.

'Hi, lovely to meet you, I'm Jenny.' She holds out her hand and I shake it when I reach her.

I follow Jenny through an office space towards a little meeting room at the back. I feel a quick lurch in my stomach as I realise that the people in here do actually appear to be working. That will definitely take some getting used to if I end up with the job. It'll be worth it, though.

Another woman with a blond ponytail is waiting in the meeting room.

'Hi, I'm Mara.' She smiles.

'Hi.' I shake her hand too, trying hard to say everything I need to in my handshake, like the online articles say you should.

'So, Natalie,' Jenny says as she sits down, 'tell us about yourself.'

When I say I remember my 'tell me about yourself' speech word for word, I really do mean that I remember it word. For. Word. It's an astonishing performance. And the realisation that I'm *giving* an astonishing performance makes me feel more confident as I talk. I have never experienced this before. I had really expected to go to pieces. Am I actually . . . performing well under pressure? Was that . . . not just a lie I told in my application?

'Do you have any questions for us?' Mara asks a while later. I *still* feel confident? This is unheard of.

'Only, I mean, how does the job actually work? With the travel and everything? Like, what's the purpose of that? Is there a lot?' I hope I come across as someone who's just wondering, and not as someone who's desperate to freeload every trip she can possibly manage.

'Well, you'll be in the office probably ninety per cent of the time,' Jenny says. 'You'll be joining my team. Well. *Becoming* my team, really. We work with the hotels to make sure they're happy, solve any issues, put through new orders, that kind of thing. But we just like to pop out and see them in person every once in a while. It really gives it the personal touch, you know. They're five-star hotels, we want to give them five-star service too.'

'Oh, of course.' I nod. I don't add that I'd give them six-star service if it meant I got to go to Bali. I don't even know what six-star service would entail, but I'd do it.

FIONA

I wonder if it's possible to bounce your foot so hard that your shoe comes flying off. I decide it probably is and I should stop. But I'm not really in control of my actions at the moment, so the bouncing starts up again. I'm really, really trying not to be nervous. I mean, this is a fun thing, isn't it? I get to talk to some people who work for a super-cool company, and we will probably chat about travelling and reading, and . . . I can think of worse ways to spend an afternoon.

I keep repeating that to myself. Because I can. I can think of worse ways to spend an afternoon. For instance, all the ways I'll spend my afternoons for the rest of my life if I don't get this job. But no. Not helpful. I'm just here for a chat. A nice, low-pressure chat.

But my thoughts keep creeping back to what my life might look like if I *don't* get this job. I'll sell ice cream and clean up other people's kids' sick until Matt and I get married, apparently a lot sooner than I thought, and we'll have a kid of our own, which I guess will also happen a lot sooner than I thought. And then we'll take that kid to the ice cream shop, and . . . It's just really hard to see how my life won't revolve in some way around children and ice cream forever.

I jump when the door on the other side of the reception desk is pulled open. I catch a glimpse of Natalie smiling and shaking hands with a brunette woman. As she walks out into the foyer the brunette woman looks at me.

'Fiona Maitliss?'

I nod and stand up, brushing down my borrowed trousers to smooth out any wrinkles. Natalie grins and veers towards me, grabbing my hand and squeezing it as she passes.

'Good luck,' she whispers, 'you can do it.'

I give her a weak smile, suddenly jealous of the relief she must feel at it all being over. Still, less than an hour and that'll be me. I tug my borrowed jacket down as I walk over to the door.

'Hi, I'm Jenny,' the brunette woman says as I reach her. She holds out a hand and I shake it.

Natalie's right. I can do it. I follow Jenny through the door and into an office. The radio plays quietly on the windowsill, and people sit at computers. A few of them glance up as I walk through. A printer whirrs away in one corner, a woman who looks like she's about my age collects the sheets it keeps spitting out. It's so weird to think that I could have been that woman if I'd made different decisions before now. Don't get me wrong, I categorically did not *want* to be that woman. But if I didn't want to be her then, do I really want to be her now? But if I don't want to be *her* now, and I don't want to be *me* now, and I don't want to marry Matt now, then . . . what *do* I want? I keep my eyes on Jenny as I walk behind her, try to block out everything else. Now is not the moment for a mid-life crisis. Stop it, stop it, stop it.

A woman with a swishy blond ponytail stands up and smiles as we enter a little meeting room in one corner of the office. She holds out a hand and I shake that too.

'I'm Mara, lovely to meet you. Please, have a seat.'

She points at the chair on the side of the table closest to me, then walks to the other side and sits down next to Jenny. It seems to take ages for the invitation to sit down to reach my brain and then turn into action, so for a second I just stand there and make everybody (myself included) uncomfortable.

'So, Fiona, why don't you tell us about yourself?' Jenny says when I've finally done as I'm told. She doesn't actually look at me, instead casting an eye down the CV Natalie helped me put together. I just stare at her until she looks up. 'Fiona?'

'Right. Sorry.' I clear my throat.

And it's so weird, because usually people clear their throats when they're about to, I don't know, *say something* instead of sitting in complete silence with their mouth hanging open like an idiot. But once *I've* cleared my throat, I simply sit, with my mouth hanging open, like an idiot.

Because I can't remember the opening of that whole speech Natalie got me to prepare. And because I can't remember the start, I can't remember the rest of it, either. All that's going on in my brain is a high-pitched noise, and visions of that ring, and ice cream, and . . .

'Ice cream,' I stammer eventually.

My interviewers look bemused, as well they should. Get it *together*, Fiona. I clear my throat again. Dear god in heaven, please let me be able to follow it with some words this time.

'Sorry,' I say (she speaks!), 'I mean, I work for an ice cream shop at the moment. Scoopz, on the high street, if you know it? I worked there straight out of school to save money to go travelling, then I went off for a couple of years, and I've been back for about eighteen months. I started working there again, just so I had some money coming in, but I'd love to work here. This job sounds amazing.'

Oh my *god* when did I start sounding so pathetic? The blouse I borrowed from Natalie suddenly feels a bit like a greenhouse, and I'm sure I must be going bright red.

'OK,' Mara says, scribbling something in her notebook. 'Thank you.'

I'm not even sure what we talk about for the rest of the interview. As soon as a question is asked, I forget the one before. Unfortunately, there are a few points where I also forget the question I'm still in the middle of answering, which leads to me rambling like a total imbecile. Eventually I seem to float out of my body and I watch myself stammering and stuttering with the same detachment I might feel if I was watching some other total dummy try and fail to stand up to even the tiniest bit of pressure.

'Do you have any questions for us?' Jenny eventually asks. I'm so grateful that this is about to all be over that I forget to say 'I actually do have a couple', as agreed with Natalie, and retrieve my notebook from my bag in a move designed to showcase how organised I am. I just swallow and shake my head.

'Well, in that case, thank you very much for coming in. We'll be in touch. Probably in a couple of days.'

Mara stands up and raises an arm to indicate that I should lead the way out. So, I do. I push the door of the meeting room, but it doesn't open. I push again, still nothing. If I am now trapped with the two people I just absolutely bombed in front of, I will die of embarrassment, I swear to god. I push the door a third time, though, and still nothing.

'Here, let me,' Mara says, stepping in front of me.

She *pulls* the door. It obviously opens because I am completely dumb. I follow her out.

CHAPTER TEN

NATALIE

'How was it?' I ask Fiona when she turns up at the flat later.

'Do you know what? I don't even want to talk about it.'

Sometimes when she says that, she really *does* want to talk about it and she's just being dramatic. This time, though, I feel like she might be telling the truth. It's a shame, because I sort of wanted to compare notes. I want to figure out if I really did as well as I feel like I might have done. I'm just very unfamiliar with the sensation, I do not trust it.

'That good, eh?' I say instead. Maybe the fact that I do want to talk about it and she does not should tell me everything I want to know.

'I just . . .' She shakes her head. 'Anyway, is this guy on his way yet?'

'I guess so.' I shrug. 'He hasn't said he's not. Do you think the place looks OK?'

'Are you kidding? It looks great. I should have left ages ago.'

I don't know what to say to that, because a 'yes' might sound like I mean 'yes, I wish you had'. But a 'no' might mean 'no, the life choice you just made was a bad one'. So I just accidentally leave an awkward silence stretching out between us. I wrack my brain to think of something to fill it with.

FIONA

Natalie's phone gives a very welcome beep. She snatches it up, reads the message.

'He's outside. I'll be back.'

I watch her leave, then walk over to the sofa. I perch on the edge of it, and then I stand up again. I wanted to be here, very much wanted to make sure that my friend didn't get murdered by a Strange Internet Man. But now I'm not really in the mood. But it's not like I'm in the mood to go home either, so . . . I'm out of options. But maybe that's actually helpful in my bodyguard role. One wrong move from this dude and I will unleash the *full* force of a woman who has already made a total arse of herself once today, who has vastly underestimated the pace of her relationship, and who therefore has very little left to lose.

I jump up as the door opens.

'I really don't know, I'm afraid,' Natalie says as she comes in. 'Fi, do you remember if they ever did a structural survey of the building?' She flashes me 'this guy will never live with me' eyes as she leads the way inside. I blink my acknowledgement.

I pretend to think. 'I'm not sure,' I say eventually. I walk towards him and hold out my hand. 'Hi, I'm Fiona. I used to live here.'

'But you won't be living here now?'

'No.' I'm still holding out my hand. He still hasn't shaken it. It's officially at the point where it's embarrassing.

'OK, then.' He glances down at my hand and steps past me. I shoot Natalie a look. She returns it. What else is there to do?

'What did you say your name was, sorry?' I ask, determined to grind a modicum of politeness out of this man.

'Richard.' He sniffs the air. 'Is that damp I can smell?'

'No, there's no damp,' Natalie tells him. 'Shall we start with the bedroom and come back out here?'

She walks towards ~~my~~ the room but only gets a couple of paces before she realises that Richard isn't following her.

'You can't know there isn't damp,' he says, staring up at one of the walls. He points at nothing. 'What about that patch there?'

'There's . . . no patch there.' Natalie doesn't even look.

'I can see a patch.'

'Really?' I stand right next to him, squinting up where he's pointing.

He scowls. 'Well, it's difficult to see, but it's there. They call it the hidden killer, you know.'

'I really don't think they—' Natalie begins, but her phone rings. She looks at the screen and her eyes widen a tiny bit. 'Oh, sorry. Let me just get this. I'll be right back.'

I flash her a look that very clearly says 'if you leave me here with this man I will never speak to you again' but she just mouths 'Sorry' and heads for her room.

'Did you know the mould that comes from damp is responsible for fifty per cent of all deaths of people between the ages of thirty and sixty?' Richard says as I hear the door close.

NATALIE

'H-hello?' I answer tentatively, because there's no way they're calling me back already.

'Hi, is that Natalie?'

'Speaking.' I don't know how I'm managing to sound normal when my heart is trying to climb up my throat but there we go.

'Hi, Natalie. It's Jenny. From CLC. Listen, we were really impressed with your interview earlier, and I'm just calling to formally offer you the role.'

I stare at the wall ahead of me for a moment. I did *not* hear that correctly. I know I did not hear that correctly. I let it sink in for a moment.

'Are you still there?' she asks after I've been silent long enough for it to be weird.

'Yes, sorry.' I clear my throat. 'That's amazing, thank you so much!'

'Do you have anything you'd like to ask me for now?'

'I . . .' Come on, Natalie, think of something. Don't let her think she's offered the job to a blithering idiot. 'Isn't it a bit . . . late? To be calling, I mean?'

'Not for me. I was finishing off some other bits and I thought, "Why not round off the night by giving out a bit of good news?"'

'Sure.' I glance over my shoulder.

'Why, is it an issue to call now?'

'No! God, no. I'm glad you did. Thank you.'

'Well, you were the best candidate we saw, it wasn't hard. So, Mara will be in touch next week with the paperwork, and we'll go from there.'

'Amazing. Thanks again!'

We say goodbye and I hang up. I lean against the wall, just because I need to remind myself that there's something solid next to me. My knees feel weird? I slip my phone back into my pocket and shake out my hands.

'I honestly don't know,' Fiona is groaning when I leave my room. I can't see her. Judging by the slight reverberation, they're in the bathroom.

'Aha, here's Natalie,' Richard says as I get to the door. 'Maybe you'll know. When was the last time this floor was taken up?' He taps a toe on the lino.

'I don't . . . think it's ever been taken up.' I'm more bemused now than frustrated, because this is the moment when I realise that I don't have to show any more Internet Weirdos around my flat if I don't want to. That salary – *my* salary – means I could just live here on my own. 'Why would we take the floor up?'

Fiona glares at me and takes out her phone. She types something, looks at me pointedly, and my phone beeps a moment later.
FIONA: DON'T ENCOURAGE HIM!!!!!!!!

I press my lips together to stop a giggle slipping out.

FIONA

This *man*. Natalie doesn't know. She *left* me with him and, honestly, I never want to hear anything about damp-proof courses ever again. I had never heard of them before this evening but, at this point, I'm too afraid to admit that. I'm in too deep.

But now she nods and actually *smiles* as he drones on to her about the dangers that might be lurking underneath the grotty lino in the bathroom. And, really, if that's the case, why would we lift it up in the first place? I obviously don't ask that, though. I didn't come here tonight to die of boredom.

'Have you seen everything you needed to?' Natalie asks when he's talked about spores for upwards of ten minutes. She's still smiling, and I just don't know how . . . unless . . . Something cold feels like it's trickling down my back.

Natalie shows Richard to the door and gives him a cheery wave. She should really be showing him back down to the door to the street. Otherwise, I think there's a strong chance I'll bump into him whenever I leave, feeling for wet patches on the perfectly fine walls in the entrance.

NATALIE

'What's going on with you?' Fiona asks as soon as I close the door.

'What do you mean?'

'Well, we've just spent the evening with the most boring man in the world. You seem . . . very happy about it.'

I open my mouth. I don't know how to tell her. Because if I tell her that I *did* get it I'm also, by extension, breaking the news that she didn't. She's one step ahead of me, anyway.

'You got the job, didn't you? That's who called?'

I pause for a second, but what am I going to do? Not say 'yes' and then lie for the rest of my life? She deserves better than that. So, I nod.

CHAPTER ELEVEN

NATALIE

I wake up on the morning of my first day with butterflies in my stomach. I stare at the ceiling for a couple of minutes, trying to pick out shapes in the Artex. Will I make friends? Will I fit in? Why are my worries the same as a kid starting Big School? But, seriously. Will they think I'm weird? Did I exaggerate my Excel skills too much and now they think I can do macros? I try to push everything down, remind myself that I'm actually excited.

I brush my teeth and my hair, and I even put on make-up. I gave up on make-up a long time ago, but maybe Natalie with The Fancy Job is Natalie Who Wears Eyeliner too. New job, new me. Not that I'm putting too much pressure on it or anything.

When I arrive I sit in reception, waiting for somebody to call my name. People trickle in while I sit off to one side, their cards beeping on the reader outside and then the door whirring open automatically. Some of them make accidental eye contact and give me curious looks and small smiles as they pass.

When Sophie arrives she trots over to me and pulls me into a hug.

'Hey! How are you feeling?'

I pull a face. 'Kind of tired. Bit nervous.'

'Oh my god, I was a *wreck* on my first day. Totally reasonable. You'll do great, though, I promise.'

I nod, and then Sophie rubs my shoulders and disappears into the office proper. I watch her go. I try to get control of the swooping sensation in my stomach and get back to giving off the vibe of being a cool, approachable colleague and/or friend.

'Natalie?'

It's a relief when my name is called and I can stop. Giving off vibes is exhausting. Much easier to use my words. I jump up.

'Hi. Jennifer. Jenny.'

'Yeah, I remember.' I smile. She reaches out a hand and shakes mine.

'Do you want to follow me?'

I don't even have time to say yes before she's walking off. I trot to keep up. We end up in a kitchen area.

'Tea?' she asks, flicking the kettle on before I even answer.

'Yes, please.'

We both stand awkwardly and watch the kettle bubble. We catch each other's eye once and I smile nervously, then return to the kettle. I scan my brain, desperately trying to find any topic of conversation, but it's just tumbleweed and dead leaves up there. Jenny pours water into the mugs, and I still have nothing. She takes a bottle of milk from the fridge, and still nothing. Then she hands me my tea and takes a sip of hers. 'Do you want to follow me?'

She indicates another door and I walk through it behind her. We walk through a small office, only maybe twenty people. Sophie looks up from her desk close to the kitchen and does an exaggerated smile at me, giving me two thumbs up. The person at the desk next to her catches her face, and then looks up at me with a smile too.

Someone's phone is ringing. A couple more heads turn as I pass, everybody checking out the new girl.

'That's your desk.' Jenny points to an empty one near the window, and then sits down at the one opposite. 'You probably remember from the interview, but I'm the account manager. It's my job to keep everybody happy once they've signed up with us. You'll be reporting to me, so that's why we're close together. And this is Tom, he does sales.' Tom, who I had barely noticed at the desk next to Jenny because he was obscured by a giant monitor, stands up a little so that I can see him over the top.

He holds up a hand in greeting. 'Hi.'

'Hi.' I nod.

I shift in my seat, trying to establish the most comfortable position. I fiddle with a couple of levers underneath it and the whole thing sinks with a hiss because OF COURSE IT DOES. Come on, Natalie. This is basic stuff. Don't fiddle with the chair in front of people, it was always going to backfire. I hover my bum above the seat while I raise it again. I *think* Tom is pressing his lips together, suppressing a smile.

'Your login's on that piece of paper,' Jenny tells me, like she hasn't even seen anything. 'If you get yourself logged on, there's a bunch of training and things you need to do before you do anything else, so you can probably just focus on that for today.'

I nod, and gratefully duck behind my monitor so that she can't see my bright red face anymore. This is awful. I'm sure one day I'll laugh at myself but, honestly, I cannot imagine when. I feel like my organs are trying to scrunch themselves up into a ball inside me.

I do eventually figure out how to act like a human being who knows how to function in the world. I manage to get myself logged on. I check my completely empty email, making a mental note of what that looks like because it will never happen again. I watch a short training video about fire extinguishers, which is compulsory for some reason.

'What are you doing tonight?' Tom leans over his screen. I don't immediately realise that he's talking to me, because why would he be? 'Natalie. You. What are you doing tonight?'

I flush. I look around to see if anybody else is witnessing this. Is he . . . asking me out? I can't believe I've been here for maybe five hours, and somebody *already* fancies me. Although I do look better than normal today so maybe I can.

'Only because everybody's going out for a drink tonight if you fancy joining,' he adds.

Oh, right. Well, still nice.

'Yeah, definitely!' I grin. 'Whereabouts?'

'Just to the beach, I reckon.' He raises his voice. 'Beach OK for everybody tonight?'

A few people call back their agreement, and as I glance towards the rest of the office I see a couple of thumbs up as well. Hanging out on the beach of an evening for no reason other than it's Monday feels *very* different to the painstakingly organised 'cupcakes and tea' parties we used to have at the school to celebrate retirements or the occasional start of a maternity leave. I've never been much of a beach bum, even though it's so close. Maybe that will be the next new facet of my personality. Natalie Starr: international adventurer who is not grossed out by seaweed and looks perfectly natural hanging out next to the sea. Natural and tanned. And good in a bikini. Maybe one day.

I take out my phone, just as Jenny happens to look up.

'Um, Natalie, we actually try not to be on our phones during working hours if we can help it.' She gives me a tight smile.

'Sorry, of course.'

I dip the phone under the desk and type out a quick text to Fiona.

NATALIE: Hey, sorry, know we were meant to meet up tonight but new work mates going out for drinks so think I should go xx
NATALIE: Can fill you in tomorrow instead?? xx

FIONA

I snatch a moment to look at my phone when I'm grabbing another box of cups from the cupboard. It is *chaos* today. Time feels like it's going too fast to keep up with and yet somehow at the same time it's slower than it's ever been. They're queueing out the door on a *Monday*.

If that wasn't enough, I keep comparing this to what I could have had at CLC if I hadn't completely blown my interview. *I* could have been where Natalie is right now. *I* could have been cancelling on *her*. But *I* apparently can't string a sentence together the one time I really need to, so here I am, being ditched by my best friend on the first truly summery day of summer.

I possibly wouldn't have such an issue with it, but I've been actively clinging to Natalie lately. Not that I've told her as much. But between spending time with her and Amy, even going to hang out with my parents, I've been avoiding the flat as much as I can. Matt has not said a single thing about the ring, so I haven't brought it up either. But I just feel its *presence* there, hanging over me. We already changed everything by moving in together, do we have to do it again so soon? And married people settle down. They have children, mortgages, paperwork. It's a whole different life, probably one I want someday, I just . . . I guess I thought 'someday' was an unspecified point in the far-off future, not something we were putting an actual timeline on.

Anyway. Today of all days, Natalie ditching me is the last straw.

Natalie

I hitch a lift to the beach with Sophie.

'It's so great to have you along for these kinds of things now!' she enthuses on the way.

'Do you do this a lot?'

'Quite a bit in the summer. Why not, right?'

I watch the dunes speed by as we head for the car park. We're only five minutes from the office and it's like we're in another world. I really don't come up here enough. Rabbits look up and race away as we crunch along the gravel road. Gaps in the grass reveal white sand underneath. Every so often there's a clump of tall, pink flowers. Then yellow. Then white. As we park, the sea shimmers below us, a few people bobbing in the water. I can smell barbecues.

Fiona

We sold out of pretty much everything at the shop and ended up closing early. Amy had to dash off so she turned down my offer of a drink. I wandered around for a little while, but I don't love being out in public wearing the uniform that very clearly belongs to Scoopz. I'm always paranoid that I'll be seen doing something bad or illegal, and I'll end up getting in trouble. I've never done anything bad or illegal in my life, but the worry is always there that I'll trip up and fall into a pile of cocaine, or something.

'Oh, hi,' Matt says, appearing at the living room door when I get in. I forgot he had the day off today, so he's home early. Just what I need. I wonder if I can head back out, but I can't think of a reason. 'Nice to actually see you. I feel like we've been like ships passing lately.'

I give a weak laugh and walk over to kiss him. 'Hi.'

He heads back into the living room, so I go into the kitchen. I take a moment to centre myself, trying to get over my annoyance at the 'ships passing' comment. Even though it's true. But I've had a shitty day, I do *not* need to be *attacked*. After a while, Matt appears in the doorway. I put my phone down on the side and wrench open a cupboard, trying to make it look like I was choosing what to cook.

'Everything OK?' he asks.

I look up, trying to keep a look of bemusement on my face. 'Of course. How was your day?'

'It was good. Yours?'

'Amazing. Inspiring. Couldn't get enough.' I turn around and hide my face in the cupboard. When I look back, I've fixed the dumb smile back on my face. Matt shrugs and takes a couple of steps out of the room. Except then he comes back.

'*Is* everything OK, though?' He leans against the kitchen door frame now. I don't think he's trying to block my way but he's still making me feel, well, trapped.

'Yes, honestly. Just forget about it. It's nothing.' I push past him and head into the living room. He follows me.

'But if you're saying "it's" nothing, then "it" must be something. Because there's an "it", right? Is that why I've barely seen you? You've been out with Natalie, or Amy, or you've felt ill and gone to lie down, or whatever else. What's up with you?'

'It's not . . .'

But you know how sometimes you'll be on the verge of tears, but still just about managing to keep it together, and then someone starts asking questions and the floodgates open? Turns out someone implying that you've been acting weird can do the same thing in the right circumstances. My eyes spill over, and I've let out a couple

117

of gasping sobs before I even know what's happening. I throw my hands up to hide my face as if that's going to make me invisible.

'Fiona, what . . . ?'

I feel Matt's hand on my back, can sense him standing right behind me. He steers me gently towards the sofa and I go with him, still keeping my hands over my face. He's seen me cry. I've squeezed out the occasional single tear at a wedding or a sad film. But this is . . . Well, there's snot. But then I feel his warm hand touch my cold one and he gently-but-firmly pulls my hands away from my face.

'What's happened?' he asks. 'Really, you're scaring me now.'

I take a shuddering breath. Then I tell him everything. I don't even really intend to tell him *everything*, it just comes pouring out. I tell him about applying for the job at CLC, and messing up the interview, and helping Natalie to get ready for her first day, and how hurt I feel that she ditched me tonight, and how shit my day was before any of that even happened, and . . .

When I start hiccupping out all of my worries he rubs my back in circles, and it's actually nice. I wish I'd said any of this sooner, because I actually *do* feel a bit better. But at some point in my rambling he moves his hand away. I don't notice immediately – it's only after I stop talking that I realise he's put some space between us. I gulp.

'Matt?'

I look up. He's frowning at the coffee table. He doesn't move for a second, and then he turns to frown at me instead.

'So, hang on.' He speaks slowly, and I can't really blame him. I did just dump a *lot* on him. 'You applied for a job?'

I nod. I sniff and wipe my nose on my sleeve because, honestly, he's seen me at my worst now, so why not? My crying jag was the death of any mystery between us.

'And that job might have meant you pissing off to other countries at a moment's notice, and you just . . . didn't think to tell me?'

'Well, I . . .' I'm about to launch into an explanation, but then I realise I don't have one. 'Yes.'

'So, if you'd got this job, you might have just been jetting off to, I don't know, Bora Bora or the Seychelles all the time and I wouldn't have had any say in the matter?'

'OK, firstly, it was never going to be all the time. And also, *say*? What kind of say? I don't need you to sign a permission slip, do I?' It's probably uncalled for, but he's caught me off guard. Wasn't he being nice to me two minutes ago? Where did *that* go? I open my mouth again but he holds up a hand and cuts me off.

'This isn't some patriarchal thing of "oh I want to control everything my girlfriend is doing". Fiona, we *just* moved in together. We were supposed to be settling down! We get to just be us, on our own. And you want to ruin that. How did you think I'd feel?'

'I guess I didn't really—'

'Look. You just should have told me, that's all. We could have talked about it together.' He shakes his head at me and something snaps.

'You're a fine one to talk about not telling people stuff.'

'What the hell does that mean?' He looks at me like I'm mad, which I am *not* having.

'Were you ever going to mention the *ring* you're hiding in your drawer? I've been freaking out, Matt! We're not ready to do something like that. And I didn't know how to talk to you about it, because that is the kind of thing you discuss with someone before you make huge life decisions! So don't you dare make it seem like I'm the only one who's keeping things to myself.'

He gapes at me for a second. 'You found the ring? So you went through my stuff.'

'Not deliberately. I was looking for washing.' I perch on the edge of the sofa while Matt paces on the other side of the coffee table. He stops, and looks at me.

'And, just to check I heard you right . . . you were freaking out?'

I look at him. He's frowning down at me, having stopped pacing. For a second I wonder how I can word it gently, but, do you know what? We're in it now, and everything's going wrong, and how is it helping either of us to keep pussyfooting round the subject?

'Of *course* I was freaking out, Matt. We're not ready for that! You're not even thirty. Do you really want to be locked in to something for the rest of your life? Are you really ready to, like, buy a house, and have kids, and never be able to go anywhere ever again? To just be trapped? And *here* of all places? Because I'm willing to bet your mum's not going to let you move away again, and—'

'Trapped?'

I falter. 'Sorry?'

'You said if we got married you'd be trapped.'

I pause. Tread carefully. 'Well I-I didn't . . .'

'That's what you think, isn't it?'

I could lie, but we've come this far already. I speak quietly now. The panicky shrillness gone. 'I mean, kind of, maybe. I don't know. I didn't realise until I saw the ring, but then I did, and—'

'And you thought I was trying to trap you.' He nearly sits on the sofa, but as soon as his bum hits the cushion he's back to standing. 'For your information, Fiona, my mother gave me that ring when she came round for the dinner party. It's some old heirloom she came across. *She* wanted me to use it. It was *her* idea.'

My god, the relief. 'Oh, well—'

'But fucking hell, it's nice to finally know how you feel. You know, I did sort of think this was at least going somewhere. Like, maybe we're not getting married now, but in a couple of years? Like, maybe one day you'd finally be ready to grow up and—'

'What does *that* mean?'

'Doesn't even matter. You feel trapped. Great.' He shakes his head. I feel a stab of panic.

'I don't feel trapped. I don't. I don't know. I just wondered – for, like, one second, just when I saw the ring – if there might be more out there and if we were closing ourselves off, or denying ourselves.' He leaves the room. I follow him. 'We're still *so* young, Matt. I didn't know if we were ready for that.' He's putting his shoes on now, grabbing a jacket, so I speed up what I'm saying even though I wasn't really making any sense at *normal* speed. 'But now I know that I *am* ready. If you wanted that, I would want it. I think. I would do it. For you. Because I love you, and maybe I needed to have that moment of doubt to really know for sure that I—'

The door slams. I don't hear him walk down the stairs right away and I strain my ears for a second, because maybe he's going to change his mind. That's what he'll do. He's standing on the other side of the door to teach me a lesson, but then he'll come back in, take off his jacket, and we'll laugh about the whole thing.

Except I hear him start walking down the stairs. I put my head in my hands.

NATALIE

People cheer when we turn up. Lots of them have changed out of their office wear into full shorts and t-shirt, and I can't believe the contrast between this and what I would have been doing even a week previously. Someone hands me a beer from a cool box. Smoke curls up from a bucket barbecue with a few sausages and some . . .

'Are those . . . potato waffles?' I ask, frowning.

'Don't knock it 'til you've tried it, newbie.' Another person whose name I can't remember winks at me. 'You'll never do them in a toaster again.'

'You can do them in the *toaster*?' someone else pipes up.

Sophie laughs. 'Oh good god, where have you been? Here, Nat, sit down.' She pats the rug next to her and I sit down gratefully. I dig my feet into the sand, trying to enjoy this for the beachy moment it is, and not think about how much sand I'm going to end up with in my shower – and, probably, bed – later.

'No Jenny?' somebody asks. Note to self: for the love of god, learn some names. And while you're at it, do not let on that you've already forgotten almost every one of the names you were told mere hours earlier. 'What a surprise.'

'I thought she'd be here,' I shrug, looking to Sophie for confirmation.

'Oh, Natalie. So naive. She was never coming.' Sophie shakes her head.

'Why's that?'

'The woman is a workaholic.' Tom plonks himself down next to me. A name I remember! I take a victory sip of my beer. 'She will, like, *find* extra things to do so that she can stay at the office for hours after we were meant to go home.'

'It's sort of how she derives her self-esteem,' the woman sitting opposite me – Meg, maybe? – explains. 'She has a pathological need to be better than all of us. And not just, like, a *bit* better than all of us. She needs to be so much better than all of us that everybody around her just *knows* she's better than all of us, so she never has to mention it and, of course, by not *mentioning* that she's better than all of us, she naturally becomes *even better* than all of us.'

'Oh . . . right.' I nod. I'm not really sure what I'm allowed to say. We are, after all, talking about my line manager. What if I'm being hazed and they go straight back and tell her that I seemed to slightly agree with something bad that they said?

'It's OK,' Tom says, nudging me. 'We won't keep bitching about her. This is a safe space.'

I smile and look down at my beer can.

Over the next hour or so I decide I'm probably going to be pretty happy in my new job. It's a brand-new feeling, but definitely one I can get on board with. People are just so chilled. Everybody's around my age. They all seem relaxed, laughing about *Love Island*, showing each other memes on their phones. Nobody is talking about their grandchildren, like people used to quite a lot at the school. I feel like I could be myself, one day. Maybe even a better version? More confident, maybe. Calmer. Like everybody here seems to be.

FIONA

I sit in the silent living room for a long time. I don't know what I'm supposed to do, now. I don't know if Matt's gone for good, or gone for a minute, or if I should follow him. And I really need to talk. And I know who I need to talk to. And I know it's an important day for her, but I think if Natalie knew what had happened she'd understand.

NATALIE

My phone makes me jump when it rings. I didn't even realise I had a signal, I have looked at it that little. I glance at the screen and feel a tiny flicker of annoyance when I see that it's Fiona. Did she not get my text? I know she did, I saw her see it. I swipe the call away. She'll get the message. She probably just forgot.

The phone rings again. That's less like her. We're both usually pretty good at getting the message if someone doesn't answer. So if she's calling twice it might mean something. It could be something bad. But, I mean, if my mum was dying, my dad would call me. If my dad was dying, my mum would call me. If Fiona was dying, Matt would call me. So, whatever it is, it can't be *that* bad, can it? I swipe the call away again.

And then she rings for a *third* time? And, honestly, any other day I would answer a *third* call immediately. But I glance up at the super-cool, fun new people I'm hanging out with. I think about the chill, beachy person I can pretend to be when I'm with them. I don't want to be the one who isn't completely present, who snubs everybody else by sneaking off along the beach to answer her phone. Just for once – for *one* day – I want to be the girl who does what she wants to do, just because she wants to do it. The girl who doesn't stop to think about everybody else. The girl who simply has a good time with the people that she's with. All of which is quite a long-winded way of saying that I switch my phone off.

FIONA

The fourth time I call (I know, I know, I can't help it) it goes straight to voicemail. I move the phone away from my ear, staring at it as Natalie's message plays, quietly, through the earpiece. Then I scream in frustration and throw the phone down on the sofa.

CHAPTER TWELVE

NATALIE

Full disclosure: several people are slightly worse for wear the next morning. I am not one of them, because as much as I aspire to be a free spirit who doesn't worry about anyone but herself, I did think it might be pushing it to get completely, publicly hammered on my very first day at work.

Still, it's fun to watch the parade of people sloping in at various points after nine a.m. looking a tiny bit jaded. Tom arrives at three minutes past, takeaway coffee in hand.

'Morning.' He nods at Jenny as he squeezes past her.

'Good night last night?' she asks sweetly.

'Great, actually. You should come along one day.'

'Not really my scene.' She gives him a tight smile and returns to poring over the pile of photocopies on her desk. Tom pulls a face at me and I have to fake a coughing fit so it won't sound like I'm laughing.

'Natalie,' Jenny says, 'could you go through the spreadsheet I'm going to send you and collate all of the non-responders from the survey in March?'

I clear my throat. 'Of course.'

I don't dare catch Tom's eye again.

A handful more people creep in over the next half an hour or so. They invariably clutch cans of coke or energy drinks. There's one case of sunglasses indoors. Every time someone else arrives Jenny tuts and shuffles something on her desk, while everybody else murmurs and giggles. I have to press my lips together to stop myself from laughing too.

'Everything OK?' Jenny asks when she catches me.

'Definitely. Just, could you send me the link for the folder with the costings in again, please?'

She nods officiously. As I'm turning back to my own work, I just *happen* to catch Tom's eye. He tips his coffee cup upside down and pouts to demonstrate its emptiness. Except he doesn't notice that he's sprinkling a few remaining drops all over his desk until I raise an eyebrow and nod.

He groans and gets up to go to the kitchen.

I can't keep my giggles in then. Jenny frowns at me as the link I asked for pings through. I make it to mid-morning before I remember Fiona calling me last night. Weird. I wonder what that was all about. Still, she hasn't tried me again so, as predicted, it can't have been anything big. Probably just annoyed that I ditched her. Like she hasn't ditched me a thousand times worse in her time. But that's not very generous, is it? I shake the thought from my head and turn back to my spreadsheet.

FIONA

By the time Natalie calls me back I regret that I ever got in touch last night. Multiple times, in fact. Look, I was on autopilot, I really wasn't thinking.

Not that it's weird for me to call Natalie when something happens. She'd call me too. I would want her to. Always. But I just . . .

I mean, in this specific situation, I can't tell her that the thing I uprooted our entire lives for might already be over, can I? In the heat of the moment, all I wanted was to tell her what had happened, have her tell me that everything would be OK. Or that even if it isn't she'll be here for me. But as I got more distance, the doubts started to creep in.

First of all, it will be very embarrassing if it turns out that I basically dropped her in favour of Matt – again – for nothing. Worse than nothing. Because it hurts. And because Natalie's been so amazing at dealing with everything. But, on the other hand, what if it's not as bad as it felt at the time? Natalie's friends with Matt too. If this doesn't end everything, I don't want to risk ruining her relationship with him because of an argument *I* caused. That's not fair.

So, by the time her name pops up on my phone, I'm having second thoughts about the whole thing.

'What's up?' she asks, without so much as a hello.

'Hi. Um, how do you mean?' I stall for time. It's not my best work.

'You called me. A lot. Is everything OK?'

I consider telling her about Matt storming out. About him not coming home until stupid o'clock in the morning. About him getting up insanely early and leaving again, clearly trying to avoid me. Yep, definitely a terrible idea. So, I lie. 'Oh, yeah, great! How was the first day?'

'You mean aside from someone repeatedly trying to call me when I was at the beach with all my new colleagues?'

'The beach? Really?'

'Can I help you with something, Fi?'

There's a pause. I can picture her right now, grinding her teeth because she's (rightly) irritated.

'Nothing. It was . . . Yeah, nothing. I just wanted to say that I hoped it was going well.'

'OK.'

We're both silent for a moment.

'So, *did* you have a good day?' I ask. I have to ask, right? It's a weird one but, what? We just never ever talk about work again because it's awkward? 'I want to hear about it.'

'Honestly? It was great.' I can hear the smile in her voice, and I'm happy for her even though . . . well. 'Was that really it?'

If I was going to tell her the truth now would be the time. But it doesn't come out.

'That was it.'

NATALIE

SOPHIE: Miner's Arms on Saturday to celebrate the new job???? X

For a split second after Sophie texts me I still half think I'll be busy doing PJ-and-movie night in the flat with Fiona. But it's been weeks since we did that. I shake my head. Get over it. I text back.

NATALIE: Sounds good!

SOPHIE: Invite Fiona, obvs. Thinking we make a night of it? Invite some other people too? X

SOPHIE: SHOULD WE DO FANCY DRESS

My stomach drops a tiny bit. It was OK when it was just going to be me, Sophie, and a low-key drink. Still a little bit cringe, but certainly doable. But do we really need to make it into a whole extravaganza? It's not really me.

NATALIE: I don't think we need to make it a big deal?

My phone rings. Sophie.

'Hi, listen, I just—' I begin.

'Are you actually kidding me?' she shrieks. I hold the phone away from my ear.

'I—'

'Of course we have to make it a big thing! It already is a big thing. Think of other people, as well. We haven't been out for ages, this is the perfect excuse. Come on.'

'Yeah, but what about . . .'

'What about what?'

I search my brain for an excuse. 'I don't want to rub it in Fiona's face.'

'I think it's about time Fiona had something rubbed in her face, don't you?'

'Soph,' I warn.

'Sorry. But, look. If Fiona's any kind of friend she'll be happy for you. Is she not happy for you?'

'I mean, she says she is, but . . .'

'Right, well, if she says she is, then she is, isn't she?'

'But . . .'

'You can't decide how other people feel for them, Nat. She says she's happy, so she's happy, so you need to dig out your nicest top, because we are all. Going. Out. Yes?'

'But I—'

'Yes?' Her voice sounds dangerous this time.

'Fine. OK. Yes. Yes. OK. We're on.'

Sophie cheers down the phone and I have to move it away from my ear again. 'Great! You invite Fiona, then. And don't worry about anything else, I'll arrange it all. At the Miner's, nine p.m., OK?'

'Sure.'

Sophie hangs up the phone and I'm left staring at it, wondering what the hell I just agreed to. But it's too late now, so I text Fiona:

NATALIE: Sophie wants to go out on Sat night. Are you in? We could meet up before, get ready? I could come to you, you could come to me? XX

FIONA: . . .

I see Fiona see the message. Then there's a pause. Then the dots start bouncing. I watch them for ages. She's typing an essay. Is she going to say she'd love to but after I hung up on her the other day she doesn't think it's a good idea? Maybe she's going to say that, actually, she has grown-up couple-y plans with Matt that I couldn't possibly understand. Or maybe she just doesn't want to hang around with a job stealer anymore.

FIONA: Sounds good.

I puff my cheeks out. I'm such an idiot. Of course she wasn't going to say any of the other stuff. I do note, though, that the dots are still bouncing. And bouncing. And bouncing. I try not to let my imagination run wild this time.

FIONA: Can I get ready at ours?

FIONA: *yours, sorry

NATALIE: Mi casa es su casa :)

FIONA

'Hey, what are you up to on Saturday night?'

Amy's cleaning the chiller cabinet when I speak. I nearly made it through an entire day without getting completely consumed by thoughts of this night out, but now that the shop's quietened down they're a lot harder to ignore. I might not have it in me to put on fake eyelashes, and smile, and pretend like I haven't put my whole relationship in jeopardy. Amy straightens up too fast and bashes her head on the top.

'Ow! For god's sake. What did you have in mind?' she asks, rubbing the top of her head.

'Just these drinks for Natalie. Because of her new job.'

'You mean the new job that should have been yours.'

'I mean *her* new job.'

'Who's going?'

'Natalie, Sophie, I think Jasmine. Maybe Alice?'

Amy considers for a moment. 'Yeah, I can do that.' She returns to her cleaning for a second, and then straightens up again. 'Why?'

'Sorry?'

'Why am I invited?'

'Why . . . wouldn't you be invited?'

She shoots me a look, which is fair. She's never seen eye to eye with Natalie. I know it, she knows it. Ever since Natalie's couple of summers at Scoopz. I don't really know why, and I dare say Amy doesn't *really* know why either. It's just the way it is. Some people don't get on.

'Fine,' I concede. 'They don't know I'm asking you. I just think it'll be hard.'

'Because she stole your—'

'She did *not* steal my job, before you say that. But she did *get* it, and everyone'll be excited about it, and I just . . . It'll just be hard. And Matt—' I clamp my mouth shut and Amy narrows her eyes a tiny bit. 'I could just use some backup.'

'And Matt what?' she asks.

'Sorry?' I pretend I've gone deaf, thinking I can buy myself some time.

'You said "and Matt". And Matt what?'

'Oh, no, it's nothing.' Amy puts her cloth and spray down on the counter and crosses her arms. 'It *is* nothing. Nothing.'

'It really seems like nothing.' Amy shakes her head.

I don't want to tell her about the argument. She's not really the person I confide in. She's the person I have a laugh with. She's the person I make stupid jokes with just to get through the day. The person I bitch with about everybody else. In a fun way. But it's not like I can talk to Natalie about it. Especially not now.

'We had a fight,' I sigh, eventually.

Amy blinks. 'And?'

'And I said some horrible things. And so did he. And now he's, like, avoiding me. Coming home late, leaving early, not talking to me. And I don't know what it means.'

'Well, it probably doesn't mean anything.' Amy waves away my concern. 'Men are such children.'

I chew the inside of my cheek. This is not the kind of reaction I'd get from Natalie. And, like, I appreciate the effort, but it actually makes me feel worse about not talking to Natalie when I had the chance. It's too late now. I feel a pang of longing for our friendship the way it was a few weeks ago, before the moves, and the jobs, and the sudden introduction of politics and protocols. And that fucking ring.

'But, look,' Amy continues, 'I will come with you on Saturday. We'll have fun. And you guys will definitely have made up by then, mark my words, and we'll have a laugh about how worried you were. Look at your face!'

She laughs and then ties up the handles of the black bag by her feet.

NATALIE

FIONA: Is it OK if Amy comes on Saturday? X

I stare at the message. It's bad enough that this thing is happening at all, and now we're inviting *more* people? I don't want to be ungrateful. It's so nice that everybody's got behind this in such a big way. But the wider the circle gets, the less I want to be in it. But that's not the spirit, is it?

I want to text her and say 'none of this was my idea in the first place'. I could suggest we sack the whole thing off, stay at mine, binge-watch something. She'd probably go for it. But then there's Sophie, and the other people she's inviting, and if I didn't want to do it, I should never have agreed in the first place. So, I'm stuck with it now. And if Fiona needs moral support, that's fine.

NATALIE: Sure! Bring Matt too, if you like. Would be good to see him xx

FIONA

FIONA: Fancy coming to the Miner's on Saturday night? Going there to celebrate Natalie's new job x

I chew my lip as I wait for Matt to answer. I see him see the message and then I see nothing else for ages. And then he's typing, and then he isn't. And then he is again.

MATT: Will see

Amy locks the shop door and flips the sign over. I glance up and she grins at me. I smile back, but it's weak.

NATALIE

FIONA: Matt might have a gym thing on Sat but if he's back in time he says he'll come and meet us :) should be good! X

I read Fiona's message and shudder.

NATALIE: Tell him that sounds awful and he should definitely just come out with us insteadddddd xx

I hope that a few extra consonants will make it seem like I'm into this whole idea. But it genuinely would be nice to have Matt there if this thing has to happen at all. He might keep everyone a bit more sane. He is, after all, a grown-up. It takes forever for Fiona to answer me.

FIONA: Ha ha

CHAPTER THIRTEEN

Fiona

When Natalie and I walk through the doors of the Miner's Arms we're stopped in our tracks by cheering coming from the group sat in the corner booth. Sophie stands up and waves, in case we couldn't tell they were there from the noise. I wish I could muster the same enthusiasm.

Instead, I keep thinking about that text from Matt. What the hell is 'will see' supposed to mean, anyway? 'Will see' you there? 'Will see' if I can bear to drag myself out when I'm still furious at you? 'Will see' if I can forgive you first? I scan the table, but if he's even coming, he's not here yet. My heart sinks. I'd kind of convinced myself he'd be here, and we'd have the kind of night we used to when our only plans for the future were to have a laugh for the next couple of hours. But he might still come. He might? He might.

He's managed to avoid actually talking to me the past couple of days. He's been out early with his gym bag in the morning, and home so late in the evenings that he just goes straight to bed. And I can't ask where he's been, can I? I think I lost that right. So, I've just been lying next to him in bed, staring at his back, wondering how this is all going to pan out. He might still come. He hasn't said he won't.

I glance at Natalie. She smiles as we walk over, but I'm close enough to see that the smile is actually more of a look of grim determination. She doesn't *love* this kind of attention, to be fair. I wish we'd both owned up to not wanting to go, sacked it off, and stayed at Natalie's for movie night or something.

The table Sophie, Amy, and a couple of others are sitting at is already cluttered with empty glasses. Everybody seems to have had a delightful time getting a head start on us. Sophie, famously this evening's ringleader, is laughing into an overfull glass of wine while Amy – looking about as different from the usual hair-tied-back, pastel-uniformed, wholesome ice-cream-serving girl as it's possible to be – nods at something Sophie is saying. Jasmine and Alice grin at Natalie and me as we get closer to the table.

'Natalie!' Sophie cheers as we sit down. 'Natalie with the new job!'

'That's me,' Natalie laughs. But is it a *genuine* laugh or is she saying it through gritted teeth? Maybe? But probably just because it's hard work to be different levels of drunk so early in the evening. You can already tell it's going to end with someone holding somebody else's hair back.

Amy nudges my toe with hers under the table as we sit down. She must be *almost* as drunk as Sophie, judging by the empty glasses in front of her. She inclines her head slightly, frowning. This is how we communicate when the shop's busy and we're not allowed to chat. I nod.

'Who wants anything? Next round's on me,' Natalie announces, getting up. It's a nice thought, but I happen to know that she hasn't been paid yet, and I still feel bad for lumping her with double rent. I put my hand over hers on the table, even though I can't actually

136

afford it either, especially if I'm in a single-income household now too. But, fuck it. If my life is about to go up in flames, the least I can do is dance in front of them, right?

'Actually, next round's on me,' I say, and Natalie shoots me a look of gratitude. 'Who wants what?'

I head up to the bar and wait for Dave, the barman, to notice me. He seems to notice everybody *around* me, but never me. Every time I come here, he seems determined to stamp out any self-esteem I might have developed since my last visit. Still, I guess it keeps me grounded. I feel someone appear next to my shoulder and turn around to see Sophie.

'Hey, I just wanted to make sure there were no hard feelings,' she says, putting her arms around me and squeezing, even though we're not normally huggers. I suppose we're not normally in this situation, either. Her breath tickles my ear. She already smells a bit like alcohol. 'I know you really wanted the job too, I just . . . With you moving out and everything, I knew Natalie needed the money, and . . .'

I pat her wrist. 'It's fine, I get it.'

'You do?' She removes her arms from around my shoulders, and I think I'm free, but then they snake around my waist and her head rests on my shoulder. For a split second Dave the barman actually looks at me and I think it's going to be my turn, but then he seems to see Sophie and decide against it. I lever open Sophie's hands which are now around my hips.

'Sophie. It's fine. Go back to the others.'

Sophie sticks out her bottom lip and looks at me. 'You're so cool, Fiona, honestly . . .' Which is a funny thing to say because I do not feel cool at all. I force myself to inhale and release it slowly. 'I knew you wouldn't mind. It's so great how you just go through life, like, not *minding* about anything. You're just, like, on your own path, and flying around the world, and not caring that you're not doing anything you're *supposed* to be doing. It's so refreshing. And one day you and Matt are going to have the *best* wedding, and I cannot wait.' She boops my nose when she says 'wait'. And I can't decide if the flare of panic I feel when she talks about mine and Matt's wedding is because I don't know if we're even together anymore, or because if we *are* still together, that wedding might actually happen sooner than I expected.

'OK,' I say, making a note to get some water for the table and trying to ignore what feels like a hundred different pinpricks to my ego because she's drunk. She's drunk. She doesn't mean anything she's saying. She's just drunk. 'Why don't you go and sit down? I'll bring everything over.'

NATALIE

'So, how's the new job?' Jasmine asks, nudging me when Fiona disappears to go to the bar.

'Oh, yeah, it's good!' I say. 'It's a lot to learn, obviously. Very . . . different to being at the school. But people are really nice. I've had a good first week.'

'She's *smashing* it.' Sophie slurs a little bit as she picks her way back to her seat. 'You're gonna be flying around the world, getting an amazing tan, seeing all the best places, and someone's gonna *pay* you to do it. It's literally the dream.'

A glass appears in front of me. And then a smaller glass goes next to it.

'We've got some catching up to do.' Fiona winks, and I hope she didn't think I was bragging, or anything. Her smile doesn't seem to reach her eyes. She gives out the rest of the drinks and puts a big jug of water in the middle of the table and adds very pointedly to Sophie, 'Just in case anyone feels the need.'

Fiona holds out her own shot glass towards me and I clink mine against it. I swallow the liquid, not even questioning what it is. It just tastes like burning. Fiona pulls a face beside me, then catches my eye. We laugh at each other.

'To Natalie!' Sophie says, holding her glass in the air. Everybody clinks theirs against Sophie's and then each other's, eyes wide. I meet each gaze in turn. It's bad luck, otherwise. Most of them sparkle, excited for any excuse to be out. Amy's is a tiny bit cooler. Fiona holds eye contact for the longest. I wonder if she seems a tiny bit less enthusiastic too, but I guess that would be fair.

FIONA

My phone buzzes in my lap as we sit and chat around the table. Sophie and Amy keep threatening to get up and dance, but so far they haven't actually taken the plunge. If I focus really hard, I can just enjoy being in the room. Nothing exists outside of here. There is no Matt (until he arrives, anyway), there is no worry about what I'm doing with my life, there is no doubt about my relationship. There is simply Jasmine somewhere to my left telling me about the amazing curtains she found online and saying she'll send me a link in case I need any. But I do not need any because this room is the entire world and there is nothing outside of it. I sip my drink. Amy comes back from the bar and puts another one in front of me, squeezing herself onto the end of the bench next to me.

'How are you doing?' Amy shouts in my ear, also shooting a glance at Natalie. I give her a thumbs up because in this room I'm great, even if the room is starting to blur at the edges a little bit.

My phone buzzes in my lap.

MATT: Not going to make it, sorry. Say hi to Natalie

I stare down at my screen, suddenly able to hear my own heartbeat. It's fine. *We're* fine. Something's just come up at work, or one of his friends needs him for something, or . . . It's too loud in here. I can't breathe.

NATALIE

'Where's Fiona?' I ask Sophie a while after I come back from the loo. I stopped at the bar, too. Fiona's drink is sweating on the table and she hasn't come back to claim it. Sophie's too distracted, flicking through Tinder on my phone.

'Look, you matched w—' she begins, leaning over to show me the screen. I am changing my passcode tomorrow. I grab the phone off her, put it face down on the table. 'Soph. Look at me. Where's Fiona?'

'I don't know.' She shrugs like a sullen child and picks my phone up again.

I find Amy, Jasmine, and Alice dancing together near the quiz machine. Nobody else is dancing. I touch Amy on the shoulder. 'Hey. Do you know where Fiona went?'

Amy looks at me and narrows her eyes. 'You know you *stole* that job, right?'

Which doesn't feel great to hear, but it's not like I haven't thought that myself. I can hear my heartbeat in my ears, but then I realise Amy's still saying something.

'Sorry?'

'I *said*, she went outside!'

FIONA

'There you are!' Natalie laughs when she finds me. I'm sitting on one of the swings in the play area, pushing the bark chips into a pile with my toes. It's nice out here. I can think. I don't want to think, but I can. There's no sound except a dog barking somewhere, and some people laughing in the smoking area.

'Hi.' I give her a weak smile. She's going to try and drag me back inside, I know she is. My hands tighten on the chains of my swing. The frame creaks as she sits on the empty one next to me.

'Why are you hiding out here?'

'Just . . .' I shrug.

'Fi, are you OK?' She turns on her swing, twisting the chains above her head. I glance at her and then look away.

'I'm fine.' I kick at my pile of bark chips, scattering them again.

'OK, because you don't seem OK, and if there's anything the matter, and if it has to do with me, then I . . .'

'Natalie.' I twist my swing to look at her too. Then I turn back, the swing jolting me as I do. 'Just leave it, it's nothing.'

It maybe comes out slightly harsher than I meant it to, but what am I supposed to tell her? This thing with Matt has gone on too long now, which is technically *her* fault for not answering the phone, but in a week's time or something, will I be telling her about a breakup, or will it all be fine and a load of fuss over nothing? It doesn't feel like it's going to end up being option two.

'Is this about the job?' Natalie asks slowly.

'About the . . . No, Nat, this isn't about the job. I've told you, I'm fine about the job.'

'Well, OK, but you don't *seem* fine and you basically just told me to shut up, so . . .'

'Because maybe you *should*?' I bite back. I hate myself as soon as I've said it. She looks wounded. But I can't exactly take it back, can I? We both know I didn't misspeak. 'I'm sorry. I didn't mean . . . You just—'

'No, that's fine.' Natalie stands up and pushes past me. I chase after her. She bumps me with her shoulder as she reaches for the door. It swings shut on me before I get a chance to go through it too. I yank it open again.

'Natalie, wait,' I say, stepping back into the warmth. I say it a little bit too loudly and people look up. I would too if I were them.

She's nearly back at the table, but she wheels around to face me. 'Why should I? You don't want to hear what I'm trying to say.'

'It's not that. It's not. It's just, you don't understand.'

'*What* don't I understand, Fiona? You're mad at me, right? That's fine. I just wish you'd talked to me about it, you know? How can we fix it if you don't talk to me?'

I make a noise of frustration. She doesn't *get* it. And, fine, she doesn't get it because I haven't wanted to bother her with any of it, but at the moment I'm too annoyed to be reasonable. 'Natalie! I am not mad at you! I'm *thrilled* for you! It's going to be amazing. Not *everything* is about you.'

NATALIE

'When was I making everything about me?' I ask, genuinely stung. I have tried *so* hard to make things right with Fiona, what is she *talking* about?

Fiona closes her eyes. When she speaks again her voice is more even. 'I don't mean . . . I wasn't . . . Look, just forget it, OK? Who wants a drink?'

Someone else in the pub cheers at this, and then his mates join in, because everybody's a comedian. Fiona pulls a face. She tries to walk past me to the bar. But the thing is now *I'm* annoyed, so I catch hold of her arm.

'You can't just accuse me of being selfish and then tell me to forget it. What did you mean? I want to know.'

Fiona throws a glance over to our table like somebody's going to step in, but everybody there is watching, rapt. In fact, the whole bar is weirdly quiet all of a sudden. I don't even care.

'I mean, I just . . . You seem to think that the only reason I could *possibly* be in any way on edge is if I'm *wildly* jealous of you and your amazing new career. And I've got *bigger* things to worry about, so excuse me if I'm not actually completely obsessed with you!'

'What bigger things have you got to worry about, then? Go on!' I demand. Because we tell each other everything, and if that were true, she would have said something.

'I don't have to tell you that!'

'You do if you're going to be a bitch about it!' I practically scream. I'm not sure exactly when I lost control of my volume.

Fiona looks at me for a couple of seconds, her eyes stone cold. I have goosebumps all of a sudden. I open my mouth to take it back but my mind is blank and then before I can say *anything*, she turns around and walks to the door.

'Fiona!' I call. I glance back at the table again. Most of the others are sitting around it in varying stages of wincing. Sophie pulls a face and shrugs. Amy narrows her eyes and shakes her head. I turn around to face Fiona again, but she's gone, and the door is just swinging shut.

For a second, the pub is completely quiet. The silence is only interrupted by the quiz machine playing a little tune. And then the chatter starts back up, and am I hearing things or is there more laughter than there was, well, before?

I feel a hand on my arm and it's Alice. I'm glad it's Alice. She's the most measured one of all of us. That must mean it's OK. I don't really know how that makes sense but I'm clutching at straws. She guides me back to the table and I sit down. Fiona left her jacket. I pick it up and fold it over my arm, hugging it to me.

'What the hell was *that* all about? She's an odd one sometimes.' Sophie leans towards the middle of the table but I can't get into it with her. Fiona said she has bigger things going on. What bigger things? If she has bigger things, why wouldn't she tell me?

'Maybe you shouldn't talk about things you don't understand,' Amy says, getting to her feet, glaring at Sophie. 'I'll see you ladies later.'

She walks away and I stare after her as she goes. *Amy* knows something? Something *I* don't know? Sophie gets to her feet next to me.

'Soph.' Alice shoots a warning look at her and shakes her head. Sophie sits back down without saying anything.

I don't last much longer that night. I'm too aware of everybody glancing in my direction. One guy tiptoes past me with his hands up on the way to the loo, as if I'm going to yell at him too, which is obviously completely *hilarious* and all of his mates laugh their heads off. Sophie, Alice, and Jasmine are very nice and completely avoid the 'what the hell just happened?' elephant in the room, but I'm still done. I make my excuses. They let me go.

CHAPTER FOURTEEN

FIONA

When I wake up, I feel The Fear before I can remember why. I just lie in bed, feeling the full force of this weird existential dread. And a pretty violent hangover, too, I won't lie. Matt sleeps next to me, facing away. I hate it, but I don't think that's why I have anxiety swooping through my chest this morning, so then why . . . Oh *god*. I suddenly remember being awful to Natalie last night. I cross my arms over my face for a second, thinking that maybe I can block out the light and go back to sleep. But it's no use, there's sunshine creeping around the sides of our inadequate curtains and my heart feels like it's trying to climb up through my body. I have to text her.

I find my phone next to my shoes, on the floor in the hall. Absolutely normal. I have a vivid flash of struggling with my key as I tried to open the front door, tripping up the stairs once I finally *did* manage to get it open. I stormed into the flat and Matt looked up, startled. I kicked my shoes off and dumped my bag and phone next to them. I didn't calm down until I'd spent far longer than necessary washing my face. I did briefly wonder if maybe Matt would want to know what had happened, would try to make me feel better. But by the time I got out of the bathroom he'd got into bed so he could continue ignoring me.

I already have a couple of texts from Natalie. One from probably half an hour after I left the bar.

NATALIE: I'm sorry! I'm leaving now. Can I call you? X

Another from a couple of hours ago:

NATALIE: I can't sleep, I feel so bad. Let me know when's an OK time to call x

And then another one from about forty-five minutes ago.

NATALIE: I know you know, but I'm sorry again x

I feel a squeeze in my chest. *I'm* the one who should be sorry. Nothing would have happened if I'd just had a bit more self-control, but of *course* I couldn't manage that. Stupid. I rub my eyes, trying to convince them to open up properly. And then I jump as my phone vibrates in my hand.

Natalie

'H-Hello?' Fiona clears her throat on the other end of the line.

'Please don't hang up,' I say straight away. She would have every right to.

'I'm not going to.'

There are a couple of seconds of silence. I truly didn't expect her to answer so I didn't really think about what I wanted to say. The words are taking their time fighting through my cotton wool brain this morning.

'I—' Fiona begins.

'I—' I say at the same time. 'Sorry. You go.'

'No, you.'

Urgh, I hate being this polite to each other. That's when you *know* we've had a spat. I just want to skip to the part where we're friends again. Where we're normal. Still, there's only one way to get there.

'I just wanted to say, I am *so* sorry about going off on one last night. I don't know what came over me. I had no right to yell at you like that in front of everybody. You hadn't done anything wrong . . .'

'Well, I had.'

'OK, fine, but I didn't have to react the way I did, did I?'

'Honestly, I think you were well within your rights.'

I can see where this is going to go, and I need to stop it before it does. 'Can we please stop competing about who was more in the wrong?'

Fiona laughs on the other end of the phone. 'Fair. OK.'

There's another couple of seconds of quiet before I break it. 'Listen, if there was something really wrong, you'd tell me, right?'

I can hear Fiona taking a deep breath because it rattles down the speaker. 'Maybe we can talk about it over breakfast? Reggie's?'

'Of course we can.' My heart sinks. I wanted her to say 'no, everything's fine'. This means I've been too wrapped up in my own stuff to notice something. And I call myself a good friend.

FIONA

I wonder about going back to bed after I speak to Natalie, getting some actual sleep. But I'm too wired. I decide to make a coffee instead. Truly what anybody needs to help them calm down.

'Morning.' Matt appears in the doorway in an open dressing gown, scratching his stomach with one hand and rubbing his eyes with the other. It's like one of those dexterity tests.

I kind of freeze for a moment. He's talking to me? I don't want to scare him off. 'Hi.'

I sit at the breakfast bar and watch him drop a capsule into the Nespresso machine. The only bougie thing we have in our whole household. I don't want to lose it. The Nespresso machine *or* the household. This has gone on long enough. I have to ask. 'Matt, do you hate me?'

'Hate you?'

I nod. 'You've been off with me.'

'I think I was within my rights, don't you?'

'I mean, yeah, but . . .'

He walks around to my side of the counter and pulls out the other stool. He curls his bare toes around the bar at the bottom.

'Listen.' He speaks slowly. 'You really hurt me.' I open my mouth and he holds up a finger. 'It's not nice to feel like the idea of being with you forever has somehow kicked the woman you love into an existential crisis.'

'Matt, I—'

He makes a noise and I stop talking. 'But listen, I've thought about it a lot. And I've decided that I get it. I would have told you that last night but you stormed in, and . . . Well, anyway. I get why seeing that ring would have freaked you out. I do. I should have told you about it when my mum gave it to me but, ironically' – he sniffs – 'I didn't want to freak you out.'

He slides the coffee over to me, drops another capsule into the machine, and gets another mug out of the cupboard.

148

'I wasn't freaked out, I just—'

'Fiona. Come on. You were *so* freaked out.'

For a second, I'm going to protest, and then I figure: why lie? 'OK, fine. But I . . . I don't see how you don't find the idea of settling down really scary. Like, we did so many amazing things. We were so . . . free. God, that's wanky. But, you know, we could just do what we liked, and we didn't care what anybody at home was doing. Half the time, we didn't even know. And it didn't matter if they were judging us, or if we weren't measuring up to people, because we were so far away and we were doing the kind of things they'd never, ever do. But now that we're back, I just . . . I work where I worked when I was a teenager, and people are miles ahead of me, and I don't *want* to be exactly like them, but it's also all I can see. *You're* miles ahead of me, for crying out loud. I have, like, two friends, because everybody got all chummy when I wasn't here. And I'm paranoid that I'll never catch up, but I'm also worried that if I do we'll just be boring.'

I lean back on the counter and frown, trying to figure out what I even just said. I sip my coffee. Matt takes his now-poured one from the machine, looking thoughtful.

'You know what I think?' he says.

'What?'

He has a mouthful of coffee, wincing as he burns his mouth. 'I think you get one pass. There's been a lot to adjust to, right? But you have to be OK with the fact that I want to take that step with you one day. I'm not here to fuck around. And I'm really glad our life might be boring one day, because you're in it.'

I look down at my coffee and nod, tears pricking my eyes. I blink. A lot.

'I'm really sorry.'

'It's OK. Just promise me you're in this with me.'

I meet his eyes. 'I am. I promise. I do.'

'OK, good.' He pulls the belt of my dressing gown so that I'm forced to stand up, then he wraps his arms around me and kisses me.

NATALIE

She's late. This is the second time in a row, now. She said she'd forgiven me. But she's still not here. And she said she'd tell me what's going on with her. So, has she chickened out? Or maybe she just . . . doesn't trust me all of a sudden?

I know when I'm spiralling. I try not to get overwhelmed by all the negative (and unlikely) scenarios in my head. I sip my orange juice and try to notice things about the other people in the room. Anything to stop my brain from running away with every possibility. There's an old man in the corner wearing a leather jacket with flames embroidered on the back. Unexpected. There are identical twins at the next table. At the table between mine and the window, a group of women are adding something from a hip flask into their orange juice. Bold. Genius. I mean, I'm only just emerging from my hangover, so maybe not one for today, but certainly something to think about for the future. One of the women accidentally catches my eye and I nod in a way that I hope conveys my respect for them. She nudges her friend, who looks at me too. I smile, and they look away, giggling.

As I stare at them, I catch sight of Fiona on the street outside, running – literally running – for the door. She looks stressed, and I'm kind of relieved. Only because that means her lateness probably wasn't a deliberate tactic.

FIONA

Fuckfuckfuckfuckfuckfuckfuck, I did not want to be late. Not today of all days.

'I am so sorry,' I pant as I drop into the chair across from Natalie. 'I was . . .' I stop, because I don't want to say 'having make up sex with Matt' because a) Natalie doesn't know there was anything *to* make up after and b) Well, gross.

Luckily, she waves my apology away. 'It's fine.' I guess I still don't look sure because she laughs. 'Honestly, no harm done.'

She pours a glass of water from the jug on the end of the table and I down it in one. Frankly, it's a miracle I don't pour it over my head like I've just finished a marathon. Natalie fills it again.

'What can I get you, ladies?' a waiter asks.

We both order pancakes and coffee. When the waiter disappears to sort the drinks, Natalie clears her throat.

'So, are we OK now? You know I'm really sorry, right. Like, really sorry.'

'Are you kidding? Of course we're OK. And I'm really sorry too. Like, really sorry.'

She laughs as I repeat her phrasing. 'I don't know why' – Natalie takes a sip of her juice and looks over at another table where a kid is climbing over the chairs – 'but I was really worried last night. I know we've fought a thousand times, but I thought this one was going to be different somehow. Worse, I mean. Like, we wouldn't just be fine.'

'Well, bloody hell, this is hardly the worst one we've had, is it?' I say. 'Remember when we were on holiday and I fried your brand-new hair straighteners when you hadn't even used them yet? We asked not to be seated next to each other on the flight home and the woman behind the desk looked like she wanted to murder us.'

Natalie smiles at the memory. Our coffees arrive at the table and she takes a sip of hers, putting the tiny biscuit that comes with it on my saucer. She makes a noise into her cup and puts it down.

'Do you remember all the way back in school when I didn't want to go to that party, and you *desperately* wanted to go because we never got invited anywhere, and you told me we couldn't be friends if I didn't support you? And then our mums had to be our intermediaries for, like, a week afterwards. But we were still arranging to meet up and go shopping, so we were never actually *not* talking to each other.'

I laugh. 'I was all "I'm never speaking to her ever again in my *life*, tell her I'll meet her outside BHS at two p.m."'

Natalie snorts into her coffee.

NATALIE

'Excuse me.'

I'm just wiping the froth off my face when one of the women who were spiking their drinks appears at the end of the table.

'Hi,' Fiona says.

'I was just wondering if you guys could settle something for us. Are you the two girls from that video?'

Fiona frowns at her and I'm just as mystified. We look at each other, pretending to consider what this weirdo is saying. And I think we actually deserve quite a lot of credit because we really do pretend to be giving it some proper thought.

'Sorry, no, I don't think so.' I stick out my bottom lip and shrug, and she disappears back to the table.

'What video do you think that is?' Fiona mutters when she's sat back down.

'God knows.' I shake my head and take another sip of coffee.

Our food arrives, and it's honestly the most beautiful thing I've seen all day. I haven't eaten since before we went to the pub last night. My stomach growls. But I only get to eat a couple of forkfuls of chocolate chip pancake and whipped cream before somebody else materialises at the end of the table.

'Can I—' I start to speak but then realise I've literally bitten off more than I can chew. I cover my mouth with my hand until I can form a coherent word again. 'Help you?'

I look up, and this time it's a different woman, also from the spiked drinks table. Maybe they're not such geniuses if this is where it leads. Learn to pick your moments, ladies.

'I'm sorry, I'm not having it,' this woman says.

'Not having what?' Fiona puts her fork down on the side of her plate.

'You're definitely the girls from the video. There's no way it's not you. We've got a bet on, and I am not going to lose just because you're liars.'

'Hey!' I protest before Fiona can. She looks at me with her mouth open. How *rude* is this person? 'We haven't been in any video, OK? And we don't know what you're talking about. We just want to have a nice breakfast in peace, please, so can you . . .' I wave her away, my fork still in my hand. I drop a piece of pancake on the table. I will get that when this stranger's left.

'No, sorry, I'm getting twenty quid if I'm right. You must be them. Look, *this* video.'

FIONA

This absolute crazy person (sorry, I know that's not very considerate language, but she *is*) holds her phone low so that Natalie and I can

153

see the screen. She hits 'play' on a video. And it is, indeed, a video of . . . well, us. This absolute crazy person is right.

My instinct, and I don't know why, is to keep a look of mild interest on my face as if she's showing me something I've never seen before, and certainly did not *take part* in. Like I'm watching a scene from a soap opera or something. But I can feel a flush rising up my face, can feel sweat beginning to form around my neck. I don't want to give my horror away, but I risk a look at Natalie. She's pressed her lips together into the thinnest line I've ever seen and looks like the girl is holding out a gun instead of a phone.

'Not *everything* is about you,' my video self shouts through the tinny little speaker, and I close my eyes. Oh god, I *did* say that. It's so much easier to put this kind of thing behind you when somebody hasn't recorded it.

Somehow, we manage to sit through until the end. Natalie and I stare at each other in horror. We need this person to *delete* that, but if we come across as too confrontational, maybe she won't. Oh god, what if she won't? No. She will. I force my face into a bemused smile.

'So, that was weird,' I say, as the girl tucks the phone back into her back pocket with a triumphant look on her face. I try to keep the tremor out of my voice. 'Funny. So, you were there last night? You know it's not cool to just film people without their permission.'

'*Me?* Oh my god, no, I would never. This is just all over Twitter. And I figured it might be someone local, I thought I recognised the Miner's Arms. Anyway, glad I was right, just won twenty quid, nice to meet you!'

She basically dances back to the table and her friends collapse into giggles. They're laughing so hard they look like they might choke. Maybe I wouldn't hate it if they did. I certainly wouldn't be in a rush to use my First Aid certificate on them. Natalie stares at me, open-mouthed, horrified.

'*You* haven't seen that before, have you?'

'God, no,' I say emphatically. And then, less emphatically, 'Although I haven't actually been on Twitter this morning, so I don't know, it could . . .' I open the app before I've even finished the sentence. Natalie gets her phone out too.

'This is so dumb.' She laughs, waiting for it to load. But the nervous look in her eye doesn't quite match the certainty in her tone. 'Nobody's going to . . .' And then she stops talking and starts scrolling.

I scroll my timeline as well. But I don't get far before I see that someone I actually really like has posted a video. I can tell from the couple of details I can make out without playing it that it's been filmed at the pub. Given all of the evidence we've had so far, what are the chances that it *isn't* of us? This person has posted it saying 'YOU AIN'T MY MUVVA! YES I AM!!!' Which, in any other situation, I'd find quite funny. Now, though, my stomach swoops like I'm on a roller coaster.

Natalie's gone awfully quiet too. I look across the table. She's still staring at her phone, her face lit ever so slightly by the glow of the screen. But her mouth is clamped shut and her jaw is tense. She looks up and meets my eyes.

'What the hell do we do?'

We try to pay for our breakfast. All either of us wants to do is leave the restaurant and the table of women who are *still* giggling. Honestly, does female solidarity mean nothing anymore? But when we ask for the bill, the waiter dismisses us.

'On the house for the local social media stars.' He winks. So that's . . . well, it's not terrible, is it? Natalie's face clouds, though. She grabs her jacket and pushes past the woman who showed us the video in the first place. That table collapses into yet more hysterics.

'Nat!' I call, and chase after her.

CHAPTER FIFTEEN

NATALIE

I had to get out of there, I just . . . I had to. Everybody laughing at us? I can't deal with it.

'Nat!' Fiona pulls on her jacket as she walks through the door, and then trots to catch up with me. 'What's wrong?'

'What do you mean, "What's wrong"?' I stop and stare at her. She nearly bumps into me.

She backtracks. 'I mean, yes, no, obviously I know "what's wrong", that's a silly question. It's gross. But are you, like, OK? You don't seem OK.'

'I am not OK.' My throat feels like it's closing when I speak, I can barely get the words out. I pick up the pace again, turning into the park, trying to stride out whatever I'm feeling that makes me want to never stop moving or see another human being ever again in my life.

'Hey, stop. Stop.' Fiona catches hold of my arm, and I do, mainly because she's holding on really tightly. I glance around, but there's nobody else here. I relax. Just a tiny bit, my shoulders just a couple of millimetres less close to my ears. 'This is OK, OK?'

'But it's so . . .' I still can't really think of the right word. 'It's icky. I feel icky. Don't you feel icky?'

The corners of her mouth twitch and she purses her lips to stop them.

'Sorry. I'm not laughing at you,' she says, 'it's the whole "icky" thing. Someone films us unawares, puts it on the internet, and all we have is "icky".'

'It is, though, isn't it?'

'Oh god, yeah. It's gross. *So* icky.'

She starts to walk, and I fall in step with her. I don't stomp away this time, I just focus on moving. Just walk on the path in the empty park and don't think about anything else. Except after a few minutes the spell of the steady steps, breathing in time with them, it all stops working. I can feel panic rising past my sternum.

'What the hell do we *do*, though?'

'I don't think there's anything we *can* do.' Fiona shrugs, rueful.

'But—' I stop.

'What would you do, then?' She looks at me, but I don't have an answer. We stand in a kind of hopeless silence for a minute until Fiona breaks it again. 'Look, what do you think other people do when they go viral?'

Another stab of panic. 'Oh my god, do you think we've gone *viral?*'

FIONA

I honestly don't know how I feel about the whole thing. Because, on the one hand, this is a huge violation. It's *so* weird. The idea that you could be out and about, living your life, and some total stranger can just film a bit of it? That's weird to start with. And then while you were sleeping they put it on the internet? Suuuuuper weird. And *then* while you were going about your Sunday morning, just minding your own business with *Sunday Brunch* on the

TV in the background or, um, *making up* with your boyfriend, or eating chocolate chip pancakes, more and more people were watching you, sharing you, talking about you, and you had no idea? A little chill runs down my spine and I shiver. It *is* icky. I still want to laugh at Natalie's choice of word but I also have no idea what else to call it.

So yeah, that's one side of it. And then at the same time . . . I kind of want to laugh? Like, this is so ridiculous. And a lot of the stuff I saw on my quick scroll through Twitter was actually quite funny. And we're all good now, so it's not like there's much harm done. I keep feeling this bubble of hysteria floating up into my throat and I want to laugh like those girls at that other table, except Natalie doesn't seem to feel anywhere near the same so I keep it pushed down. Not the time. We'll laugh about it one day.

But I don't know what counts as going viral, I don't know if we *have* gone viral, and I don't know if we're supposed to take some kind of action now? It feels like we probably should, but what? Honestly, all the time we spent learning about Pythagoras at school, when how to act in this exact situation would have been way more useful.

Natalie and I stare at each other. She looks almost like her teenage self again, just totally lost.

'Hey!' someone yells, and we both jump. Jasmine and her boyfriend are walking towards us, her little terrier running rings around them as they cross the grass. 'I was going to text you when we got home,' Jasmine says. 'Jason's just been telling me about this video. You've heard about it, right? Please tell me you've heard about it.'

'Yeah, it's come up,' Natalie says, weakly.

'Isn't it so weird? Everybody's talking about it.'

'And who's . . .' Natalie swallows. 'Everybody?'

'Oh, I don't know, just some people we've seen while walking Titan. That's why Jase had to explain. It's been great, actually. Nice not to talk about the weather for once!'

'Oh god.' Natalie puts her head in her hands. 'That means it's everywhere, doesn't it?'

NATALIE

I am going to lose my job. That's the main thing I keep thinking. I am going to lose my job. And then the second thing is, if I *do* lose my job, I will need to find a flatmate after all, and who on *earth* is going to want to live with the absolute lunatic who called someone a bitch in a YouTube video?

This might be the end of . . . I mean, everything? I'm really trying to stay calm, to not be melodramatic. But I also can't see a single way that this could pan out that doesn't end in me losing everything and being completely humiliated. I can tell Fiona's secretly a tiny bit amused, but it's alright for her. She has her life together already, it's not like Matt's going to leave her any time soon, and if she lost her job, she'd probably be secretly glad.

I can see *objectively* that it might be funny if it was a video of someone *else* that *we* were laughing at over pancakes. But, like, it's not, is it? So it's so, so, so much worse.

'Hey, it's not that bad,' Jason, Jasmine's husband, says. He pats my arm. 'If it helps, a lot of people are on your side.'

'They're taking *sides*?' Fiona gapes.

'Oh, big time. I'd say more people are on Natalie's at the moment, but you never know, the longer it goes on, they might come around.'

Fiona and I stare at each other for a second, and then she asks the question I also want to ask, even though I have a horrible feeling the answer isn't going to matter.

'And I don't suppose anyone's bothered that we're actually still friends?'

'They don't seem to be.' Jasmine at least has the decency to look a little bit sorry for us. 'Look, it's a Sunday, there's nothing else going on, no other news, you both just have to ride it out, it'll all blow over.'

FIONA

It's just so. Incredibly. Weird. But I will say I'm starting to wonder if it's as icky as I first thought. Only because . . . I don't want to sound like a twat, but it's kind of *nice* to think someone's talking about me. Before this, the only people who even knew I existed all lived in, like, a five-mile radius. So, in a weird way this makes the world feel a little bigger.

I wave at the people who beep at me because it feels like the right thing to do.

My phone buzzes when I'm nearly back.

MUM: Hi love, someone sent me a video of you and Natalie. Is everything OK?

I'm just typing out an answer when it buzzes again.

DAD: Mum's worried about you.

'So, you've been busy,' Matt says when I get home. His eyes are twinkling. It's mainly amusement, but there might be a tiny bit of concern in there if you look really hard. I decide not to look really hard.

160

'I honestly don't even know what's happening,' I tell him, and it's the truth. 'Who sent it to you?'

'I think the better question is, who *didn't* send it to me? Tim, Chris, Ryan, my *boss*. He remembered you from Christmas a couple of years ago.'

'I didn't know I was so memorable.'

'Of course you are.' He plants a kiss on the side of my head. 'Anyway, don't worry. They'll all move on to something else soon, I'm sure.'

'Right.'

I walk into the kitchen and pour myself a glass of water. I lean on the sink as I drink it.

'You guys are OK, though, right?' Matt appears in the doorway, leaning against the frame. 'You and Natalie?'

'Yeah, definitely. We had matching breakfasts. All good.'

'It's not breakfast if it's two p.m. We've been over this.' He gives me a lopsided smile.

'It is if it's pancakes.'

I nudge him playfully as I pass him in the doorway, then head back to the living room and pick up my laptop. I'd love to pretend I'm not going to google this video for the rest of the day. But I accept myself for who I am, and would ask everybody else to do the same.

NATALIE

When Fiona and I have parted ways I turn towards home, put my head down, and walk as fast as I can. I'm about halfway home when I hear what I would describe as excessively loud exercise. Like, yes. You're jogging. Congratulations. I glance up without thinking and catch sight of Roger Newcombe, the local vicar, running towards me. I recognise the face straight away from the many, many school assemblies we had to sit through where he bored us out of our minds with Bible stories. The shorts he's wearing are certainly surprising. You simply never expect to see so much of a clergyman's thigh.

He slows down as he gets closer. I dip my head again, staring extra-hard at my shoes. But then I look up, worried I'm actually just in his way. He's frowning at me. I give him a weak smile and pick up the pace as I walk past him.

'Do I know you?' he asks. I grudgingly stop and turn round, clenching my fists in my pockets to stop my hands from shaking.

'I think you used to do assemblies at my school,' I offer, because I am not about to help him with the other thing. He can't have seen the video anyway, can he? Surely he has better things to be doing than watching videos on the internet. Especially on a Sunday.

He takes a couple of steps closer and squints at my face. Which, by the way, is turning redder by the second. Then he suddenly makes a noise like he's figured out a difficult crossword clue.

'No, I know! You were in that video.'

For a second, my instinct is to feign confusion, pretend it wasn't me. But, I mean, there's literally a video, so I'm not sure that's going to work. I could pretend I have a twin who also lives locally . . . But maybe things are bad enough without bringing more chaos into it. So, I concede.

'Oh. Yeah, there was a video.'

'Well' – Reverend Roger bends down to pull his socks up and then picks up each foot in turn and rolls his ankles – 'we have the half marathon in a couple of months. Maybe we'll get you to start the race if all of this is still going on then. You can be our celebrity guest!'

He starts jogging again before I can let him know how little I want to do that.

162

I get about two paces down the road when my phone goes off.

MUM: NATALIE WHAT IS THAT VIDEO

MUM: HOW DO I GET OFF ALL CAPS

MUM: ARE YOU OK???

How do you say 'no' in a way that won't worry your parents?

CHAPTER SIXTEEN

NATALIE

I spent the whole of the rest of Sunday scared of my phone. When I finally got home I had a message from Sophie saying 'have you seen this????????' and of *course* it was the video. And in a way it was good because I hadn't actually seen the whole thing, just the clip that the (I assume) tipsy girl had shown us both while we were out. So, thanks to Sophie, I could watch the whole thing and see what I was dealing with. Rip off the Band-Aid and all that.

So, I did watch it. And then more messages started coming through. My parents – well, my mum, but my dad was definitely looking over her shoulder while she tapped it out with one finger – texted *again* even though I'd already tried to shrug the whole thing off. A couple of ex-colleagues from the school sent me the same thing. My auntie, who I did not realise even had my number, messaged me too.

I looked at my phone, more out of muscle memory than anything else, and I seemed to have become a magnet for every man in a hundred-mile radius with a paid Tinder subscription, because I had *not* matched with any of the people in my inbox.

LUCAS: You're that girl off that video! Like a feisty one ;)
OLLY: LOL as if anyone'd go out with you after that

In the end, I turned my phone off. I spent most of the evening sitting in silence. I even tried to read an honest-to-god book. Except I just kept reading the same sentence over and over again without it ever going in. In the end, I stopped. And then I just stared into space and tried to stop my stomach lurching until I could reasonably go to bed.

I *am* only human, so I *did* turn my phone on one last time, just to check that nobody had died. Still only my dignity, as it turned out. But another batch of 'IS THIS YOU???' messages came in, mainly from people I used to work with or people I'd met once.

JAKE: Love me a fiery woman <3

LEWIS: Hey, just wanted to say, saw the video and I think you're really fit. You usually only see skinny women online!

MILES: Yet another hysterical woman, hope you manage to find some peace.

I turned it off.

But then I turned it on. Again. And, this time, I deleted Instagram. I deleted Facebook. Twitter, too. I wondered if I should do Tinder. In the space of mere minutes another message had come through.

MILES: Your friend is way better looki—

So Tinder went too.

I got up. Sat back down. Got up again. I went to the bathroom and did my skincare more meticulously than I have ever done it before. And then I lay with my eyes closed but my mind whirring for basically the entire night.

What I'm getting to is that I arrived at my desk an hour early today and am already staring blankly at my third cup of coffee when other people start arriving. There're still some names I'm trying to connect to faces, but I look over my screen and smile in greeting as they trickle in. One man – he might be a Tim or another Tom? – makes eye contact, frowns, and then widens his eyes. When he sits down at his desk he immediately whispers to the woman next to him – a Becky or a Becca or a Bex, I think? – and she turns around and stares at me too. I smile at them both in a manner that I hope says 'I know exactly what you're whispering about and, believe me, I am not proud of it.'

'Morning, Natalie,' Jenny says, pulling the strap of her bag over her body and putting it down on the desk. She shrugs off her jacket and hangs it on the back of her chair. 'You had an eventful weekend, then.'

I shrug. 'Um . . . yeah. You could say that.' Which is dumb and obvious, but at least it's words. She seems satisfied and disappears behind her monitor.

Tom arrives shortly afterwards. 'Oh my god, Kim Kardashian, I thought you'd be too famous for this place.'

'Oh, ha ha,' I deadpan, fake-glaring at him. As I look away I realise Jenny's looking at me coldly.

We have a meeting at eleven a.m. It's the first time I've seen the Big Boss, John Stait. I think I would have been nervous to meet him anyway but *now* when I've become some kind of social media sensation overnight and everybody knows it. Nightmare.

People around the office begin to shuffle papers, stand up, and file into the meeting room in the corner. I glance over at Sophie and she grins and gives me a thumbs up. She's already told me I don't need to be nervous about this, and Tom has confirmed it too. But I did not come from the kind of place where we ever had meetings, so I've managed to make myself nervous anyway.

I don't want to sound ageist, but I do relax slightly when I follow Jenny into the room. I'm not saying Mr Stait is old, but . . .

well, he is. He's not *elderly* or anything, but he has a thick head of salt and pepper (vastly more salt than pepper, if you catch my drift) hair, and he definitely looks like he has better things to do with his weekend than scrolling through Twitter watching viral videos. He's wearing pastel-coloured chinos, so I assume he will have been drinking fine whiskey or roasting a pheasant, or something. He waits at one end of the table, near the door, and greets people as they come in.

'Aha, you must be our new account coordinator!' he booms with a plummy accent when he catches sight of me. He strides over and holds out a hand. I shake it, and then wonder if I'm allowed to sue for broken bones.

'Natalie Starr, Mr Stait.'

'Please, call me John.'

I nod, wondering if I'm allowed to move on and find a seat. Tom appears at the doorway and John Stait (I'm sorry, he really doesn't seem like a first-name-only kind of man) corners him instead. I sit down at the horseshoe-shaped table and puff out my cheeks.

Once the meeting starts, everybody gives updates on their mostly one-person departments. But even though they're the only people in them they still call themselves by the name of the department, so 'Marketing has done this', 'Finance has achieved that'. Very weird. Jenny does our 'Customer Success' update, and for a moment I wonder if she's about to say 'half of Customer Success has completely humiliated herself', but she doesn't. I purse my lips and exhale through them while Tom shifts in his seat next to me and begins talking about what 'Sales' has done.

'Lovely stuff, team. Thank you very much. And, before I forget, emails will be coming around soon about the CLC Family Fun Day. Please make sure you save the date. It's outrageously expensive to put on, so invite lots of people. Can be friends, too. Can

167

be strangers you meet in the street if you're prepared to vouch for them. Just make sure you're there. Now, any other business?'

'Just one more thing,' Jenny calls as people are starting to gather their things and stand up. My heart sinks as she places both hands on the table and gets to her feet. We were so close to making it without the video coming up. But, somehow, I suspect we haven't quite managed.

'I think it's worth reminding everyone about the social media policy we have at CLC. Basically, do whatever you like, but don't bring the company into disrepute. It's all in the handbook, obviously, I just think some people here would do well to remember it. Especially if they only got the handbook recently in the first place.'

Eyes start flicking my way and, really, if the building collapsed on us all now, I wouldn't hate it.

'This is about the video with Natalie in, isn't it?' Tom asks, shifting in his seat beside me. His arm brushes against mine, and I wish I was familiar enough with him to thump him in it so he'd shut up.

'I don't think it's appropriate to single anybody out in this.' Jenny shrugs. 'I'm just saying, we should all remember that what we do reflects on the company we work for and be a bit mindful of how we behave.'

'OK, so how does somebody being filmed without their knowledge or consent fit into that?' I steal a glance at Tom. His ears have gone red as he narrows his eyes at Jenny. 'Are we supposed to walk around for the rest of our lives behaving like saints just in *case* somebody happens to violate our privacy? Just in *case* a million different circumstances collide and we end up going viral?'

I try to make myself smaller in my seat, while Jenny and Tom bicker over my head.

'Well, it would probably be nice if we could all generally behave, yeah.' Jenny sounds casual, but there are pink spots on each cheek that suggest she might not have been prepared for follow-up discussion.

'So, let me get this straight.' Sophie's chiming in now. I widen my eyes at her across the horseshoe of tables, will her to shut up, to let this be over, but she doesn't pay any attention. Why is nobody letting this *go*? I mean, I appreciate the principle of them all coming to my defence, but you know what I would appreciate more? Being able to run away and hide in the toilets. Sophie isn't done, of course. 'I have to basically behave like a nun now because some total weirdo might film me against my will? And *I'm* the one with the problem in that scenario?'

A couple more people start murmuring and Jenny holds up her hands. 'I'm not saying that anybody has a problem. I'm not. I'm just saying that it would be nice if people could think about their actions, that's all.'

'That's not all, though, is it?' Sophie argues. 'Because you're blaming the victim. And you should also be saying that *someone* has a problem, but the person with the problem is clearly not Natalie.'

'But if she hadn't been . . .'

Sophie's got people riled up now. Everybody starts grumbling. Beside me, Tom says something that sounds like 'arsehole' under his breath, but I can't be sure. A few seats down, somebody says, 'Hang on!'

For a second an expression flashes across Jenny's face that suggests she'd love nothing more than to sit back down and never have said anything. But she covers it almost immediately, choosing one instead that looks cool, unbothered, like she's some kind of superior being to all of us. She glances at John Stait, who, to be honest, I had actually forgotten was there. Shit.

'Thank you very much, Jenny,' he says, getting to his feet and holding up a hand to quiet the room. 'It's actually quite an interesting debate, but one that I don't really have any interest in getting into, if I'm being very honest.'

Jenny looks thunderstruck. 'But—'

'But nothing. Look, I can't pretend to know what all of you are getting so het up about. You know social media isn't my thing. So, all I'll say is, Jenny is right about the social media policy we have at CLC. And if anything ever gets so out of hand that *I* end up hearing about it outside of . . . whatever's happening right now, then we might have to consider further consequences. OK. Good? Good.'

Jenny pushes out of the room while everybody's still getting to their feet and picking up their mugs and notebooks. Sophie pulls a face at me. I grimace back.

'Alright?' Tom murmurs behind me as we file out.

I nod.

FIONA

The first day back at the shop after The Unpleasantness wasn't actually as bad as it could have been. Natalie had me worried, mainly because she was worried. When she texted me in a panic multiple times on Monday morning, she managed to plant the seeds of a hundred 'what if's that never would have occurred to me if I was left to my own devices.

But Angelo, my boss, greeted me with the same 'raised hand and no eye contact' combo he uses for everyone when I arrived. I don't think he'd even *seen* the video, let alone had any feelings about it. And Amy gave me a hero's welcome when I came in. It was nice to finally be able to laugh about it. No customers seemed to recognise me or, if they did, they kept it to themselves. I think the postman might have winked at me when he came in but worse things happen at sea. He might just be a flirt, I don't know. I wish Natalie could see that all of this is only as big an issue as she allows it to become.

NATALIE

I get an email after lunch which somehow sucks all of the air from
my lungs.

> FROM: Gemma Worthing
> TO: Natalie Starr
>
> Dear Natalie,
>
> I hope it's OK to email you on this address.

– (Which, incidentally, I feel like if that's something you have to
say you almost certainly know that it is not.) –

> My name is Gemma Worthing and I'm a reporter
> for the *Crostdam Chronicle*. I understand that
> you're one of the women who featured in this
> viral video recently. I was just wondering if you
> and your friend (if she's still your friend?) would
> be interested in giving an interview? Would
> love to chat to you about what you make of
> everything, and how you feel about becoming
> an overnight sensation!
>
> Please do get back to me.
>
> KR
>
> Gemma

I mean, I don't know what about this is worse. Someone who doesn't know me in real life having my name and knowing it was me in that video? The fact that I was just starting to think it was dying down and now here we are again? The idea of being interviewed about it? The fact that this person emailed me *at work*? Especially when only a couple of hours ago I was warned not to let this whole thing get any bigger. I inhale sharply to try and stop the panic from rising in my chest. I must do it quite loudly, because Jenny's head pops up above my screen.

'Everything OK?' she asks, smiling sweetly. It's like the whole 'social media policy' thing this morning didn't even happen. And I'm willing to go along with the pretence for a quiet life, but I do find it a bit weird.

'Yes, fine, thank you.' I smile. 'Have you got anything you need me to do, or . . .'

'Not at the moment, thanks. I'll let you know.'

I nod, and Jenny disappears again. Tom catches my eye. He frowns in a way that seems to say 'Are you OK?' I nod. But then I stand up so fast my chair crashes into the shelves behind me and hurry out of the room.

FIONA

'Nat, slow down,' I say, finger pressed to my free ear in the alley behind Scoopz. I have to get back – we're rushed off our feet. I glance nervously towards the door. 'Say it all again.'

'Oh god,' Natalie groans. 'This is such a mess. Oh god, oh god, oh god.'

'Natalie,' I prompt. 'I need to get back. What happened?'

'Some journalist emailed me. At work! Where I've only been for a week! Where they warned us, *literally today*, to, like, be on our best behaviour. I don't think this counts. She wants to do an interview, and I don't . . . What do I tell her? I mean, no, obviously. But if she knows who I am doesn't that mean other people might know who I am too? How did she even get my name? You didn't tell anyone, did you?'

'You know I wouldn't do that.'

'Yeah, no, I know. Sorry. I just . . . Fiona, what do I *do*?'

'I wish I knew,' I say. Because I do.

'I should just ignore her, I think. She can't be emailing me at work, I don't want any part of this.'

I watch a couple of seagulls trying to tear open one of the bin bags I just left in the overfull dumpster. I can hear another car door slamming outside the front of the shop. I need to get back.

'Can't you just . . .' I try to think how to phrase it without freaking her out. '*Do* the interview?'

'*What?*' Natalie demands. I hold the phone a tiny bit further from my ear. I guess I did not phrase it right.

'Well, if someone knows who you are they'll keep emailing you, won't they? So maybe you just need to get it over with. And then everybody will lose interest. Someone actually famous will do something dumb soon, and then we're in the clear. So in the meantime, you just get it done and it gets people off our backs, right? Or, well, your back.'

'Fi, I love you, but I would rather die. Someone from work would see it. This is the first job I've ever had that I might really like, I can't lose it already, you know?'

'I don't know.'

'No, I know. I didn't mean . . . I just . . .'

Amy sticks her head around the door and beckons me frantically, pulling a face. I need to hurry. I wrack my brains at twice the speed. And then I hit on something. It's brilliant.

'Give her *my* name.'

'What?'

'I'm in that video too, give her my name, tell her I'll do it. I don't mind.' In fact, and I would never tell Natalie this, the idea gives me a little thrill.

Natalie is quiet for a long time. Well, a long time in the context of me needing to get back inside and her holding me up. I kick a stone while I wait for her to speak again.

'You wouldn't mind?'

'Are you kidding? It's fine! I wouldn't care if anyone from work sees it, for one thing. Angelo would probably be thrilled. If they do photos, he'll want them done here. He definitely won't fire me. He can't, I'm the fastest employee he's got.'

What an achievement, Fiona.

'Only if . . . Look, I don't want you to feel obliged.'

'Honestly? It'll be fun. Give her my name.'

NATALIE

When Fiona hangs up, I clench my fist around my phone and take a couple of deep breaths. They echo around the fire escape. I lean my forehead against the breeze blocks on the wall. They feel pleasantly cool. It's OK. She'll handle it. Someone will handle it and it doesn't have to be me. I breathe in again. Hold it. Let it go. It's all going to go away.

I can hardly bring myself to look at the email when I'm back at my desk, I just want to delete it forever, pretend it never happened. Instead, I am a big, brave girl, and I reply like a big, brave girl.

FROM: Natalie Starr
TO: Gemma Worthing

Dear Gemma,

I hope you're well.

– (I begin, even though I have never hoped anything less.) –

> I'm pleased to say that Fiona (my friend from
> the video) is, in fact, still my best friend. I'm
> afraid I won't be able to meet and talk to you,
> but she'll be happy to. I've included her con-
> tact info below.
>
> Thanks!
>
> Natalie

I sigh, shaking out my hands to release some of the tension, and Tom looks up.

'You sure everything's OK?' he asks. I glance at where Jenny usually sits, but she isn't there.

'Yep. Thank you.'

I give him a very formal nod as if he didn't try to stand up for me earlier, then look back at my screen. I am a strong, confident Business Bitch, and the world is my oyster, and—

An email pings through.

> FROM: Gemma Worthing
> TO: Natalie Starr
>
> Great! Jenny said she didn't think you'd be too
> keen but this is fantastic. I'll get in touch with
> Fiona.

Gemma

And, just like that, this strong, confident Business Bitch is heading back to the fire escape.

Fiona

'Is everything OK?' I demand when my phone rings a second time in one work day. We're still run off our feet because it's been, what, fifteen minutes since she last called me? My patience is wearing thin. Even *I* think it's unprofessional to spend *this* much time on the phone in the middle of the day and I don't have a literal dream job.

'I . . . Do you know what? Yeah. It's fine.'

Natalie hangs up. She didn't sound fine.

'Fiona, could I trouble you to do some work at some point today?' Angelo calls from the office and I don't have time to think any more about it.

Natalie

I don't know what to do. I *do not* know what to do. I just . . . *Jenny* gave her my name? Jenny of 'don't bring the company into disrepute' fame? I feel like I'm losing my mind. What does she *want*? That is basically my question. If I knew what she was playing at I might know what to do next, but I'm at a loss. All I can do is stare at the breeze block walls and try to stop panicking. Because it's not like I can tell anyone about this, can I? Oh god, it's such a mess, and I don't . . .

'Natalie?' A voice echoes down from somewhere above me, jolting me out of my looping thoughts. Tom. I freeze, and then creep backwards until I'm pressed against the wall and I can't go any further. I hold my breath so he won't hear me. But he doesn't seem to be going anywhere. 'I know you're in here. Are you OK?'

Eventually I have to exhale, and of course it echoes up to him, and then suddenly his feet appear at the top of the stairs, and the rest of him follows.

I shake my head to stop my brain from constantly whirring, then paint a fake smile across my face. 'Hi! Of course. Just needed to stretch my legs, I'll be back up again in a—'

'She's done something mad, hasn't she?'

'No.' I don't know why my immediate reaction is to lie. I don't know why I feel the need to let her off lightly. But I guess it's not so much the need to protect her as the desire to not make things awkward. Like, yes, she did a weird, bad thing. But if I make things awkward then that also makes things awkward for me. And haven't I dealt with enough?

'You're lying.' Tom narrows his eyes at me.

I glance up the stairs, wondering if I could just make a run for it. The thing is, it would also be quite awkward to run away from someone and then have to sit opposite them for the rest of the day while pretending you aren't extremely childish. So I kind of don't think I can win here. In the end, I give up and sit on a step.

'She wrote to a journalist about me. They want to interview me.' I huff. '*She* was the one who was all "Oh no, don't do *anything* to hurt the company."'

Tom laughs at my impression of Jenny and then sits next to me. 'Look, you know what everybody said about her at the beach the other night. She's so attached to being the best one out of all of us. She obviously feels threatened by you. If anything, I'd take it as a compliment. I've sat next to her for, like, eighteen months and she has never once tried to take *me* down. I'm actually quite offended.'

I smile and then drop my head into my hands. 'I just . . . What's she going to do next? I don't want to lose this job.'

'You won't. You heard everyone in that meeting. People have your back.'

'Yeah, but . . .' I look at him. 'You've all only just met me.'

'So maybe we just get off on thwarting Jenny, is that so wrong?'

'I mean, depends what you mean by "get off on it".'

Tom throws back his head and laughs. It echoes around the stairwell. We sit on the steps for a moment longer and then I start moving. We should go back, really.

'Hey,' Tom says. 'So what's the deal with you and this friend?'

I open my mouth. Big question. In the end I settle for the easiest answer. 'Her name's Fiona. And she's my best friend.'

'Still? Even after you . . .'

I wave a hand. 'Please, that was nothing. We once had a fight over a fluffy pencil that lasted for days.'

'You've been friends for a while, then. I hope. If not, I need more info on the fluffy pencil thing.'

'Forever.'

He shifts, trying to find a more comfortable spot on the concrete step. Which, let me tell you, does not exist. 'That's nice.'

I move too, trying to bring my own numb bum back to life. 'Yeah. We were going to go travelling once. Didn't quite make it. But it's the thought that counts, right?'

'Why didn't you make it?'

I pause before I speak. 'We were saving up to go together, but we were still quite a way off. But then her boyfriend's dad died – he didn't really know him – and he was left some money. And then he decided that *he* wanted to go. And then she went with him instead.'

178

'So she just left you?'

'Well, that makes me sound pathetic. But, I mean, kind of. Like, I don't blame her. All of the stuff with Matt's – that's her boyfriend – dad was kind of tough. And you can't be like "no, screw him, you *have* to hang out with me", can you?'

Tom pulls a face. 'I don't know, I'd probably say something if I had a plan and then my friend dumped me to do the same thing with someone else.'

I stand up. 'OK, well, that is because you don't understand the beauty of a simple life.'

Tom stands too. 'Is it a simple life, though? She left you and you've just, what, never addressed it?'

'No, she said she was sorry. I just chose to take her at her word quickly, instead of giving both of us a really hard time for ages. And I got to go and see her in Florence, that was nice.'

'Yeah, but you could have—'

I hold up a hand. 'I'm going to stop you there. I could have done a lot of things. I could have been a pop star, who knows. But I didn't, and I'm not, and what's the point in dwelling on anything anyway?'

I start walking back up the stairs, and it takes a minute to realise that Tom isn't with me. I look over the banister and he's still standing on the same step, looking up at me, a slight frown on his face.

'Are you coming?' I ask.

He shakes his head and starts walking.

CHAPTER SEVENTEEN

FIONA

'So you'll just make it go away and then you'll get out of there?' Natalie asked when I went round to talk tactics with her.

'Yes,' I promised. Not that I would ever have pointed it out to her, but it was a *tiny* bit funny how much of a panic she'd worked herself into. It's only the *Chronicle*, for goodness' sake. We've all been in it before. You couldn't so much as draw a picture when we were at school without it ending up in the *Chronicle*. Everybody's parents stuck the clippings on the fridge the first time, and the second. Then, by the third, they realised this was going to be a very regular occurrence and stopped. But anyway. My point is, I don't think she needs to have her knickers in *quite* so much of a twist about it.

'Because I have a life now!' she said, when I made the mistake of asking what she was worried about. 'I have a job I want to keep, sorry' – I felt a *tiny* flicker of annoyance, because I do wish she'd stop apologising *every* time she mentions work, it makes it very hard to keep being happy for her – 'and, I don't know, neighbours who I don't want talking about me. What if they see you've moved out and think I forced you? What if I still need to find a flatmate one day and they google me? What if I date someone one day and *they* google me?'

'People don't google each other.'

'Fiona, with all due respect, you have no idea.'

I'm meeting this reporter lady, Gemma, in the new coffee shop that just opened in town.

'I saw your video,' the owner says as she puts a cappuccino on a tray. She puts a cookie on it too, with a wink. 'On the house.'

'Thanks!'

'So, how's life as a viral video star?' she asks before I can take the tray away.

'Well, I'm not exactly a *star*, am I? Nobody even knows my name. Except,' I concede, casting a surreptitious look around the café and lowering my voice, 'I mean, I *am* here to meet a journalist. She wants to interview me about it.' Well, Natalie originally, but I don't have to say that.

'That's exciting!'

I think about this for a moment. All I've really heard about it so far is Natalie freaking out in person, on the phone, and via text message. She's sent me long lists of what I can and can't talk about. She's given me lectures about tone of voice, read me lists of facts about body language she found on the internet. Last night was *long*. Any inkling of excitement I felt since I agreed to this has been well and truly stamped out. But you know what? This woman is right.

'Well, anyway, back to it.' She turns around to adjust something on the coffee machine and I take my tray and find a table. I sit down and eat my cookie, which tastes all the sweeter for being free.

'Hi, Fiona?'

Someone appears in front of me. I jump to my feet, my chair scraping on the tiled floor.

'Hi! Yes.'

The woman holds out a hand. 'Hi, I'm Gemma. So nice to meet you.'

'You too.'

'Are you OK for a drink?'

I nod, and Gemma heads for the counter. I sit down. And then I stand up again, because will she think I'm rude? But, no. That's mad. I sit down again, but I still keep myself primed to jump out of my seat if that does turn out to be the vibe after all. When Gemma turns around and smiles at me, holding up a finger to say she'll be one minute, I smile back like I'm not being completely neurotic.

When she comes back to the table, she puts her coffee cup down gently and takes out her phone.

'Are you OK with me recording this?' she asks. I nod, and she opens her voice notes. 'So, you've had an eventful few days.'

I laugh sheepishly. 'You could say that.'

'So, what's it been like? Going viral, I mean.'

I puff out my cheeks. 'I don't even know. I'm sorry, that's a terrible answer, but it's so bizarre.'

'Do you find it weird that so many people are talking about you?'

'God, absolutely. But, like, the weirdest thing isn't even that. It's the fact that all of these people have decided exactly what they think was going on between Natalie and me. I've read the comments. Everybody just deciding, without even knowing who we are, that we're "too emotional", or that our whole *generation* is? Because of one video? I just think that's mad. Isn't that mad?'

'It does seem kind of mad,' Gemma agrees.

I take a sip of my flat white while she writes a couple of notes.

We talk for twenty minutes or so, and the more we do, the more I feel myself relaxing. I can do this. It isn't scary. It's just a chat with another person. I tell her all about travelling, we talk about

Crostdam and how it's changed (or hasn't), and we talk about being on the internet and what that's like in this day and age. I sort of forget that I'm even being interviewed. The little Natalie in the back of my head reminding me to be on my best behaviour completely disappears.

'So, Fiona, tell me. I know people will be dying to know the background of this video. What is your relationship like with Natalie normally?'

'Oh, god, she's my best friend. Easily my best friend. We live . . . *lived* together. Up until very recently.'

'But that wasn't . . . because of the argument?' I can see the hope in her eyes. She's very nice, but she'd still clearly love it if she got that scoop.

I laugh. 'God, no. I moved in with my boyfriend.'

'Nice! And things going well there? Wedding bells on the horizon?'

'What? Why?' I snap. My collar suddenly feels too tight. Way to play it cool in front of the journalist, Fiona, jeez.

'No reason?' Gemma waves away my panic. 'Just gives a bit of colour, nothing major.'

'Oh, well, no. Not quite ready for the ball and chain yet.' I laugh before I notice that she's wearing an engagement ring herself. 'Not that if someone was they'd be . . .'

But she's not even paying any attention, she's reading from her notepad. 'So, can you give us any insight into what the argument was about? I know that's a big topic of speculation.'

'So I've seen.' I pause, wondering what to say. I guess I don't really know myself. 'Honestly, just one of those things, I think. There's been a lot of change lately, with me moving, and it was just a lot of upheaval and stress. You know what it's like.'

'Sure.'

Gemma looks a tiny bit disappointed with my answer (so am I) and starts packing her stuff back into her bag.

'Oh, what, so that's it?'

'That's all there is to it.' She smiles. I can't believe Natalie was so freaked out about this, really, the woman's a delight. 'I'll arrange for someone to take a quick portrait sometime, if that's OK? It should only take a couple of minutes. It's a surprisingly quick business!'

She gives me a cheery wave and seems to be out the door before I've even lifted my hand to return it.

NATALIE

I rush out of the office kitchen when my phone buzzes in my hand.

'Hey, how'd it go?' I whisper as I hold a hand against the fire escape door to stop it closing too quickly and slamming. I swear I might as well move in here at this point. At least it'll all be over soon and I'll be back at my desk trying to figure out what the hell my job's supposed to be.

'It was good.' Fiona sounds relaxed. How can she be relaxed? It's probably an hour before I expected to hear anything. There's a bowl of soup in the microwave that proves I still expected the interview to be happening. I didn't expect to be able to *eat* the soup either. Just keeping up appearances.

'You're sure?' I ask. 'Was it OK? Did they ask anything horrible? You don't think they tried to trick you, or mislead you, or—'

'Natalie. Chill. You know they're not all like some parody in a TV show or something.' Says the PR expert who's met all of one journalist ever for less than an hour.

'OK. Sorry.' I don't really know what to say then. I try again. 'So, was it? OK, I mean?'

'Honestly, it was nice. If we have to do any more you should come along.'

'*What?*'

'I'm just sayi—'

'Fiona, there won't *be* any more. There can't be any more. That was *it*, remember? Just to make it go away. And now it's gone away, and we can leave it.'

'No, yeah, I know.' Fiona speaks quickly. 'I just. It wasn't as scary as you were thinking, that's all I meant.'

'And no more.'

'No more.'

'Well, I owe you one, anyway.'

'You can take me out for a drink to celebrate. I'll have my people call your people.'

'Ha ha,' I deadpan.

FIONA

I lean back in my chair when I've hung up on Natalie. That was officially my last duty as Media Spokesperson. Funny. I was starting to enjoy it for a second. But, OK. I owe Natalie this, don't I? I have to give her this one.

NATALIE

In all of the kerfuffle over the interview, it takes me a while to remember that I'm supposed to be inviting people to this CLC family thing. But, I figure, it's a nice way to get back to normal. Try to, at least.

'What's up?' Fiona answers when I call her at lunch.

'Hey, are you busy?'

'I mean, the shop is busy. *I* am hiding. Very important that I get the stock room organised in order of date, I think.'

'Totally. What even is a shop without an organised stock room?'

I watch a sparrow hopping along the other picnic table out the back of the office. I squeeze a crust of bread between my fingers.

'So, what's up?' Fiona prompts again. 'More public appearances for me?'

'What? No. Of course not.'

'Alright, well, it was only a joke.' She sounds stung.

I clear my throat. 'Sorry.'

'No no, carry on.'

'OK, well . . .' I'm not sure how to begin. I don't want it to be weird. 'CLC are having this, like, family day thing. It's next Saturday. It's in someone's field, like a festival or something. We're all allowed to bring a few guests, and I was just wondering if you fancied coming along? My parents are going, and Sophie'll be there too. It's sort of food, and games, and things. I think a bit of music? It might be a bit twee but there'll be drinks, and it's free.' It comes out in a rush, but at least it's out. I hold the now-squashed crust out towards the sparrow.

'Next Saturday?' Fiona repeats.

'Yeah, is that OK?' The sparrow hops closer.

'I can't make it,' Fiona says, after a pause. 'I'm helping Angelo somewhere. Like, a wedding or something? He's literally getting the van out.'

'Gertie!' The sparrow flies away, startled.

'Gertie.'

'I didn't know he still *had* Gertie.'

'Neither did I. But she's riding again. Sorry. But you know how much money we bring in on those, I can't really turn it down.'

'No, of course.'

FIONA

I stare at the boxes lined up on the racks in front of me. I feel a kind of warmth somewhere in my chest. Because it was nice of her to ask me to come. And I genuinely would have said yes if it weren't for this wedding. And it just feels like we're finally getting back onto a more even keel, like we're finally managing to get past some of the awkwardness. Do not get me wrong, I cannot imagine anything *worse* than spending an afternoon living in fear of bumping into people who've witnessed me completely bombing a job interview. I probably would have made up an excuse if I didn't already have one. But it's the thought that counts, right? And the thought was there.

NATALIE

In a way, it's a relief, anyway. The idea of mixing work life with the rest of my life is already making me uncomfortable. It definitely won't be the end of the world if I don't get to add *more* people to that mix.

At the back of my mind, I'm also conscious that the interview with Fiona will have come out just before the family day. I'm very aware that I don't really know what she ended up saying. I know she told me it was fine, but it might work out better if people don't see the two of us together. It's not that I don't trust her, I don't think she'd actually let me down. I just . . . I mean . . . And I *hate* myself for thinking it, obviously, but this is really, really big. And, well, she's got form.

FIONA

'Hey!' Matt calls on a Thursday evening as I get home and close the door with a slam.

'Hi!' I shout back, tucking the *Crostdam Chronicle* under my arm so I can take my shoes off.

He appears in the kitchen doorway, drying his hands on a tea towel even though I bought us hand towels for that exact purpose. Men. 'I saw the interview.'

'What did you think?' I ask, sitting on the hallway bench to take off my shoes.

'I thought it was really good! You came across really well, great pictures. I bought a few copies. Got one for my mum. Got one for your parents too, I thought they might want it. Natalie must be pleased?'

'I think so. She's taking me out tonight, actually. We agreed she would after the interview. You should come too.' Matt's face drops. 'What?'

He sighs. 'It's . . . No, do you know what? It's nothing. It's fine. I just thought maybe I'd cook for us tonight. You know, celebrate? I spatchcocked a chicken.'

It's really lovely. I do know it's really lovely. But I also . . . don't understand when we became middle-aged and stopped going *out* to celebrate good things when they happen? I want to go *out*. I feel like people need to see me go out.

'I could eat first, though, right? And then go?'

'I haven't even put the oven on, it'll be ages, just . . . Look, go and hang out with Natalie. We can have it for lunch tomorrow.'

'You're sure you don't mind? Why don't you come?'

I can tell from his posture that he definitely minds, and I really do feel bad. But he also didn't mention *any* of this to me, so I'm not really sure it's my fault.

'No, look. I've got some work I have to finish – I should stay home. But you go, it's fine.'

'Thank you.' I grin and step forward to kiss him on the cheek. As I pull away I think he *might* reach a hand out to pull me back towards him, but if he does he's snatched it back before my brain makes the connection. And I have to run, anyway. I need to get changed.

CHAPTER EIGHTEEN

NATALIE

This feels like such a bad idea. Or maybe not a *bad* idea, but certainly a weird one. Why would we return to the scene of the crime to celebrate the newspaper article about the crime? I don't want to celebrate it at all, as it happens. This is very much not the definition of 'make it go away'.

'You can't put it off forever,' Fiona reminds me as I pause outside the door. I can hear laughter from inside, and shadows move in the light that spills from the windows onto the pavement. And I could go home now and nobody would even know. Except Fiona. And I owe her because she saved my arse. I look at her and I'm obviously not hiding my trepidation well enough because she adds, 'Where else will you ever go out again if the one pub in town is off limits?'

She does have a point, so I fall behind her as she opens the door. It takes a minute for people to start noticing us, to start nudging their friends, and for a whisper to make its way around the room. Then there are a couple of moments of complete silence, during which I can hear my heart hammering in my ears. And then the place erupts into cheers. It's like we've come back from winning the World Cup or something. For a second, we're frozen to the spot. Then Fiona throws back her head and laughs. She raises an arm in the air and does an exaggerated bow, practically to the floor. People start cheering all over again. It's so disappointing. It really felt like it was all going to go away for a second. Is this what everything going away looks like? I think not. I think everything is back and bigger than ever.

'Drink?' I call to Fiona over the noise of people's excited chatter. She shakes her head, frowns, points at her ear. 'Drink?' I basically yell directly into the side of her face. She gives me a thumbs up and is dragged off to talk to a group of people before I've taken another step.

'What can I get you?' Dave the barman asks. Dave the barman is paying attention? To me? That's new.

I order a bottle of wine because it works out cheaper than buying glasses, and rifle through my bag to find my purse. When I pull out my card he waves it away.

'What's up?' I ask. I really have to shout. It is *loud* in here today. If it'd been like this last time there wouldn't have been a problem because nobody would have been able to hear a word we'd said anyway.

'This one's on the house.'

'Why?'

'Look around you! It's been busy in here ever since that video. And then getting a name check in the paper as well? You're the best marketing team I've ever had. So this is on the house.'

'I'd really rather pay,' I say, quite pathetically. Maybe if we act normal things will *become* normal again? And the first step to being normal again very much does not involve being given free drinks.

'What?' Dave shouts, pressing his ear forward like that might help.

I put both hands on top of the bar and lift myself onto the very tips of my toes so I can basically scream into his face. 'I said I'd prefer to pay!'

'Not a chance, young lady. Legends drink free!' He shouts the last part like he's geeing up troops in a film. The cheering starts up again and I cringe but try not to show that I'm cringing. Dave slides the wine bottle towards me, as well as two glasses and four (?!) packets of crisps. I have to carry the crisps in my teeth as I balance everything else in my hands. A couple of people slap me on the back as I squeeze through the crowd. Deeply unhelpful in my precarious situation.

FIONA

By the time Natalie reappears from the bar a small crowd has gathered around me to hear the tale of the viral video. I'm sitting on one of the tables, which I thought would get me told off, but so far I'm getting away with it. I don't even recognise most of the people sitting on chairs they've pulled here from all over the pub. More people are leaning against the walls. I think you might say I'm 'holding court'. It's fantastic.

Natalie pushes her way through everybody, juggling a bottle of wine and two glasses, and has some bags of crisps clamped between her teeth.

'Pushing the boat out?' I ask with a raised eyebrow. 'I should do your PR more often.'

'Dave loves us now apparently. Gave it to us for free.'

I crane my neck to look back towards the bar and Dave gives me a thumbs up. I wave back. I didn't even know he knew who I was, not really. This is mad.

'Hey, Fiona.' Someone taps my knee. 'Carry on. You were saying, you were at breakfast and then you heard about the video.'

I glance at Natalie and she shrugs, twisting the cap off the wine bottle and picking up a glass. I turn back to my audience.

'Right, so, Natalie was freaking out about it, of course, and—'

'Why "of course"?' Natalie laughs as she tears open each of the crisp packets and lays them flat on the table. I know she wants to seem like she's amused, in on the joke with all of the rest of these people. But she's blushing too hard and, if you know her like I do, it's enough to give the game away.

'"Of course" because it's just weird, right?' I say. I'm treading a difficult line between entertaining my public and not throwing her under the bus. Natalie motions for me to continue.

I think I . . . *love* this? I wait for the whispering to die down before I continue, and I'm about to open my mouth when my phone buzzes.

MATT: Hey! Finished the work thing now, you still at the pub? Could come hang out? XX

I read the text a couple of times as a hush falls over the people waiting for me to continue the story. I glance up. And then I look back down at my phone.

FIONA: Hey, kind of dead here so might come back soon. Don't think it's worth it tbh x

I'm a terrible person. I know. But if Matt comes here, he'll want me to hang out with just him and Natalie and I'm not sure I'm willing to sit quietly in a corner again. Not yet, anyway.

I glance up at Natalie. I know she won't be enjoying it like I am. But I *did* do her a favour, so maybe she can make an allowance just for tonight. She perches on the table next to me, sipping her drink and desperately trying to avoid eye contact with anyone.

'Natalie?' Someone comes up to her. I don't pay a lot of attention.

Natalie

Fucking Jenny's at the fucking pub. Of course fucking Jenny's at the fucking pub. Because it's not excruciating enough to have all of these people *looking* at me while Fiona rehashes easily the most embarrassing period of my life. And I'm happy she's happy, but it's also awful. So, obviously Jenny would be here too. The shit cherry on top of the shit cake.

I clear my throat. 'Hi.'

Fiona cocks an eyebrow when she sees Jenny. She looks at me. I look at Jenny. Jenny's face remains impassive. For a moment none of us says anything. I was paranoid that someone from CLC might turn out to be here, but *Jenny*? I'll never live this down. And maybe I shouldn't technically *have* to live anything down, but I would still like to have the chance. My ears are ringing, and I've lost the thread of what's happening anywhere outside of the square of floor where Jenny stands and smiles at me benignly.

'Nice to see you, Natalie,' she says. 'And Fiona, right? I remember you. Nice to see you again too.'

She walks away. I watch her walk out of the door, and even though I know she's gone, I still feel like she's here somewhere, watching me.

Once she's left, I shake my head, tuning back in to the room. Someone opens a copy of the paper and I can't listen to it, I just can't. I know it's not terrible. But I can't sit in this room full of overexcited people, drunk on something a tiny bit different from the norm (and many of them also just drunk), and laugh along. This is not making everything go away.

I glance towards the door. I need to get some air. I stand up and Fiona frowns an 'are you OK?' at me. I nod. As I walk past, people bicker over who should get to read out the article about the most embarrassing thing that's ever happened to me. We're literally trapped in my nightmare.

I lean against the wall when I get outside. I can still hear the laughter from the pub but it's at a remove, so I can, at least, pretend it's about anything else. The air is chilly, and my breath mists in front of me as I focus on inhaling slowly, clearing my head.

A couple of men walk past me on the way back from the smoking area.

'Alright, love? You looking for your next opponent?' one of them says. The other one laughs.

Fiona

'Fiona Maitliss is a normal woman.' A guy I don't really know reads from a copy of the paper. We actually laughed at that in the shop earlier once I'd finally read it. Like, cheers for the vote of confidence, Gemma? 'And the Miner's Arms in Crostdam is a very normal pub.'

The man who's reading pauses for effect here and everybody in the place obliges with another raucous cheer.

'I'm getting that put on an advert!' Dave the barman laughs. '"A very normal pub".'

Everybody laughs, but then Reading Man clears his throat and they fall silent again.

'But what happened on the night of the thirteenth of June was anything but ordinary.'

It's maybe *slightly* melodramatic? Like, it sounds as if I survived being held at gunpoint or something. I shake my head.

'Hey,' Natalie says, reappearing near my elbow. Her voice is hoarse. 'I'm going to head off.'

NATALIE

'We can't leave yet, we've only just got here,' Fiona complains, grabbing my wrist to keep me where I am. She says it loudly so that other people can hear. They start protesting too, and her eyes twinkle in amusement.

'No, not . . . I said *I* might head out. I'm not really feeling it. You don't have to come.'

Fiona frowns. She keeps hold of my hand as she jumps up from the table, and then she pulls me towards the door.

'Oi oi!' someone shouts. 'Here we go again.'

She laughs and flips the bird in the general direction of that person, when all I can do is get flustered and turn even redder.

'Seriously, are you OK?' she demands.

'Fine!' I say. It's maybe a touch too emphatic, but the pub was so loud, and it's so quiet out here that I think I get away with it. 'I just . . . I think I'm getting a migraine or something.'

Fiona peers at me. 'So, not fine, then?'

'Well, you know. Fine with everything that's happening in there. Fine with' – I gesture towards Fiona's little fan club – 'the situation. I just don't feel well.'

'You're sure?'

'I'm really sure.'

'And you can get home OK?'

''Course.'

FIONA

I lose track of how long I stay at the pub after Natalie goes home. Amy pops in for a while, taking full advantage of the 'legends drink free' policy. Dave rings the bell for last orders and I still have a little group of people sitting at a table with me. At some point they all introduced themselves, but I'm not sure I could remember any of their names now. Not after an entire night of free drinks.

I sway slightly as I stand outside the door of the pub. I look up at the sky. The stars are bright and the moon is a perfect crescent. It's a hundred per cent the alcohol talking, but I feel a bit emotional. I don't know. Everything just feels like it's Coming Up Fiona a bit at the moment.

'You OK getting home?' one of my new friends calls.

'Yeah, it's not far, thank you,' I say.

Whatever this girl's name is pulls me into a hug like we've been besties forever.

'It was so nice to meet you!' she says as she walks away.

'You too!'

I take out my phone to check the time. It's far too late. And there's a text from Matt.

MATT: Guess it was a better night than you thought? Going to bed now.

I am a bad girlfriend.

CHAPTER NINETEEN

FIONA

'Fiona.' Angelo makes me jump when I'm hiding out by the bins, looking at tweets about the video again. They've slowed to a trickle at this point and, if I'm honest, it's making me feel twitchy. Not that I *want* them to start up again, I just . . . It was nice while it lasted, that's all. And it's amazing how quickly it was over. I wasn't ready. I snatch up the bin bag closest to me from the ground just to look like I'm doing something. 'How's it going?'

'Yeah, great. Just have to . . .' I sling the bag into the dumpster.

'OK, well, could you do it quicker, please? One of the newbies just put a jug of ice cream in the microwave to make a milkshake. I can't believe they let these kids into university, honestly.'

He shakes his head and pinches the bridge of his nose, sighing extra-loudly. My favourite thing about Angelo, without question, is how much he dramatically, comically, hates everything to do with running an ice cream shop. He's just so *theatrical* about it. Definite 'hating your job' goals.

I smile. 'I'll be right there.'

'Oh, and arrangements for tomorrow,' he says, pausing on his way out the door. 'A couple of crossed wires, not that it makes much difference to us, but it's not a wedding, it's some kind of corporate fun day. If that's even a real thing. Some local company's hired a big field and they're putting on a festival, basically.'

I feel cold pooling in my stomach because this is ringing a bell. 'That wouldn't be . . . a company called CLC, would it?'

Angelo clicks his fingers. 'CLC. Yes. That's the one.'

I nod. And I keep nodding. Nod, and nod, and nod. Wait for the implications of that to truly land.

'That an issue for you?'

'No! No. It's fine.' I sling the other bag into the dumpster and let the lid slam. 'Great.'

'Good. Amy's going to do it too, since it's bigger than we thought. You'll need backup.' I laugh derisively. No kidding. 'So, you're OK with that, then? Looking to get there for nine a.m., so it'll be about an eight a.m. start.'

I nod again. Nodding is all I have, it seems. Angelo is distracted, looking back out towards the shop floor. I jump when he yells, 'Sam, I swear to god, if that goes in the microwave too you will be out on your ear, I don't care if you *are* going to be a doctor one day!'

NATALIE

I can't believe my eyes when we turn a corner and I catch sight of what can only be the CLC Family Fun Day. For one thing, I swear there's not that many people in the company, and yet the field seems to be packed with cars. And for another thing, the setup in the adjoining field looks *amazing*. Bunting flutters against all of the fences, and brightly coloured inflatables dot the grass. I can see carnival games with giant cuddly toys tied to their awnings. I can hear the music from a carousel. I can smell fried onions, fried dough . . . a lot of fried stuff generally. And this is all to thank people for our hard work for the company? I can't get over it. Here was me thinking that's what our pay cheques were for.

The issue with anything fun at the moment is that the thought of the video is never far away. It all seems to be dying down now, and that's a huge relief, but you never can tell, can you? What if someone in there recognises me and kicks up a fuss in front of John Stait himself? What if someone films me doing something *else* dumb, like going arse over tit in a cow pat or something? Or what if it just all kicks off again online while I'm stuck in a field and not looking at my phone? And then I don't realise that it's happened? And then this time it's so big that John Stait actually does see it and he fires me on the spot to save CLC's reputation? I know that all of these things are a bit mad, but so was any of this in the first place. It's much harder to believe something mad isn't going to happen once you've seen that it can.

I immediately regret bringing my parents, too. They don't know how precarious this all is. And I'm not about to *tell* them, obviously, but my hopes that maybe they won't be too excited are quickly dashed.

In the driver's seat, my dad whistles through his teeth as he parks in the spot he's directed to by someone in a bright orange hi-viz. 'This is some setup, Natalie. Very impressive.'

'I mean, it's—'

'No, I'm serious, Nat.' He shifts in his seat, turning to look at me. That's how you know it's serious. My palms feel clammy all of a sudden. 'Your mum and I are really proud of you, getting this job. It bears repeating. Especially now. You can deflect all you like, but it's a big achievement. You've done so well.'

It's difficult to know what to say when your usual response is to deflect and you've literally been told you can't do that. I fidget and look out of the window at the flags flapping from the top of bouncy castles. It *is* big. This *is* better than anywhere I've worked before. But it *might* still all go away.

'It's incredible.' Mum nods beside Dad. 'I can't believe they'd put on something like this. You must do a brilliant job.'

'Well, *I* don't . . .'

But before I can remind her that it's not just *my* work, someone knocks on my window and I jump. I look out and Tom is standing there, waving. I am not ready for Family Fun Day to start right this second. I still need to give my parents a lecture on how they shouldn't embarrass me. Which is a bit rich given recent events, but I need to maintain the illusion that I don't already think I killed my own chances of keeping this job. It's just very confusing and tricky, and Tom can stand out there until I am prepared to . . .

'Friend of yours?' Dad asks.

'Just . . . Can you just be cool for a minute?' I plead. I wind down the window and smile. 'Hi.'

'Hi. Alright? Are you heading in?' He looks like he might be about to reach for my door handle.

'Yep, in a minute. Just need to go over a couple of things. I'll catch you later.'

Mum's window whirrs down because apparently people in this family don't know what 'be cool' means anymore.

'Hi there! Do you work with Natalie?' she asks. 'I'm her mum. This is her dad.'

Tom grins, sidestepping along to Mum's window. 'I do. I sit across from her. My name's Tom. Are you coming?'

'Yeah, we'll be there in just a second,' I call. 'You should go on ahead and we'll—'

But Mum pops her door open. Tom grabs it and holds it for her.

'Such a gentleman.' She smiles, slamming the door shut.

My dad gets out of the car as well, slamming his door shut too. And, for a second, I am sitting on my own, in the back of my parents' car, still with my seatbelt on, feeling like a ten-year-old waiting for Dad to nip in to the shop and get the paper. I do briefly wonder if maybe I could stay here with the radio on and opt out of all of this. My mum's started what looks like a *delightful* chat with Tom. She might not even notice I'm gone. But then my dad pulls open my door.

'Come on, you.'

I climb out grudgingly and look around. To the left of the field we've parked in is a patchwork of purple, brown, and bright yellow fields, all the way down to the cliffs. And then it's just the sea. It's breezy up where we are, and little white peaks flash and disappear on the water. I can hear gulls mingling with the carousel now, a few chords strummed by someone who must be warming up on the stage. Everybody's left me behind. For a moment, I'm tempted to let them go. But then I remember that I can't police what my parents are saying if I can't hear it, and I also can't manage their expectations, so I run to catch up.

'So, you haven't brought any family with you today?' my mum is asking Tom as I fall into step with my dad.

'Well, my sister's bringing her kids. But they live a while away, so they come separately. I might not see them at all if there's as many things to do as last year.'

'And no children of your own?'

'*Mum!*'

Mum shoots me a look over her shoulder. 'I am just making *conversation*, Natalie. You should try it some time.'

'I didn't know Scoopz was going to be here today,' my dad interrupts. 'Isn't that Gertie?'

I peer in the direction he's pointing.

FIONA

'I thought you were doing a wedding today.' Natalie appears at the window of the van. 'Hi, by the way.'

She looks lovely in a blue and white sundress, with her hair tied up, and bright pink sunglasses. I, on the other hand, am a sweaty mess because I'm wearing the same old polyester shirt and am slowly being cooked alive in a metal box in the full sun. I really try to push down the thought that our places could have been swapped if things had just . . . No. Stop it.

'Hi.' I give her a tight smile. 'Honestly, so did I. But you've met Angelo. Big surprise, he didn't have all the details clear when he booked me in.'

I can only see Natalie's head and shoulders from here, but she moves from side to side, and I can tell she's shifting from foot to foot.

'Natalie,' Amy says, appearing next to me. 'Fancy seeing you here.'

'Hey!' Natalie says, her voice immediately jumping an octave as per usual. 'So, you're both here. That's . . .'

'You don't need to worry about a thing,' Amy says, putting an arm around my waist and smiling at Natalie. Maybe baring her teeth? Hard to tell. Whichever it is, I feel on edge. 'I will make sure Fiona doesn't cramp your style.'

'No, she wouldn't be . . . That's not . . .' Natalie looks at me. 'You know I don't . . .'

Her face is turning red. It's clashing with her sundress. I have to put her out of her misery. I elbow Amy. 'It's fine. Don't worry, it's not going to be weird.' Natalie doesn't look sure. She glances behind her. I can see her parents talking to some guy, Sophie's on her way over too. I shake my head. 'Honestly, Nat, it's OK. I didn't have to come, did I?'

203

'You bloody did,' Amy mutters under her breath. I step on her toe to shut her up.

Natalie seems to weigh this up for a second. 'OK. If you're sure. But, hey! If you guys need any help or anything, you can just text me, and I'll come and get involved, how about that?'

I laugh. 'Don't be stupid, you're a guest. We'll be fine. Honestly.'

NATALIE

'Oh my god, Nat's doing *so* well!' Sophie is enthusing as I rejoin my parents. Tom is still hanging around as well. How are they *gathering* so many people when I just want to stay under the radar? But I can't wonder about that now. I need to stop Sophie from overselling my performance to my parents. I can't have them thinking I'm about to get promoted or something, when I still might get fired. I look around nervously for Jenny, but I can't see her. Sophie is still going. 'Honestly, she's found her feet really well, and she just—'

'Maybe we shouldn't talk about work right now,' I suggest. It would be a more effective suggestion if we weren't literally at a work event, but I've said it now.

'Don't be dumb.' Sophie frowns at me. 'I was just saying how well you're doing.'

'Yeah, but' – I scrabble around for a reason to stop that isn't 'I'm worried if my parents get too proud of me they might scare it all away' – 'it's not very interesting to talk about *me* all the time, is it?'

'Is Fiona in the van today?' my dad asks.

'Yeah.' I cast another glance over there. They've already got a queue. Tom glances at me with interest as I look back to the group.

'Well, we should go over and say hello. We've hardly seen her since she moved out,' my mum says.

'No, Mum. She's busy. And I just . . . It's all a little bit sensitive. I think you should just leave her to it.'

We're interrupted by a small, red-haired girl running through our little standoff and throwing herself into Tom's legs. She head-butts him in the stomach.

'Uncle Tom!'

He makes a sound as all of the air is knocked out of him. Then he laughs. 'Well, that's my cue. Have a lovely day, everybody. It was nice to meet you, Eleanor, Rob.' He nods at each of them and then carries on, 'Sophie. Natalie.'

He holds his niece's hand and lets her drag him towards the Hook A Duck stand.

'He's very nice,' my mum says, watching him go.

'He is,' Sophie says, nudging me and cocking an eyebrow. Absolute stirrer. And the terrible thing is, I'll let her stir that instead if it means she'll stop stirring up my parents' belief that I'm suddenly some kind of wunderkind.

'Look, they have a tombola,' I say, which might be the lamest distraction tactic anybody has ever used, and I do mean *ever*. 'Come on, we should have a go.'

FIONA

I don't even have eyes on Natalie, but I still hear her shout.

'Mum! Leave her alone!'

I steel myself for what I think is coming next. I might be being presumptuous. I've met her parents, though, so it seems a pretty safe assumption.

'Hello, Fiona, love,' Eleanor says, appearing at the window as I suspected she might. She shuffles along and Rob appears too.

'Fiona! Nice to see you.'

I smile. You can't really help it with them, they're the cheeriest people known to man. Blithe. I think that would be the word. I feel like they make sense of how reserved Natalie is a lot of the time. She's learned to be the sensible one. Anyway.

I grin. 'It's good to see you too.'

'We miss not seeing you when we come to the flat now. How's life with that young man of yours?' Eleanor winks at me.

'Oh, it's . . . Yeah, good.' I shrug, because who needs to get into the intricacies of it all? It is, primarily, good.

'I just can't believe our Natalie's got herself into a place like this, can you? Isn't it so nice to see her coming into her own?' Rob says with a proud smile.

I open my mouth. To say yes, obviously. Because of course it is. And, like, did I think for a moment that maybe *I'd* be the one who was going to come into my own first? Sure. And is it a little bit disorientating adjusting to your oldest friend just blazing past you in seemingly no time? Of course. And am I wondering if there are things I could have done differently? *Should* have done differently? Naturally. But . . . My mouth is still open and I've forgotten the question. I change my expression into a generic smile.

'I'll have a couple of scoops of rum and raisin, love, if you're serving,' Rob says.

The morning moves surprisingly quickly, considering time often doesn't do that when we're working. It's nice being out of the shop, people seem to largely be on their best behaviour because it's a corporate event, and if anybody *was* to throw up, they wouldn't be doing it on the shop floor, which immediately removes a lot of the tension.

I don't really know what to do when I take my break. It's been fine up until now. Surprisingly so, really. I know Natalie finds it weird that I'm here like *this*, and I can't say I blame her, but all either of us can do now is make the best of it. She texted me about an hour after she came to say hello.

NATALIE: Give me a text when you get a break, we'll get candy floss or something :) xx

And I do think about letting her know I'm free, but I just . . . These people aren't my people. And it's not just the fact that they literally turned me down for a job mere weeks ago, although that obviously doesn't help. But it's the fact that they get all day here while I get a snatched half hour wearing clothes that mark me clearly as an outsider. It's the conversations I've overheard while I've been piling ice cream onto cones and sharing looks with Amy, it's the fact that this – this whole event – is something they're just used to. I don't fit in here, and that's *fine* by me, but I don't want to make things hard for Natalie by forcing her to straddle the line between her old world and her new one. Today, she's Natalie from CLC. She should just feel free to be that.

So, I wander around and take everything in, wondering what I'm actually allowed to do considering I'm merely staff. I half-heartedly throw some balls at a coconut, taking the roll of love hearts I'm offered as a consolation prize for being crap at throwing. I stand at a distance and watch someone on the stage with an acoustic guitar. They're not exactly holding the crowd's attention, but at least they're giving it a go, right? And I duck behind the First Aid tent when I see Natalie's parents strolling along the grass splitting a tray of chips. Not that I need to hide from them, I just . . . It's easier to keep everything separate. It's only for a day.

I hear quiet sobbing and look a little bit further around the tent. There's a little girl there in a pink checked dress. She's pulling handfuls of grass out of the ground, twisting them around, then letting them go and watching the blades float back down, sniffing and gasping for air in that hiccup-y way that kids do. She could be anything from three to ten years old. I truly do not know how you're supposed to know.

'Hey,' I say, keeping my voice soft so I don't scare her. I sort of forget that I'm literally dressed in candy-pink stripes and therefore couldn't scare somebody if I tried. The little girl looks up at me with big, wet eyes. There's a bit of a snot situation as well, which I do everything in my power to ignore. 'Are you OK?'

'I . . . Can't . . . Find . . . My . . . Mummy.' She hiccups, and then dissolves into fresh tears.

I look around to find a grown-up, but quickly have the terrible realisation that the grown-up in this scenario would be me. God. OK.

'Well, that's OK,' I tell the girl, crouching next to her. 'How about if you come with me, and I'll help you find her?'

I hold out the half tube of Love Hearts I still have left and try not to think about how thin the line is between Good Samaritan and Child Catcher. The girl takes her finger out of her mouth, touches every sweet in the tube, and eventually takes one. I smile and try not to look disgusted.

'I'm Fiona. What's your name?'

She sniffs. 'Florence.'

'And what was your mummy wearing? Do you remember?' I ask as I get to my feet and offer my hand to the girl. 'Was she wearing trousers? Or a skirt? Do you remember the colour?'

We eventually narrow it down to a red dress (bold, I like her mother's style) and go looking. Florence's hand is clammy in mine, and all I want in the world is to let it go, but that doesn't seem like the done thing, so I keep my grossed-out-ness to myself. We scan the crowds for any sign of a red dress for a good ten minutes, and I know Amy'll be expecting me back, but I can't exactly leave a defenceless, surprisingly sticky child in a field, can I?

'Oh my god, Flo, where have you been?' A woman about my age races up to us. She's wearing a white top and jeans, which, of *course*, I should have expected. For a second I wonder if I now have a duty of care to make sure this woman is who she says she is, but Florence throws her arms around her neck and buries her face in it, so I take that as a good sign.

'Sorry,' I say, feeling an urge to clarify that I am not a weirdo, 'I found her behind a tent. She was upset, so we were—'

'God, don't apologise, honestly. She wanders off all the time. And this is what happens, isn't it?' She gives Florence a stern look, and the child hides her head in her mother's shoulder. 'My name's Isla. I'm John's daughter. John Stait? Sorry for this one. She's a bit of a madam.'

'Oh, no, she's fine,' I lie, dismissing the apology with a wave of my now-sticky hand.

'Do you have any of your own?' she asks.

I laugh involuntarily. I try to hide it, pretend it's a cough, but I don't think I do a very good job. But that's an insane thing to say to somebody, right? I mean, I suppose she probably does look about the same age as me, and I suppose that is what people do, so . . . Everything spins. It's hot. Probably just because we're standing in the sun. I cast my eyes around for an escape route. But this woman – John Stait's daughter, did she say? Whoever that is – is still looking at me.

'Sorry,' I say, shaking my head as if I'd got distracted by my phone or something, not had my life flash before my eyes in a field. 'No. No, none yet. As far as I know!' I add. Honestly, why am I the way that I am?

John Stait's (whoever that even actually is) daughter gives me a weak smile, clearly regretting getting into this conversation with me.

'So, have you had a good day?'

'Well, you know. I'm working, so . . .'

'Really? On the weekend? God, Dad's a bit of a slave driver, then?' She laughs. Possibly barks? It's quite hard to tell. 'What team are you in?'

I gape. 'Oh. No. I didn't mean . . . I'm working. Here, today. I work in the ice cream van.'

'Oh, I *see*.' She tightens her hold on Florence a tiny bit, which is almost definitely a coincidence but it doesn't feel like one. 'Well, it must be *lovely* to be up here on such a nice day, isn't it? Anyway, I should probably be going.'

I nod towards Florence and hold out the half packet of now-spitty Love Hearts. 'She can have these if she likes, I'm probably not going to—'

'Oh, no, honestly, that's OK. She doesn't really go for refined sugar, do you, baby?'

Florence nuzzles her head into her mum's shoulder and they head back towards the stage, where lots of people have spread picnic blankets. I look at my watch. Shit. I am so late to get back to Amy. I trot towards a bin to get rid of the tainted sweets.

'Fiona!' someone calls. It's Sophie. She's standing by a Pimm's bar with Natalie. They're laughing with a couple of people I don't recognise, because why would I? Because Natalie has her own fancy group of friends now. And I'm just a woman who looks like she could have children and also a member of staff when everybody else is here to have fun. They're upstairs, I'm downstairs, and never the twain shall meet. Or should meet.

'Come and have a drink!' Natalie calls.

I shake my head, tap my watch. 'I have to get back!' I reply.

NATALIE

I think I've done very well for most of the CLC Family Fun Day. I *was* kind of hoping we could get away without my parents meeting any of my colleagues. So being escorted in by Tom was, admittedly, not the best start. But it went well for a while. Once Mum and Dad ran out of ways to freak me out by telling me how proud they were, I managed to get my panic under control a bit. I wandered round the craft tent with Mum while Dad trailed behind us moaning about how everything was tat. We got hog roast rolls. We had a go at a couple of games.

But then it started going downhill. As the day wore on and we kept going back to the Pimm's cart and the beer tent, Dad got louder and more effusive with his praise again. Mum sat beside me and watched with an indulgent smile, occasionally chipping in with a 'he's right, you know'.

And on paper it was all very nice. Again. And I know there are women my age who would kill to have their parents be that supportive. But it's also a little bit embarrassing when they start drowning out performers using literal amplifiers on stage and drawing amused looks from people I have to see at work again on Monday. Whose own parents were sitting with them and somehow managed to just. Be. Cool.

I also wish they'd think about how embarrassing it's going to be if they have to take it back one day. I don't think I'm out of the woods yet. I've forgotten what 'out of the woods' even feels like. Even *now* someone could be posting that video again with some fresh take and everything could kick back off. I am a child of the internet. I know how it works. And it's not like I want them to *know* that I'm on shaky ground while I'm still on probation. I just want to gently encourage them to talk about something else occasionally. But every time I've tried all afternoon, my dad's been telling me to stop being so modest, have a bit of pride, my generation's always like this.

So, what I'm saying is, I tell them I'm going to the loo and then I duck behind the beer tent. It's only for a moment, just to give myself a couple of minutes of silence where I can slow my thoughts and exist without my parents being proud all over me. Except I do not find the solitude I was hoping for.

'Oh.' I stop dead, surprised to see Tom hiding here too. Even more surprised to see him sprawled on the grass, smoking a rollup. He seems very much the opposite of the man I often only see the top half of in the crisp button-down shirts.

'Great minds,' he says, finishing the cigarette and stubbing it out on the grass. He pats a patch next to him.

'Yeah, something like that.' I frown and look behind me. Maybe I can dash over to one of the other tents without anybody spotting me. The crowd *is* quite distracted by a puppet show. I might be able to make it.

'How are you enjoying your first Family Fun Day?' Tom asks.

'It's . . . weird. I didn't know you were a smoker.'

'I actually prefer "legend".' He cocks an eyebrow and I laugh in spite of myself. 'Nah, I'm not really. I'm one of those "smokes when he drinks" wankers.'

'Oh, I'm sorry to hear that, how embarrassing for you.'

'It really is. So who are *you* trying to hide from, huh? And would you sit down? You're making me uncomfortable in my one moment of peace and quiet.'

'I'm not trying to hide,' I say. But I do sit down.

'Look, no judgement. Every single person here has tried to hide at some point today, I guarantee it. It's very nice of them to put this on, but it has a *very* parents' evening vibe about it. Every year.'

'Oh my god, that's what it is!' I hit him on the arm. 'Worlds colliding. Awful.'

'Terrible.' He sips beer from a plastic cup.

'Your niece was excited to see you, though.' It's a bit of an assumption, but I think I have it right.

'Oh, and I'm excited to see her. She's just seven years old with the energy of a seven-year-old, and I'm thirty years old with the energy of someone in their sixties.'

'That'll be all the smoking and drinking.'

'I know, I'm a time bomb.'

FIONA

John Stait's (whoever that is) daughter's words ring in my ears when I get back to the van. Luckily, the customers have slowed to a trickle so I have plenty of time to obsess over them.

'What's up with you?' Amy asks, thrusting a box towards me. 'Put this on that shelf.'

'Nothing's up with me.'

'Really? Because you seem like something's up with you.'

'*Nothing* is up with me.'

Amy holds up her hands and turns back to the unfeasibly tiny sink in this van.

It wasn't even John Stait's (literally whoever that is) daughter's words that hurt. It was more the change in her attitude when she realised I wasn't an employee of this stupid company. Or related to an employee of this stupid company. Which I *know* is her issue and not mine, but the change in her demeanour when she realised she'd accidentally talked to someone outside of her little circle still stings. Like, I *tried* to be in her little circle. Is it my fault they didn't let me in?

My phone buzzes.

MATT: What time are you home tonight? Don't forget we have that BBQ with Tiffany & Michael x

I close my eyes. I like Tiffany and Michael. I do. But recently they make me feel like a child. Or, more accurately, they make me painfully aware of how much of a difference there is between Matt and me. I just don't know if I can face a whole evening of listening to who messed up what report and then occasionally having them remember that I'm in the room too and asking me how work is. We all know you don't want to hear about the backache I got from spending my entire Saturday on my feet, guys. It's fine.

My phone buzzes again, and I assume it's going to be Matt asking me if I can pick something up on the way home. But it's someone calling me.

I motion to Amy that I'll be a minute and hide around the back of the van.

'Hello?' I hold a finger to my ear to muffle the sound of the carousel.

'Oh, hi. Is that Fiona? The Fiona who was in the viral video and then the *Crostdam Chronicle*?'

'Um . . . Yeah? Speaking.'

'Oh, great. Hi, my name's Leonie. I work for *South West Tonight*. You know, the news show? Derek Jordan, one of our hosts, read your interview in the *Chronicle*. We'd love to invite you on if you'd be at all interested? We're looking to have you on today if we can. We wouldn't be talking so much about the video as your experience of going viral, what that felt like, that kind of thing. What do you think?'

I open my mouth to say yes, but I close it again straight away. Because, I mean, I *can't* say yes, can I? I want to. I really want to. It sounds like fun. And maybe it would make people take me seriously . . . I really feel like I need that after today. But Natalie would murder me, and I don't even think I'm exaggerating when I say that. She would actually kill me. But then, if it's not *about* the video, and it's just about my experience, maybe that's OK? But I still don't know if . . .

'Fiona? You still there?'

'Yes, sorry.' I clear my throat. 'Listen, would you mind if I called you back in, like, ten minutes? I just need to check something first.'

'Sure. But I really do need to know ASAP, we'll have to make alternative arrangements if not.'

'Of course.'

I hang up and immediately call Natalie. She doesn't pick up, so I try again. I chew the inside of my cheek as the phone rings this time, trying to keep my temper under control as I wait for her to answer. I know she doesn't *know* that I need her. I mean, she would if she would answer the phone, but— No. Stop it. Unhelpful. I get her voicemail. Of course I do, because I really needed not to, and that's just the way things are going for me at the moment. I make a noise of frustration.

But she *is* around here somewhere, right? So, rather than try to call her a third time, I put my phone away and run. And I have not run since I was at school, so that should tell you everything you need to know about how seriously I'm taking this. I have to find Natalie, have to get her blessing. I don't know much, but I do know I can't do this behind her back. I see Natalie's dad as I run from tent to tent.

'Rob!' I call. 'Have you seen Natalie?' He shakes his head and does a pantomime shrug. I keep running.

I know her well enough to know that she won't be coping well with the praise her parents are no doubt giving her, so when I can't see her anywhere obvious (the bar) I decide to do a lap around the backs of all the tents. I'm still a couple of tents away when I spot her. She's sitting in the grass, legs out in front of her, leaning on her arms. And she's not alone. Natalie Starr is sitting with a man. I stop dead.

A couple of thoughts cross my mind. First of all, I don't want to disturb her. And, secondly, why do I not know that there's a man on the scene? Why would she not have told me that? Is it a new thing? Is it a real thing? I just . . . She told me everything about Tinder Nigel and she basically hated him from the off. But she didn't mention this?

I hop from foot to foot a couple of times, and then I head back to the van.

'Where the hell did you go?' Amy asks.

'Sorry.'

NATALIE

Tom and I sit in silence for a moment. I can still hear the carousel. They must have run through every tune it can play at least twenty times by now. The puppet show's still going. I can hear the high-pitched voices, the children screeching.

'Your parents seem excited for you.'

'That is . . . accurate.' I shrug. 'And understating it. It's really nice. I kind of wish they'd have a bit of chill.'

'Why do you think they don't?'

'I guess just because . . .' I look at him. 'We really don't have to talk about this.'

'No, I like them. I want to know.'

'I guess I was just always quite directionless when I was younger. Like, I was smart, but I didn't know what I wanted to do so I took the first job I could get after uni, and me and my friend Fiona, you know, from the—'

'From your starring role.'

'Exactly. Well, I told you we were meant to go travelling together, and when we didn't . . . I just think my parents just want to feel like I'm heading somewhere, rather than just floating along in my own life.'

'That's fair.'

'I suppose. I just . . . Sometimes I wish they'd be interested in me for me, not for what I'm doing. Or not doing. I don't know.'

We both watch a bird hopping through the grass towards us. It investigates a discarded chip tray which has blown against the fence.

Jenny appears out of nowhere while we're sitting in comfortable silence. She walks over to the fence at the edge of the field. In fact, she almost seems to stagger. She has her phone in one hand, her other on her sternum. If she was a Victorian lady she'd be clutching her pearls. She looks back at the crowds, and then down at her phone again. Definitely in a panic over something. I wonder about sneaking away and leaving her to whatever bad news she's just had. Or maybe we should talk to her? I look at Tom.

'Word of advice.' Tom's regarding Jenny with an expression of pity. I look back at her too. 'Never let this place get to you so much that you look like that when you're reading your emails.'

'You think that's what she's doing?'

'I will bet you a thousand pounds that she's reading her emails. Someone probably used the wrong-sized font in a document or something.'

I smack him playfully on the leg. I push myself up to standing and I swear more joints than I realised I had in my body click as I do. When did I get too old to sit on the ground? Doesn't matter. I walk over.

'Is everything OK?' I ask. Jenny jumps when I speak. 'We were just . . .' I turn around to point to where Tom and I were sitting, but he's disappeared. Wow. 'I mean, I was just sitting over there, and you don't—'

'I don't *what*?' Jenny snaps. Oh god, are her eyes going red?

'Nothing! You just . . . looked a bit upset, is all.'

For a moment, Jenny draws her head up, making herself a couple of inches taller. She flicks her hair over her shoulder. It's amazing to watch the facade come up right in front of me. But then it all comes crashing down just as fast and she seems to deflate.

'Do you have time to come to the office?'

It's probably as close as I've ever come to being in a car chase as Jenny races down the hill towards CLC. I glance over at her as she glares at the road. The car goes ever so slightly faster. I can see the muscles in her jaw working. Her cheeks and the tips of her ears are pink.

'I'm still not sure what we're supposed to . . .'

She huffs and tightens her hands around the steering wheel. 'I told you, Hotel Dérive emailed. They got a pallet of . . . erotica and they think it's my fault.'

'No, no, I know that.' I suppress a smile because, look, I'm only human and it's not *not* a funny thing to have happen. 'I just don't know what we're supposed to do about it on the weekend.'

She groans. 'John's going to check his email later. He likes getting all of the family day thank yous' – I make a mental note to send a thank you because I had not thought of that before – 'and he'll see it, and, I don't know. We need to find proof that it wasn't us. Or something. Get it in ASAP. Otherwise he'll have the whole rest of the weekend to get really worked up at us.'

'*Us?*'

Jenny gives me a look. At the same moment a van appears around the bend.

'Mind!' I shout, and she swerves at the last minute.

'Do you ever think this might not be worth dying for?' I grip the handle on the door with one hand, the side of my seat with the other.

'Nope.'

FIONA

I call Natalie a couple more times. And she should really thank me, because I could have just gone over there and ruined whatever moment she was having with whatever man she was having it with. But I didn't. Even though this is pressing.

I listen to the phone ring. And ring. And ring. When I finally get her voicemail message each time ('Hi! It's Natalie! Nobody makes phone calls anymore, why don't you try texting instead?') I make a noise of frustration and hang up.

I dial for the third time. I know I'm being annoying, but it is imperative that I get an answer *right* now, and she needs to know it's important. And, honestly, I'm so excited I could happily keep doing this. Some people all sat around in a TV studio today and talked about *me*. Maybe at exactly the same time as John Stait's (honestly, who even is that?) daughter was looking me up and down and trying to get out of a conversation with me. These total strangers want to put me in front of other total strangers and hear what I have to say. I'm sorry, but that is an honour, even if the audience is small.

This time there's no ring. It just goes straight to voicemail. She's calling me back. We've called each other at exactly the same time. Bloody typical. So, I hang up and wait for my phone to ring.

And then it . . . doesn't. And I wait for a really long time. Like, even if Natalie and I had had a bit of a psychic moment and both decided to wait for the other to ring at exactly the same time, she would still have thought it was too long and tried me again. I decide to be the one to dial. And it still goes straight to voicemail. She's switched it off.

NATALIE

'Fucking inbox zero!'

I choke on the water I'm sipping while I perch on the edge of the desk behind Jenny's. I have never heard her sound so unprofessional. 'Sorry?'

'Inbox zero. I read an article about inbox zero, so then I zeroed my inbox, and now my inbox has zero proof that I *didn't* send a crate of . . .'

'Porn.'

'Yes, thank you. *That* to one of our biggest clients.'

She sits back in her chair and holds her hands over her face and groans.

'I don't think you're supposed to *delete* everything when you do inbox zero.'

'Well, I know that now.' She huffs. 'I'm going to get fired.'

I look at her for a second, the cogs whirring in my brain. Because, I mean, would that be the worst thing? She is the only thing about this place that's been anything less than amazing since I started. If she wasn't here, wouldn't it be better? Wouldn't my life be easier? And it's not like she wouldn't deserve it after . . . everything. But, on the flip side, do I really want to be the one who does that to somebody? It felt awful when I thought it was going to happen to me. She hasn't coped very well with me starting here, but can I honestly say *I've* coped very well with any of the changes in *my* life recently? So maybe this is where we both get over everything. We just act like grown-ups, and I take the high road.

I slap my hands on my thighs and stand up, striding around to my desk.

'What are you doing?' Jenny asks, looking up.

'You copy me in to stuff. I've never deleted an email.'

'How have you nev—'

'Is this about that right now?'

Jenny stands up and walks around to my desk. 'No, you're right. Carry on.'

FIONA

I try to be a decent person. I do. I try to put myself in Natalie's shoes and give her time to get back to me. Because if her phone actually just froze or something, I'd look like a right arsehole. I honestly wait for, like, half an hour. I go back to the van, I dish out ice creams, and I try not to be completely impatient.

But when my phone rings again and I jump, it's still not her. It's Leonie from *South West Tonight*, chasing me for an answer.

NATALIE

We found the email in the end. I've only been at CLC a matter of weeks and my inbox is already a cesspit. And thank god it is, because who's laughing now? Not Jenny, that's for sure. Right up until the moment she dropped me back at my flat, she refused to admit that a fancy hotel receiving a box of erotica instead of a collection of leather-bound classics was even a tiny bit funny.

'You saved the day, though. Thank you,' she said as I got out of the car.

'It was nothing. I'll see you Monday.'

I'm inside and pouring myself a wine when I remember I basically abandoned my parents in a field. There's a beer tent, though. They might not have noticed yet. My phone is still switched off. And then I remember that Fiona tried to call me while I was risking death in Jenny's car. So, OK. Deal with that first.

CHAPTER TWENTY

FIONA

'Natalie' my screen reads later as she finally – *finally* – calls me back. And, I mean, it's too late. Far too late. Amy drove me here in Gertie the second we were free to leave the CLC event. I texted Matt to let him know I couldn't buy taco shells. Everybody who needs to know knows, and it serves Natalie right for ignoring me. I glance up at the clock on the wall in the green room they've put me in. Someone'll come and get me and take me to make-up soon, which gives me a little thrill. I just hope they can make me look less sweaty after a whole day sweltering in a van in the sun. And then there's a bunch of other stuff that Leonie told me about when I arrived. And then I'll be live. On Actual TV. Natalie didn't want to talk to me earlier? Well, guess what. I don't have time to talk to her now. You don't get to be involved in the decision if you don't answer your phone. It's my turn to switch mine off. I tuck it into my bag.

I stare around the room as I wait to be picked up. The walls are painted white brick, the sofa is a bit shabby, with a few scuffed marks in the leather. There's an ironing board, and the kind of tea-making facilities you'd get at a not-very-good hotel, and that's about it. Which I'm not saying to be judgemental. It just makes this whole world seem more . . . achievable, maybe. I would have thought of being here as something unattainable even a couple of hours ago. But this is actually within my reach. I wonder what else could be.

There's a knock on the door, and someone I haven't seen before sticks her head in. She looks young, she must still be at school. How does someone who must still be at school even get into this? That's what I should have done. I flash her a smile, and it must be slightly too wide because she looks alarmed. I take it down a notch.

'Hi, are you ready for make-up?' the girl asks. I nod. She escorts me down a shabby corridor with stained ceiling tiles and points into another door. 'Here you go. Leonie will come and get you and take you to the studio after.'

I've wondered before what a professional hair and make-up experience might be like. I always assumed that when I finally got to have my make-up done by someone else, I could get them to go to town. Apparently not for an early evening current affairs show.

'You want what, darling?' the make-up woman asks, tightening her pinny as she talks.

'Um, glitter? And, like, a smoky eye?'

'Oh, sorry, no can do. Too early. You have to look natural. Or, like, *enhanced* natural. Still yourself, just a bit smoother. Nice try though, I like your style.'

I nod, trying not to be too flustered by my mistake. I'm learning. That's all. I'm learning for my future. 'Oh yeah, didn't think.'

'You're all done, sweets,' the make-up woman says when she's finished. She shields my eyes and sprays something in the air around my face.

I stare at myself in the mirror. I look radiant. I can't wait for people to see me. And I feel another leap of excitement as I remember that people are, in fact, going to see me. Looking like this. I honestly think the last time I felt this confident was when I naively thought I stood a chance with the job at CLC. Like, I had a *purpose* when that was happening. And I'm not saying I want to be on TV forever or anything, I'm just saying it's nice to have that back again.

NATALIE

'Hey!' Matt opens the door and looks surprised, maybe a tiny bit put out, to see me. Rude, quite frankly. How many times did he show up unannounced at *my* front door over eighteen months? 'What's up? I guess you've heard?'

'Heard about what? Is Fiona home?'

'You don't know.'

'I don't know what you're talking about, no. She tried to call me earlier and I was busy, and then I tried to call her, and she didn't answer, so—'

'Oh shit, I think it's starting.' Matt grabs my wrist and pulls me into the flat. I try to stop so I can take my shoes off, but he drags me right through to the living room. If Fiona ever finds out, I want it on record that I *tried* but I was *overpowered*. Tiffany and Michael are in the living room as well. They nod politely when I come in, but they seem twitchy, as if they'd quite like to leave. What on earth have I walked in on?

Matt releases me and perches on the edge of the sofa, staring at the screen. The opening music of *South West Tonight* starts. I wouldn't say I'm a regular viewer, but I sometimes catch the first five minutes if I happen to leave the TV on while I'm doing the washing-up. Matt gets up, paces up and down on Fiona's excellent rug for a minute, then does a weird pirouette and sits down again. Then gets up. Then sits down again. It's like he's doing a modern dance performance. Weirdo.

'Are you . . . OK?' I ask, still hovering in the doorway.

'Yeah. Yeah, it's . . .'

I shoot a querying look at Michael, but he just shrugs and pulls the slightest face. I turn back to glance at the shoe rack, because if Fiona comes home and realises I crossed The Rug with my shoes still on, I will never live it down. I pop out of the room and am just sliding one heel off when I hear the voiceover.

'On *South West Tonight*, she became a viral sensation against her will. We speak to Fiona Maitliss about what life has been like ever since.'

You *what*? I kick my loose shoe off as hard as I can, and it thumps against the wall. Then I race into the living room with one still on, and no regard for the rug, and plonk myself on the sofa next to Matt.

'What's she done?' I ask in a whisper.

'I don't even know.' Matt shakes his head.

I barely even hear a word Fiona says when her interview starts. I can't even . . . I don't believe . . . I just . . . I don't want to sound like a *total* child, but she literally promised this was over. She *promised*. And it doesn't exactly look like she was dragged there against her will. There's a tiny voice in my brain suggesting that maybe if I'd answered the phone when she'd called, she wouldn't be on screen right now. But she knows how I feel, it's not like there's any ambiguity there. It is incredibly easy to not be on TV, I literally do it every day. This is just her only thinking about herself. Again.

I sit on the sofa with Matt and we both watch Fiona flick her hair and laugh with the presenters as she downplays how incredibly stressful the last couple of weeks have been.

'Oh, no,' she says at one point, 'everybody's been super-supportive. To both of us! It's been really lovely.'

I can't even begin to describe how not-true that is, so I just sit there in silence. I glance at Matt. He has his legs crossed as he perches on the edge of the sofa. He's kicking his leg and chewing his thumb nail. Tiffany and Michael look like they regret being here at all, and I think that's fair enough.

'So, describe a normal day for Fiona Maitliss,' one of the presenters is saying.

Fiona pulls a face and giggles. 'Well, it's pretty boring, I'll tell you that for free.'

'Great,' Matt whispers.

'Well, she doesn't mean *you*, does she?' I say, bumping him with my shoulder. *He* doesn't have anything to be miserable about. But he doesn't even answer me, just scoffs.

I really try to act positive enough for both of us after that. At least for a while. I try to have some perspective, to take the path of least resistance. Because, look. She's already on TV. That has happened. It can't be undone by me getting mad about it. Even if I secretly am. I can shove that down. I am very well practised. I have good things of my own happening now, and yes, those good things are mostly contingent on the video being gone forever, but Fiona's only talking about herself so maybe it's fine. And the more I think it, the more I start to believe it. But then they play it again.

FIONA

I'm not bragging, but when the show ends and the red lights on the cameras go out, *everybody* tells me how great I did. OK, fine, I *am* bragging. But I think I'm allowed? And I'm not naive, I do realise that they probably tell everybody they did a great job. But that doesn't mean it's not nice to hear.

I feel this swell of pride, and this time it doesn't just recede again. It fills me up. I did a good thing. *I* did a good thing. Something that sets me back apart again. I can imagine everybody I know sitting at home, watching me and thinking about how impressive I am. Or, maybe that's strong. But they certainly won't think of me as the one who's trailing behind Natalie, will they? My parents are probably jointly composing a text as we speak. Amy will be cheering at the TV, assuming she got Gertie back to the garage in time. Natalie probably hasn't realised it's even happening. But what she doesn't know won't hurt her. I'll tell her about it first thing tomorrow. I do enjoy a good dramatic reveal.

The people I served at the CLC day today, the John Stait's (I repeat: who?) daughters of the world, the people who interviewed me and didn't pick me, might be sitting at home thinking 'well, we underestimated her'.

NATALIE

FIONA: Hey! Fancy breakfast tomorrow?? Have something to tell you x

I get Fiona's text when I'm walking home. I do not answer.

CHAPTER
TWENTY-ONE

FIONA

'I'm back!' I call into the apparently empty flat. I'm not sure what I expect when I announce my arrival back home, but it isn't dead silence.

It seemed to take ages to get away from the TV studio. In a good way. People I passed in the corridors kept stopping me to tell me I'd done well, so it took ages to get back to my stuff. What a hardship. And then I hung around in the green room because, well, I didn't really fancy going back to being someone who does *not* get to hang around in a TV studio with a load of people who a) know who she is and b) seem to think she's done a great job. Leonie found me there.

'Hey, you about ready to go? I've arranged your car – it should be here soon.'

'Thank you, that's really great.'

'All part of the service. Oh, and here.'

She handed me a *South West Tonight* tote bag with a few bits in it. There was a t-shirt, a water bottle, a pen, and one of those fluffy monster things with the ribbon. I wanted to look like I was too cool for a bag full of freebies, but I definitely snatched it from her a bit too eagerly.

Now, I sling the bag onto the bench in the hall while I take my shoes off.

'Matt?' I call. The place is completely dark. No light in the living room. Nothing. Maybe he's gone out? Maybe everybody went somewhere after the barbecue. Kind of rude that they wouldn't stick around and celebrate with me, but we can talk about that later.

I walk through to the kitchen, turn on the lights, and switch the kettle on. The microwave tells me it's ten p.m. I would definitely have expected Matt to be back by now. But, hey, it doesn't hurt us to do our own thing every once in a while, does it? I can hear my footsteps it's so quiet. I can hear the fridge whirring away, until the kettle drowns everything else out.

'I'll have a tea if you're making one,' someone calls. I nearly drop the mug I'm holding.

'Matt?'

'In here.'

What the *hell*? I march across the hallway to the living room. It's still completely dark. I can just about make out the shape of Matt on the sofa, but I genuinely wouldn't if he hadn't said anything.

'What are you doing?' I ask, flicking on the light. Matt blinks in the sudden brightness. 'You nearly gave me a heart attack. Why are you sitting in the dark? Breakfast or camomile?'

'Breakfast.'

I go back to the kitchen to make the extra cup. When I come back again, I put it down on the coffee table. As I sit down Matt jumps to his feet.

'Everything OK?' I ask. This is not the hero's welcome I was expecting. I mean, not that I was expecting a *hero's* welcome, necessarily. But a 'well done' wouldn't go amiss. A 'you look nice in your professionally done make-up', maybe. 'Did you see . . . ?'

'Oh, I saw,' Matt says through . . . is that gritted teeth? I peer at him. This doesn't feel correct. I can see the vein in his forehead that only shows up when he's really mad or lifting something very heavy, and there's a flush slowly creeping up the back of his neck that I honestly might not have seen since I sat behind him in the exam hall when we did our A-levels.

'Did you get my message?'

'Yes, Fi. I got your message. I got your message and I saw you on TV.'

'OK, good. You just seem like you're kind of—'

'Kind of what? Boring?'

'What? No. Kind of angry.'

Matt looks at me in *very* sarcastic surprise which, considering I still don't know what his problem is, I do not appreciate. 'Angry? Me? No. Why would I be angry? It's not like my girlfriend went on TV and told everyone I'm boring or anything.'

I open my mouth as I rewind my brain through the past few hours. 'I literally never said that.'

Matt picks up the remote and switches the TV on. I'm on the screen, paused mid-gesticulation. Matt hits 'play' and the version of me on the screen comes to life.

'So, describe a normal day for Fiona Maitliss.'

'Well, it's pretty boring, I'll tell you that for free.' On-screen me laughs.

Matt presses 'pause' again, then turns off the TV. I stare at him, nonplussed. *That* is what he's *this* annoyed about?

'And?' I prompt. 'That wasn't about you. That was just about life.'

'Oh, well, I'm so sorry I overreacted, then. Here was me thinking I'm a part of your life, but I guess I must not be.'

I stare at him for a minute. I'm just not sure why he's got his knickers in a twist about one innocuous comment. But I'm not about to *say* that. I still shudder sometimes when I think about the argument we had before. I don't want another one. I shake my head.

'Matt, look, I'm really—'

'You know Natalie came round here?'

'Did she?'

'Yeah, she was looking for you. She couldn't get hold of you on the phone, so she thought she'd try here. You didn't even tell her you were going to do that, did you? You know how much she wants all of this to go away, that was a dick move too.'

Matt starts doing laps of the coffee table. I pull my legs up onto the sofa so he can get past, crossing them under me.

I scoff. 'I *tried* to talk to her about it. I looked for her at the thing, I called her a million times, and then she switched her phone off on me. And this isn't about Natalie, anyway, is it?'

'It's not *not* about her. You just treated both of us the same way.' I wish he'd stop pacing and look at me.

'And how's that?'

And then he does stop pacing and does look at me. And I wish he hadn't. He just looks so . . . *hurt* and I feel a squeeze in my chest. But then the squeeze in my chest puts me on the defensive for reasons I can't/don't want to work out.

'With, I dunno, disdain. Like you're so much better than us, somehow. Like we're holding you back.' For a moment he fixes me with a look, and then he shakes his head. 'Never mind. We can't talk about this.'

'No, we're going to talk about it.' I get half up from the sofa and Matt stops in the doorway. 'We should talk about it.'

'OK. Talk.'

'I-I'm not . . . *You* talk.'

'OK. Fine. I feel like you've been incredibly selfish.'

'What? But . . . *I* haven't been—'

'OK, well, we had plans tonight, and you ditched them. You didn't even tell Natalie that you were going to do what you did tonight, and you were literally talking about her. What would you say that is?'

'Why are you taking Natalie's side over mine?'

'I'm not taking—' he begins, but I cut him off.

'Really? Because it feels like you are. And I'm sorry that I'm not Natalie, that I'm not, like, better, and more inspiring, and that I don't have a better job, and I'm not going anywhere. I wish I could be more like her for you. I do, but . . .'

Matt screws up his face. 'What's that supposed to mean?'

'I don't know, you just seem so obsessed with whether I've talked to Natalie or not.'

'Because she was here! And she's my friend too, and she was really upset. And you did that to her.'

'Oh, well, I didn't know you cared so much.'

'Of course I do. She's my friend.'

And then a switch flips in my head and I start saying things that I know to be completely mad but I can't seem to stop myself. 'I don't know, you keep saying that, but maybe you secretly wish you were with her instead of me. Maybe she fits in better with your life plan, with your secret rings, and your careers, and . . .'

He shakes his head. 'You sound crazy now. You must be able to hear yourself.'

'Yeah, but, am I, though? I know I'm not as grown-up as you and your friends. It's not like I'm not *trying* to be, but I get it. Maybe you want someone like her who doesn't make things awkward every time someone asks them how their day at work was. Maybe you want someone who can talk about spreadsheets and reports. Maybe that's not me.' I shrug. 'You know I've had a shitty time lately, and I can't believe you'd—'

'Having a shitty time is no excuse for how you're treating people at the moment! And if you've had such a shitty time lately, you should have told me. You promised you would tell me. How can I help you if you don't talk to me?'

'I don't want you to help me, Matt. I don't need help. I don't know what I need. I just—'

'Fine. You don't know what you need. But what do you *want*, Fiona? Do you still want to be in this relationship at all? Because I have to be honest, you're really not acting like you do.'

'I don't . . . I can't think about this now.' I take a shaky breath.

'Well, I think that's my answer, then, isn't it?' He shrugs.

'No! I don't mean *that*. I just . . . It's all really confusing, and so much has happened and—'

'But it's not a difficult question, is it? You told me you were ready.'

'And I thought I was! I did. And maybe I am. But then, things keep coming up, and I wonder if everything I have now is actually what I want. Because, I mean, I always thought that maybe I'd be special somehow. Or, like, different.' Matt makes a noise. 'I'm sorry, I know that's gross, but it's true. You know, everybody else was finding jobs and we went off travelling, and it was so amazing. And it's just different, having to settle down. Fun – so fun – but you couldn't keep that up forever, it'd be insane. That's why people say they're settling down, right? Because it all settles. No more highs. But also, no more lows. And I *am* settling down with you, it's just taking me a minute to get my head around it. I just need to adjust to that, that's all. But I'll get there. I will.'

I look over at him. He's still leaning on the living room wall, arms crossed, back hunched, staring at his feet. I can tell he's grinding his teeth because I can see his jaw working. It seems to take him ages to lift his head.

'And what if I don't want to wait around for you to get there?'

'Well, I mean, you have to,' I say, a tremor in my voice now. I never thought about this. How did I never think about it? What kind of *monster* wouldn't think about it?

'Why do I have to?'

'I-I don't know. You just do, right?'

CHAPTER TWENTY-TWO

NATALIE

My phone rings, like, *rudely* early the morning after Fiona ~~stabbed me in the back~~ went on TV, and of course it's her. I've calmed down a bit since last night but that still doesn't mean I want to talk to her. If anything, the fiery anger I initially felt has cooled now, and become something much more solid. It sits in my chest and prevents me from going back to sleep once she's woken me up with her phone call. And it's only just gone five a.m. on a *Sunday*, of all days, so that isn't helping her case.

I roll over, pulling the covers right over my shoulder, trying to burrow down into the mattress and get comfy again. I close my eyes and try to imagine I'm sinking into the mattress, hoping I can drop off again. Nothing doing.

I just don't understand in what world she thought I'd think doing that was OK. She might have cost me my job for all I know. She probably has. She's certainly cost us both a friendship. And for what? Ten minutes on local TV.

I pick up my phone and it burns my eyes as it lights up. I have messages from Fiona too. Lots of them. I swipe them off the screen without reading them.

I huff into the darkness and punch the pillow as I turn over. I glare up at the ceiling, even though it's dark. I can just about see some of the Artex picked out by the early morning light that's seeping through the cheap curtains.

I turn over again, even though I know that sleep is a lost cause. I do it again, pull the duvet tighter over me, close my eyes. But I can't relax anymore. Can't imagine myself sinking into the mattress or whatever else they say you're supposed to try. Because she was *supposed* to have my back. That's what it all comes down to. I needed *one* thing from her. And she couldn't do it. And haven't I done enough for her over the years?

I'm just turning onto my back again when there's a knock on the door. I sit up, pulling the covers up to my chin and holding my breath. All the better to hear the burglars with. Except, burglars don't knock, do they? I hug my knees and strain my ears in the silence. But there's nothing. Weird. I settle back down to continue quietly seething about Fiona, and then there's another knock.

This time, I pull my dressing gown around me and tiptoe towards the door. I wonder about bringing a knife with me, but I only have the two that survived Fiona moving out and they're so cheap and blunt they can barely get through an onion. As I get into the hall, whoever it is knocks again. And then the letterbox opens, which, let me tell you, feels like the stuff of horror movies when your mind is already going a mile a minute with murder scenarios.

'Natalie,' Fiona whispers through the flap.

For crying out loud. I glare at the letterbox for a second. I'm not in the mood. I consider creeping away again, denying all knowledge. But then she adds, 'I can see you.'

I roll my eyes and unlock the door.

'Do you know what time it is?' I hiss. I've started speaking before I get a good look at her, but then the light from the hall spills out of the door and . . . Yikes. Her face is blotchy, and her eyes are red. Her hair is everywhere. She's still in her pyjamas, she's just thrown a pair of tracksuit bottoms on over the top. She has a backpack with her. 'Did you . . . walk here like this?'

I actually do not want to know. I don't care. I'm still mad. She has no right to turn up here, out of the blue, when she's probably caused me to lose everything. But I'm also only human and she is my best friend, and if someone's died or, I dunno, she's been attacked, it's not like I wouldn't still listen.

So, I get out of her way. She takes her shoes off by the door and then goes over to the sofa. I close the door and pause for a second, refusing to look at her, trying to decide if I'm more mad or more worried. I think it might be a tie. I shake out my hands.

'Are you coming?' Fiona asks. I turn around and she's curled up against the arm of the sofa, on her favourite side, the throw we – well, I – keep over the back tucked around her legs. That didn't take her long. So, I think I'm more mad after all.

'What do you want, Fi?' I don't come any closer, I still have one hand on the door.

Fiona looks taken aback. She really does look a state. She has mascara streaked down her cheeks as well. She opens her mouth, then closes it again. Then she opens it. And then her eyes well up and spill over.

'I think Matt's broken up with me,' she says eventually.

'OK.' I nod. On any other day this would be a shocking turn of events. Right now, though? I can kind of see his point.

'*OK?* Is that it?'

'I don't know what else to say,' I shrug. Which is true.

'I told him I've been having a really hard time since we moved in together. I don't know, it's been a really difficult adjustment, feeling like maybe I don't measure up and—'

'Are you actually kidding me?' I demand. Fiona looks up, shock on her newly tear-stained face.

'S-sorry?'

'I'm just trying to figure out what you want. What can you possibly have to be upset about?'

'I don't—'

'Because I'll tell you what *I'm* upset about, shall I? My best friend went on TV last night and basically guaranteed that I'm going to lose my job. So that's the first job I've ever loved, just gone. And that means I'm probably going to lose my flat, too, and my savings – literally everything – and it would be really, *really* thoughtless of you to come in at god-knows o'clock in the morning and start complaining that *you* are upset about something.'

For a moment, Fiona just stares at me. Her eyes are wide. The room is so quiet I can hear a car passing on the street below.

'You're mad at me too,' she eventually says. Her voice shakes but I can tell she's trying to keep it even.

'Please give me literally one reason why I shouldn't be. You knew I wanted that whole thing to go away.'

'I tried to call you. I wanted to ask you first. You switched your phone off on me.'

'And what did you think I was going to say? We've talked about it a thousand times, the only thing I've ever said was how much I hate that video being out there, how uncomfortable it makes me. Did you really think that you were going to call for my blessing and I was going to say "Oh, yes, *please* drag all of that up again, it was *just* starting to go quiet, I'd *hate* for everybody to forget."'

I've got her. I can tell. 'I thought you might—'

'No, you *didn't* think. You *don't* think. You wanted to be able to say you'd asked, but you were going to do it anyway. If you actually cared about my feelings, you wouldn't have needed to ask.'

'And what about *my* feelings?'

Is a sentence I didn't think for a second I'd hear her say right now, but here we are, apparently.

'I spent all day yesterday being talked down to by people I might have ended up working with if things had gone a little bit differently. But they couldn't *see* that, they just saw someone who was there to serve them. Every single day, I'm just someone who's there to serve other people, and then I go home and I'm just, like, one half of Fiona and Matt—'

'Which you were excited about!' I interject.

'Yeah, but . . . I just . . . Sometimes I don't even feel like I exist as my own person. I used to feel good about myself and now I'm just less good than you, and I'm less good than Matt, and I'm less good than everybody I see, and honestly? I loved last night. I got to be myself. I got to feel like I had valid things to say. I'm sorry you're upset, but . . .'

I feel the anger rising inside me and all I can do is make a noise of frustration at even having to listen to this. Fiona looks at me coolly.

'You know what,' I say. 'This is just like the travelling stuff all over again.'

'What do you mean?' Fiona swallows. I suspect she might actually know what I mean.

'It's just . . .' But I'm not sure I even want to dredge it all up again. Not now. It wouldn't have done anything then. It's not going to do anything now. 'Do you know what? Forget it.'

Fiona shakes her head. 'No, go on. I want to hear.'

'OK, fine,' I huff. 'You do this, Fiona. You make plans, or you promise things, and then you change your mind, or you back out, or you decide that people are some kind of inconvenience to you, and you leave them behind as soon as it suits you. And you just seem to expect the people around you to accept anything you decide and just deal with the consequences. We were going to go off travelling together! It was going to be amazing! And you flaked on me as soon as you got a better offer. How did you think that was going to make me feel?'

'Yeah, from a . . . I thought you were . . .' Fiona stands up and goes to look out of the window. I carry on, even though she won't look at me.

'I mean, I get it – I did get it. But that didn't make it any less hurtful.'

'But you never said it was hurtful.' Fiona wheels around to look at me, leaning on the windowsill. 'I said I was sorry and—'

'What good would it have done if I said I was upset, though? You were still going to go. Would it have made any difference if I'd said anything?'

'I don't . . . I didn't—'

'Exactly. You would still have gone and I would have been left at home having told you how hurt I was. I would have been left behind knowing that I told my best friend exactly how I felt and it wasn't enough for her to change any of her plans. How do you think that would have made me feel?'

'But if you told me—'

'We talked about it for months, Fiona. You knew how excited I was. I shouldn't have needed to tell you. You should have realised—'

'How was I supposed to—'

'By having the tiniest bit of consideration for literally any other person in the world!' I throw my hands up in frustration. 'Any time you want to you could think about anyone other than yourself. But you never do. You literally *never* do. And sometimes I wish I was more like you. I can't imagine what it must be like to go through life never once worrying about how something you do might affect somebody else. It's basically your superpower.'

'That's not fair.'

'But it's true. And the fact is that last night was just you treating people like you've always treated people, and maybe it's high time those people told you they were sick of it. Maybe you've brought all of this on yourself. Maybe we're not going to be there to let you walk all over us all the time anymore.'

Fiona shuffles, crossing her arms. 'And how does your new dream job come into all of this, hey? How is that not you walking all over me to get what you wanted?'

'Because I got that fair and square!' I shake my head and rub my eyes. I can't believe she isn't getting this. 'And I didn't even know you'd applied. And when I *did* find out, I think you'll remember that I offered to withdraw my application. You didn't do that for me, did you? Me getting something I wanted isn't me taking it away from you just because you wanted it too. It is not the same as you completely ditching me. It is not the same as you actively doing something you knew would upset me, just because you feel a little bit insecure, or whatever's going on with you.'

'Yeah? Well, if I'm such a nightmare to be friends with, then why have you bothered all these years?'

'Do you know what, Fiona? I'm honestly asking myself the same question. Maybe I just won't anymore.'

I take a couple of steps towards the front door before I remember that this is *my* house, actually. I spin on my heel and then march off towards my bedroom. I slam the door when I get inside.

It's only after I slam the door that I realise my hands are shaking. There are tears on my cheeks, but I don't remember crying. I take a couple of deep breaths. Or, at least, I try. I have to force the air past the lump in my throat, which isn't easy. I walk from the door to the opposite wall and back a couple of times, trying to work out this energy that's come from somewhere. It obviously doesn't help, it's three paces each way if I'm being generous.

FIONA

When Natalie storms to her room I stand in the living room for a moment, just taking everything in. I try to absorb anything that's happened to me, but everything's gone so monumentally wrong in the last few hours that I don't even know where to start.

My heart is hammering in my ears, and I try to listen out for any signs of life from Natalie's room over the top of it. But I don't think there are any. And what the hell am I supposed to *do* now? I can't believe it was only a couple of hours ago that Matt was choking out that maybe we'd made a mistake moving in together after all. And then I screeched back that it was a bit late now. And then he said it didn't have to be, he could easily move back in with his mum. And then I lost it, told him not to even bother, and came here because I thought . . . Well, I guess I thought I had a friend here.

I let out a hollow laugh in the now-silent living room, and then my knees feel shaky, and I sink onto the edge of the sofa. I drop my head into my hands, just for a second. The darkness is a relief to my burning eyes. I always hated the big light in this room. Unnecessarily harsh. Not that it's mine to have opinions about anymore.

I just . . . How did I go from having everything to having nothing in one night? Who manages that? I lift my head and look around the living room again. We laughed here. We talked about boys here. We ate bowls of buttercream icing with spoons because why bother with a cake? And now she just hates me for no reason? I haven't even done anything, I . . .

I close my eyes. I can't go round in another circle. Not here. So, I put my hands on my knees and push myself up to standing. Just about every muscle in my body protests as I do. Destroying your entire life when you're not even sure how it happened is a good workout, it seems.

I cross to the front door in a couple of paces and then I just want to be out. I'm suddenly convinced that the longer I'm here the more likely it is that Natalie will come back out and want to talk and I can't do it anymore. Not now. So, I grab my shoes and leave the flat with them still in my hand.

NATALIE

I can't catch any of my swirling thoughts for long enough to figure out what I should do now. I am *furious* with her, but if she's broken up with Matt, where's she going to go? I huff with resignation as I decide she can sleep in the spare room as long as I do not see hide nor hair of her until I'm ready. But just as I reach towards the door handle to open it and bark that information at her, I hear the front door slam.

FIONA

I stand outside my parents' house and stare up at the window of my childhood bedroom. Great.

CHAPTER TWENTY-THREE

FIONA

'Morning!' my mother trills as I stare at the ceiling in my childhood bedroom. The pictures I cut out of many and varied magazines over many years look down from the walls as if to say 'we knew you'd be back one day'. The sun glows through the window and makes my head pound. I can hear Mum climbing the stairs. 'Come on, sleepyhead.'

'Morning,' I say as her face appears around the door.

'What's happened?' Dad asked an hour or so ago, squinting against the sunrise that was busting into life behind me.

'Nothing. Can I stay here?'

I don't think I'd normally get away with so obviously avoiding a question, but he peered at me and then nodded, stepping aside to let me in. I went straight up the stairs to my room without even looking back. Because looking back invites questions. And I did not have answers. I still don't.

'Who was it?' I heard my mum ask through the wall.

'Fiona. One for you, I think.'

So, it's not like I didn't know this was coming, but I still don't know what to say. There's a pressure on the end of the mattress, and I glance down to see Mum perching there. She puts a hand on my ankle. The weight of it feels reassuring.

'Have you and Matthew had an argument?'

I hold her gaze for a second. Then I stare at the wall instead. Then I shake my head. And then my chin wobbles and my eyes spill over, and I nod.

'David!' my mum calls. 'Put the kettle on!'

NATALIE

I get to the office super-early on Monday. I figure I might as well. I couldn't sleep last night. My brain kept whirring, churning out comebacks that would have been perfect when Fiona was still here. Wildly unhelpful afterwards, of course. And the adrenaline from replaying our argument over and over again made me twitchy. So, I went to bed early on Sunday and then just glared at the ceiling until daylight started creeping through the curtains.

Which explains why I'm standing in the car park staring up at the splashes of early morning sunlight across the side of the building. I can't tear my eyes away. Either it's very beautiful indeed, or I am far more tired than I realised. I blink a couple of times.

'You OK?' someone says behind me, and I jump. I turn around to find Tom standing next to a blue Nissan, looking bemused to find me frozen to the spot in the car park. Fair.

'Morning!' I smile, snapping into 'not a total weirdo' mode. I'm not sure why, considering the man saw me hide behind a beer tent in a field not two days ago. Was doing the same thing, in fact.

'Morning,' he replies. As he gets closer to me, I can see his smile turn into a look of concern. So, that gives me some feedback about how I must look following my very early start. Lovely stuff. I pull my face into a smile. 'You never answered me. Is everything OK?'

'I—'

I don't even know where to start.

I would love to say that the day gets better after that. But, guess what? No such luck. Of course I find an invitation to a meeting with John Stait in my inbox. Of *course* I do. And that would be scary enough if it was just a one-to-one, but Jenny's invited too.

'Mr Stait?' I knock on the door of the meeting room, my heart hammering. For a minute this morning I let Tom convince me that everything was going to be OK. But now John Stait glances up from his phone for about a second, before looking back at it. He beckons me in, eyes still on the screen. I hesitate, not sure if he's angry or just, well, a bit rude. Oh god. If he's both then I have no chance. I dart over to a seat as close to the door as possible and try to sit down without making any noise. He doesn't look up.

I swallow. 'H-How are you?'

He keeps tapping away on his phone for a moment before he looks up at me again. 'Very well, thank you. How are you?'

'Yes. Very good. Thank you.'

I sound like such an arse-licker, it's almost painful. And then we're sitting in silence again. Why are we sitting in silence again? If my whole job depends on the outcome of this meeting, why can't I think of a single thing to say to get him on side? This is literally my chance. I wrack my brains but—

'Wow. Quiet in here, isn't it?' Jenny appears in the doorway. She shoots me a glance and I can't read her expression.

'Come in, Jenny. Shut the door.' John Stait turns the screen of his phone off and puts it face down on the table as Jenny closes the door and sits down. I glance through the glass wall at everybody just working away, apparently unaware that something terrible is about to happen to me. Or maybe they don't care. Little Miss Attention Seeker getting what she deserves. I feel like a spider that's been trapped under a glass.

'Now' – John Stait interrupts my spiralling – 'Natalie. You'll remember the meeting we had a little while back when we discussed – well, Jenny discussed – the CLC social media policy.'

'Y . . .' My voice isn't working, so nothing comes out. I clear my throat and try again. 'Yes.'

'And you'll remember me saying that I didn't mind what anybody was doing, as long as they weren't making so much noise that it ended up getting back to me?'

I nod, staring at the desk. I can feel the flush working its way up my face.

'My daughter texted me last night, told me I needed to watch the latest episode of *South West Tonight*. She thought she'd seen someone she recognised from the family day. Can you think who that might have been?'

That's when I know it's all over. I swallow. 'Me.'

'You. On TV.'

He holds my gaze until I'm actively uncomfortable. My face can't get any redder, so I don't know what he expects to gain, but I also don't want to be the person who speaks first. We end up in this eye-contact battle I can't see a way out of.

'Mr Stait,' Jenny interrupts.

Takes me a second to register that she's even spoken. I thought she'd just sit in the corner and enjoy the spectacle, revel in the fact that she's finally got rid of me and secured all of the glory for herself. Don't get me wrong, after our little escapade during the family day I would have thought she was a bitch for doing it. But I wouldn't have put it past her. It's so unexpected for her to interrupt that I whip my head around to stare at her. She has her eyes shut, her fists clenched in her lap.

'It's my fault,' Jenny continues. My mouth drops open, and I know I look like a complete idiot, but I think that's fair under the circumstances. 'I set her up. Or I didn't, you know, set her *up*. But, I mean, I did . . . I told a journalist how they could get in contact with her. It was only local, and it was only because—'

'Jenny.' John Stait sits back in his chair. I seem to be out of the spotlight for a second, so I take the opportunity to fidget in my seat.

Jenny pinches the bridge of her nose now, rubs her eyes. 'It was a stupid thing to do. I know I shouldn't have done it. I just . . . John, you know I've really struggled with the idea of giving up some of my workload and, I don't know. I wanted things to go back to how they were. I thought this was a way to—'

'You realise our clients might have seen some of the coverage?' John Stait leans back in his seat and folds his arms, regarding Jenny coldly.

'John, with all due respect, a five-star hotel in Sri Lanka isn't going to be reading the *Crostdam Chronicle*, are they?'

'Wait, this was in the *Chronicle* too?'

'See? And you didn't *know* that, so . . .'

John Stait sighs. Heavily. 'I really don't know what we're going to do with you, Jenny.'

'No, I know.' Her voice quivers. 'I went a bit mad for a second, I know that. I didn't cope with the change very well. And I deserve anything you decide I do. Just . . . Don't punish Natalie for something she didn't do. And she didn't even *talk* to the journalist. She wasn't the one on TV. She seriously hasn't done anything.'

I stare at her. I turn my head to look at John Stait, but he's also just . . . staring at her.

'I'm sorry,' she says. Then she turns to look at me. 'I'm sorry. Like I said, I think I went a bit mad, that's all. Just give everyone another chance and then—'

'Jennifer, you risked the kind of . . . of . . . reputational damage that you yourself were—'

'I know. I was such a hypocrite. And now I want to fix it. Please. It'll never happen again.'

John Stait creases his brow.

We leave the room ten minutes later, and all of the people who were definitely only pretending to work whip their heads up to look at us.

'Yes?' Jenny asks mildly as we head back to our desks.

Sophie frowns at me and I smile back.

FIONA

For a couple of days so far I've dragged myself out of bed, feeling terrible. I've pulled on the stripy blouse that now smells different because my mum doesn't buy the cheapest laundry detergent available. And I've forced myself out of the house after pulling one sickie, because the ice cream isn't going to sell itself. I really try not to think about . . . well, anything.

Pros of being back at home with my parents are: my mum washing the ice-cream sick off my work shirt because she knows I'm sad, home-cooked food, and watching property programmes into the night. I've never spent so much time with Phil and Kirstie. And cons? Where do I start? Humiliation, obviously. Existential dread. Panic that I've wasted my entire life up until now. And trouble sleeping. Or, *no* sleeping, really. Also, the knowledge that I've hurt everybody who was important to me by being a thoughtless, self-centred arsehole. But, aside from that, it's great.

CHAPTER TWENTY-FOUR

NATALIE

I pop to the supermarket one evening a few days after The Incident. I've subsisted on cereal dinners for as long as possible to avoid having to leave the house in the evenings, just in case anybody recognises me. But there's a real risk of scurvy if I don't see a vegetable soon, so I chance it.

My heart pounds on the walk to the supermarket, I'm so paranoid I'm going to bump into someone who recognises me. Or, oh god, what if I bump into Fiona? I might die of embarrassment. Or what if it all kicks off again?

But I don't see anybody. To be fair, it's nine p.m. and nobody in their right mind does a weekly shop at this time. Which makes it perfect for me.

I'm lugging the heaviest basket in the world out of one aisle and into the next, fast losing the will to live and wondering if there's any way I could just abandon it here and go back home, when someone bumps into me.

'Sorry.'

'Matt?'

He raises an eyebrow. I cringe, shooting a look past him towards the end of the aisle, wondering if I could just run away. He's going to go back home and tell Fiona that he saw me, and I am wearing what is tantamount to pyjamas. With a bra, at least, but still. She'll know.

'Hi,' he says, giving me a rueful smile.

'Hi,' I return. I take a couple of steps past him. 'Sorry, I—'

But he grabs my arm. 'Where are you going?'

I really want to get out of here, but I also don't want to *look* like I want to get out of here if that's something else he's going to go home and tell Fiona. So, I change tack, examine the backs of a couple of jars of peanut butter.

'How's things?' I ask.

'Well, you know, not great. Obviously.' He sounds weary. I look up, suddenly curious.

'Why not great?'

'Where have you been?'

'No, I just . . . I know why they're not great for me. Why are they not great for you?'

In the end, we pay for our stuff and buy shitty hot drinks in the sad café by the door.

'So, you didn't make up with Fiona, then?' I ask, unnecessarily.

'No. And . . . she's not gone back to live with you?'

I laugh bitterly. Matt frowns. 'Sorry. She did show up after you guys argued but I wasn't in the mood after the . . . y'know. And, yeah. We had a massive blow-up too. Don't think anybody was there to film it this time, though.' I pull a face and wave crossed fingers, but I can tell Matt doesn't think my joke is funny. I don't either. We both take a sip of our horrible drinks.

'Do you know where she is, then?' Matt asks. 'She'll have gone to her parents', right?'

'Probably.'

He sighs. 'I just don't think I have it in me anymore.'

'What do you mean?'

'Just, like, the drama. After she found the ring—'

'You had a *ring*?'

He holds up a finger. 'No, I did not have a *ring*. She just thought I did. And she freaked out, which I did understand, but then she told me she was done with it. And you know what? If she's not, that's her problem, not mine. So we'll just have to see. I hope she comes to her senses, but I'm tired of waiting around for that to happen, you know?' I nod. 'I can't believe she never told you about the ring, though. I thought you guys told each other everything.'

'So did I. I guess not, though.'

He fiddles with his coffee cup for a second, spinning it round until the seam up the side lines up with the hole in the lid, then taking the lid off and putting it on the other way again. I watch, because I can't think of what else to say. I can't figure out when it all fell apart. I mean, Fiona and Matt, just not a thing anymore? It doesn't make sense. I try to rewind back to whenever things started to go wrong, and I can only come up with one answer.

'I should never have taken that job,' I sigh.

Matt whips his head up. 'What?'

'The job. I'm sure that's what did it. No job, no argument. No argument, no video. No video, no TV. No TV, no . . .' I wave a hand in the air. 'Whatever's happened now.'

'That's not it.' Matt looks at me more intensely now. 'You can't put it on yourself.'

'I'm not . . .'

'You saying "if I hadn't got this job everything would still be OK" is one hundred per cent you putting it on yourself.'

'OK, but—'

'No, Natalie, look. I know you guys have been a package deal forever, but you're not responsible for this one, OK? Neither of us are.' He sighs and drops a crumpled sugar packet into his still-half-full coffee cup. He snaps the stirrer in two and puts that in as well. 'I don't know what the hell her problem is, but it's *her* problem. You didn't do anything. I didn't do anything. All we've done is live our lives. If she can't deal with that, if our lives aren't good enough for her anymore, then that's on her. I'll see you later.'

He pushes his chair back with a squeak on the laminate floor, picks up his bag, and is gone before I can figure out what to say.

I drive myself crazy thinking about what Matt said. I realise he's right, then feel terrible for Fiona, because I'm sure she didn't mean to push both of us away. But then I realise Matt's right, but then . . . It's hard to stop when you start.

'Do you think he's right?' I ask Sophie a couple of days later. I invited her to Sunday Morning Brunch and now she sits opposite me in Fiona's usual spot. She nods as she absorbs everything. Which is fair because I did just dump a *ton* of angst about Fiona, our argument, and everything Matt said.

'I think . . .' Sophie starts, and then takes a sip of coffee. 'Christ, do you know what? I don't know. It's such a mess, isn't it?'

I nod, glancing over her head and towards the front door. I'm so nervous Fiona's going to decide to show up and be furious that Sophie's here instead. But she also didn't answer any of my texts, and I was going crazy trying to figure out what to do. I needed to talk to *someone*.

Sophie stirs a sugar cube into her coffee and then looks up at me. 'Look, I'm not saying you shouldn't talk to her, but—'

'That sounds like something you might say just before you tell me not to talk to someone.'

'I just think maybe she needs to come around' – I open my mouth and Sophie holds up a hand – 'not that you've done anything wrong that she needs to come around *to*. But there's obviously a lot of feelings and maybe you both need to just chill out for a while. Get your heads on straight.'

I nod, then sigh. God, adulthood is shit. It's so annoying when one of you can't just demand that the other one join in with a playground game and everything's immediately forgotten.

But then our food arrives, which does help temporarily.

FIONA

I don't know what I want to get out of going to the restaurant, honestly. Natalie's either going to be there, in which case there's a strong chance I'll run away immediately. Or she won't be there, in which case I might actually feel worse because it'll mean I messed things up even worse than I realised.

It's just so weird. Like, I am *mad*, but I'm also probably the saddest I've ever been. And it's not just the things we said, either. I didn't realise how much of my life Natalie and Matt (but mainly Natalie) have taken up until now. It was the time spent together, obviously. And the calling, and the texting. But also just the looking at their Instagrams, liking posts on Facebook, the making mental notes to tell one of them something the next time we talked, the wondering what they think about everything I say or do. If only I'd been thinking when *South West Tonight* came calling.

There's just so much *time* now. It stretches on forever, completely empty, and I don't know how to fill it. Which is why I decide that I should just have a *look* through the window of Reggie's. It's like pressing on a bruise. How do you know how much it hurts if you don't test it?

I try to keep my face casual as I walk towards the restaurant. I know nobody cares what I'm doing but I want to save face anyway.

As I get closer my pace slows. Like I said, I don't really know what I want out of any of this. My breath hitches in my throat as I get closer to the window. All I have to do is face forward and walk confidently past, glance inside, and not slow down.

Easier said than done.

I immediately hate myself for looking. She's there. My heart leaps for a split second and then I notice . . . Is that *Sophie* with her?

Look, the logical part of my brain knows that I haven't been replaced and that this is really all my fault. Unfortunately, the logical part of my brain is too small and too quiet to have any say in my reaction. I feel like somebody's stabbed me between my ribs. I can hear my heart in my ears, my eyes prick, and then they brim over, and then I'm turning around and running away before either of them see me. I can't face being humiliated on top of everything else. I already *am* humiliated, but at least neither of them knows it. I wipe my nose with my sleeve and push past a couple of slow walkers. Just get home.

The worst part of all of it is that I'm halfway there before I realise I'm actually heading towards Natalie's flat. I scold myself as I change direction. Realistically, I know it's just muscle memory, but that doesn't make me feel any less dumb in the moment. If that's not bad enough, once I've changed direction, it doesn't take me long to realise that I'm running towards mine and Matt's. Just Matt's? Well, still mine and Matt's, I *think*? I hope.

Anyway, I change direction again and head for Mum and Dad's. Third time's the charm. What a mess.

NATALIE

I do feel better for talking to Sophie. I do. I do. If I keep saying it enough, maybe I'll believe it. No, but seriously, I do. It was nice to put the world to rights. It was nice to have someone confirm that I'm not crazy to be angry with her, or hurt by the way she's behaved. Although as soon as Sophie started confirming that I was, in fact, not being unreasonable I wanted to jump in with all the reasons I really might be. And now I have a stomach ache, which might be the pancake stack I ate to bury my discomfort, or it might be the discomfort not allowing itself to be forgotten so easily.

CHAPTER TWENTY-FIVE

Fiona

I am actually settling nicely into my new life as a lone wolf after a few days. Do I wish I didn't have to do it? Obviously. But Matt will quite rightly never want to talk to me again. And I don't want to try, because if I have to actually hear him say it, if I have to look at him while he tells me all the ways I've ruined things, I will wish I was dead. So, I will simply live in this weird purgatory, with Schrödinger's breakup hanging over me. It's better than the definite answer I'll be given if I ask.

And it's basically the same with Natalie. If I try to see her now all that will happen is she'll tell me she can't be friends anymore. And she'd be right to. But that doesn't mean I'm ready to hear it. So I'm learning to live with the unresolved issues. Because I don't consider them to be unresolved at all.

And, by the way, it's fine. So far, I've used the time productively. For instance, I now know it's possible to finish a whole sharing bag of crisps on your own in an evening if you apply yourself. And I know that I can go from being in bed at my parents' house all the way to Scoopz in twenty minutes if I run. You really do learn new things every day. Yes, some of those things will make your father think you might be depressed. But dads are supposed to worry, it's their natural state.

I'm manning the counter at the shop while Amy takes the rubbish out when Roger Newcombe walks in. Well, I never. I blink and, for a second, I'm back in the school hall, picking a scab on my knee while he tells us about the Good Samaritan. It stings a bit when I blink again and I'm back in the here and now. At least people still liked me when Reverend Roger used to bore us senseless.

'Hello. Fiona, isn't it?' he asks.

'That's me.' I give him a sad smile because it's all I can muster.

'Hello, Fiona. I'm not sure we've met.'

'We have, actually. Or, at least, I used to go to St James' when you were doing the assemblies there.'

'Ah. Yes. Well, we have met, then. Yes, I remember now.' There is no way in hell he remembers but it's nice that he's pretending. 'I've seen a lot of you recently, of course.'

'I can imagine.' I give him a sheepish smile. I cannot imagine where this is going. But it's not like I have anything left to lose anymore if it turns out to be video-related.

'Now, I'm not sure if you'll be familiar, but I'm with the Crostdam Harriers. You know, the running club? And I was hoping to discuss something with you.' I raise my eyebrows. Is he lost?

Amy reappears through the door behind Reverend Roger. He looks at her and she gives him a curious smile, picks up a cloth and a spray bottle and bustles over to the tables. I can tell she's eavesdropping because she starts cleaning one spot and doesn't move on.

'What did you want to, um, discuss?' I ask.

'Well, it's the half marathon soon. We have a couple of hundred people signed up, and we've been looking for someone who might be able to start the race for us. As a local – well – "celebrity", your name has come up as an option. I was wondering if you might have any interest.'

I can practically *hear* the inverted commas around the word 'celebrity' when he says it, but I still feel a little thrill. Enough to distract me from everything else I have going on, anyway. I open my mouth to speak but Amy gets there first, walking towards him with her hand outstretched.

'Amy Sinclair, nice to meet you. And your name is?'

'Roger. Newcombe.'

'Roger. Hi, Roger. I'm Fiona's manager. Could I ask what the fee would be for her making a public appearance?'

'I . . . Well. We don't really have a budget for—'

'Because obviously it's only reasonable to pay her for her time and effort, wouldn't you agree?'

What is she *doing*? I shoot her a look that says 'stop this immediately', but she completely ignores me. Reverend Roger chews his lip for a second, frowning.

'We could do fifty pounds,' he says eventually.

'And will there be catering?'

'Fifty pounds and a pasty?'

Amy opens her mouth again, but I cut in first, because I do not want her shaking down a vicar. 'That sounds great. Shall I give you my email and you can send me the information?'

He disappears a couple of minutes later with my details on the back of a piece of till roll, and a single scoop on a waffle cone, which I suspect will go in the bin as soon as he gets out of sight.

'Oh my god, isn't that awesome?' Amy says, standing up from the edge of the table she perched on while I wrote down my email address. She sprays the part where her bum was, giving it a quick wipe. 'Fifty pounds, and for what? Waving at some runners for a few minutes? That's one hell of an hourly rate.'

I mean, she's got a point. Right?

'And you don't think it's out of order to ask them for money? I don't know, is that . . . OK?'

'Babe' – Amy catches hold of my hand as I move to pick up the nearly empty box of plastic spoons from the counter – 'he could have said "no". He didn't say "no". So, it must be fine, right?'

'I guess so. It's just—'

'Have you ever heard of imposter syndrome?'

'Yeah, it's the thing people make up to get praise.'

'Oh, no. It's real. This is it in action. You are *worth it*, Fiona. Remember that.'

She looks at me so fiercely that I immediately believe her.

NATALIE

I am at my desk minding my own business when I receive an email from Tom with the title 'FWD: You might want to see this'. I catch Jenny's eye as I glance up, and she gives me a little smile. I return it. It still feels shaky, but we're definitely on some kind of better ground. I slide my eyes across to Tom and he looks pointedly at my screen and nods. So, I open the email.

From: Crostdam Harriers
To: All

Hi Harriers,

I know we've been talking for a while about how to get more publicity for the half, and I just wanted to let you know that Fiona Maitliss has agreed to start the race. She's a Crostdam local, so it feels appropriate, and you might have seen her on *South West Tonight* recently. Or, for followers of pop culture, I believe she was also in a video online. Anyway, we'll reach out to some local press and see if we can't use this to raise awareness of our event. If you have any more ideas let me know!

Thanks,

Rev. Roger Newcombe (Secretary)

I absorb the information for a moment. It stings, but I think that's more because we haven't spoken in, what, a week or so now? It's weird that there's this thing I didn't know about her when I'm used to having a front row seat. But then I take a moment to adjust to the new reality where I don't get included in stuff.

And, I mean, realistically they're not going to play The Video, are they? I have never attended, nor will I ever attend, any kind of running event. But I imagine there's not a screening session beforehand. So, like, it's fine. Fiona can do what she wants now. I don't get to have feelings about it. It's none of my business, because I made it none of my business, and that hurts, but it is what it is.

I look up at Tom again. He gives me an 'are you OK?' frown. I give him a rueful smile and a nod in return.

CHAPTER TWENTY-SIX

FIONA

If there is a worse feeling than an alarm clock going off at five a.m. I've never experienced it. People on the internet have literally said I look fat in a video I didn't know was being filmed (yes, I read the comments) but I would have every one of those guys say that to my face before I would willingly drag myself out of bed at this godforsaken time. I simply do not believe the people who try to suggest it's a positive, productive thing to do. Of course they would think that, there's something wrong with them. The only time this was ever OK was back in the day when I was catching a flight or something. And even then I tried to avoid it.

My first thought as my alarm terrifies me awake is 'Who starts a half marathon at nine a.m.?' But I am going to get paid, and all I have to do in return is stand around, so I force myself out of bed. The least I can do is look good.

'Oh,' Reverend Roger says when I meet him at the church hall for the safety briefing ninety minutes before the race is due to start. 'Morning.'

I've gone quite glam, if I do say so myself. But, I mean, people are going to *see* me, so . . . I felt I had no choice. I'm the celebrity guest. Isn't that what they do? Outfit wise, I've gone for leggings and a plain top with an oversized blazer because, frankly, I do not know what one wears to an athletic event. I've added a little neckerchief action too. Amy and I talked about it, and we thought it might be a cute, *Grease*-esque thing to do to take the neckerchief off and wave it to start the race. Although I'm not sure that Reverend Roger, in his cargo shorts and bright yellow 'Crostdam Harriers' hoody is really going to care about our cute start idea. He ushers me inside and sits me at a table with a black box on top.

I honestly thought the safety briefing was going to be a formality. Like an 'if there's a fire, run away' kind of thing. The safety briefing I actually end up sitting through feels very much like an exam. Except I didn't get up at five a.m. before any of my exams, so my brain actually worked for those. This morning I just blink at Reverend Roger as his mouth moves.

'Are you with me?' he asks, sitting on the other side of the table, one hand on the box.

'Sorry.' I shake my head. Wake up. 'Yes.'

He flips the lid on the box and there's a *gun* in there? My eyes widen. I look up to meet his.

'You look scared,' he says, as casually as you might say 'it looks like rain'. 'That's good. This is your starting pistol, and it needs to be treated with respect.'

Holy. Shit. I really, really try to listen to everything he's saying to me, but it's difficult. My brain wasn't working because of the early morning, but now there's a *gun* involved as well. I wish Amy really was my manager because I might be tempted to call her and ask her to get me out of this.

But, no. It's fine. I am a professional. I look great. If anything, firing a gun into the air is much more badass than waving a neckerchief, so that's a fun development. It's going to be fine. So fine. I'm a pro. I know what I'm doing.

'OK?' he says, and only then do I realise I haven't paid attention to a word he's been saying.

I shake out my hand to stop it trembling. 'OK,' I agree.

Reverend Roger closes the lid of the box, tucks it under his arm, and holds out a hand to indicate that I should lead the way out of the hall. The start line is a fifteen-minute walk up a hill. And, if we needed any more proof that I'm not qualified to be involved with a running race, I'm out of breath by the time we get there.

Natalie and I actually watched the start of the London Marathon last year, so I thought I knew what I was getting myself into, but this . . . is not like that. There's probably only a hundred or so people here, mostly men, all wiry as anything. This looks like the boring, professional start, when Natalie went off and made us both bacon sandwiches and builder's tea. I feel a pang of something as I remember joking with her about running it one day. But anyway, where are the people dressed as rhinos? Or the ones carrying appliances on their backs? Someone could have mustered up a pair of fairy wings or some face paint at the very least. But no. These people are all in shorts, vests, and that's it. There are barely even any spectators. I had vaguely thought that this might be some kind of exposure for me, but now I see how wrong I was.

I stand quietly next to Reverend Roger, feeling more and more like a bellend in my outfit, while he discusses trainers or something with another very-fit-looking running person.

'Anyway, I should go and line up,' this very-fit-looking running person says, clapping Reverend Roger on the shoulder. Then he looks at me. 'Hi, by the way. I'm friends with Natalie. It's nice to meet you.' He flashes a bright smile and jogs away.

He's *what* with *whom*? I've never heard anything about a very-fit-looking running man in Natalie's life. Why have I never heard of him? Unless maybe he's the man from the CLC event? For a second, I feel another wave of hurt wash over me before I remember that I have no right to know stuff about Natalie's life anymore. I made sure of that. And now I have a stomach ache. Lovely.

Reverend Roger steps up onto a little platform with a microphone and starts speaking. I'm tired, and now I'm also distracted, but I *force* myself to nod along as if I have the same authority as him. It's lots of stuff about trying not to get hit by cars, and what to do if you twist your ankle in a deserted lane and need help. It honestly sounds terrible.

'And now, to kick this thing off properly, it's my pleasure to welcome Fiona Maitliss!'

There is a smattering of unenthusiastic applause and I step towards the platform. Reverend Roger steps down and then holds out a hand to help me up. Which I need because did I mention I'm wearing heels? There is not a single part of my outfit that I got right.

Anyway, I make it up onto the platform in one piece and then stare out at the . . . 'crowd' seems too strong a word. A handful more people have joined in the last few minutes, but not many.

'Hi,' I say into the microphone, and feedback squeals in my ears because of course it does. People wince. I take a step back and nearly topple off the back edge of the platform. I can hear the collective gasp as I flap my arms to get my balance back, but then I do, and all I want is to get this over with. My heart pounds. I take everything back. I'll never take Scoopz for granted again. I want my tiny life back. This is – what – maybe half a step up from where I used to be? Probably not even that. But, anyway, I hate it, and I hate me, and I wish it was a month ago again and nothing had happened.

'Fiona!' Reverend Roger hisses. I look down and he's holding the open black box up towards me. Right. My hand shakes as I pick up the literal gun. I'm sure my trembling is encouraging for everyone. I start to raise it in the air, keeping my eyes on Reverend Roger. Since I don't remember a word of the safety briefing, my best hope is that he'll pull some kind of face if I'm doing something wrong. But there's nothing. So, full steam ahead, I guess.

'Good luck with the race, happy running!' I call, because I do not know what you're supposed to say to runners, but I feel like I should say something.

I hold the gun as high up as I can and squeeze the trigger. And nothing happens. So, I squeeze the trigger again. And nothing happens. I glance down at Reverend Roger, but I don't think he realises what's happening because he just nods at me as if to say 'Go, you dumbass in the oversized blazer and unnecessary lipstick, what are you waiting for?' I squeeze the trigger one more time, and still nothing.

I literally do not have the first clue what to do now so I lower the gun again, which, on paper, does sound like a really stupid thing to do. Even more stupid with hindsight because the gun finally does go off when it is only just directed above the runners' heads. People duck, there are screams. For a second, I think I must have shot someone. It's terrifying.

That's not even the worst thing, though. Because I jump so much that I take a couple of steps and then I fall. Off. The platform. And I drop the pistol as I do, and that hits the ground and goes off *again*. And I try to stand up to save my dignity, but my ankle is on *fire* because I twisted it when I fell and, long story short, I really do wish for death. It's carnage. And it's all on me.

NATALIE

TOM: You are NEVER going to believe what has just happened.
    NATALIE: Aren't you supposed to be running?

TOM: Absolute chaos here. Restarting in an hour. F tried to shoot everyone and then fell off the stage????

NATALIE: . . .

I type 'Is she OK?' and then delete it a few times. Because, really, I probably don't have any right to care, and I'm not sure I even do, and my pity is probably the last thing she wants anyway. So, I dither. Maybe I should just go right now and see her, give her some moral support? But I don't think me showing up at the moment would make it better. Or would it? No. No, it wouldn't. Also, very importantly, I am *done* with putting myself out for her. Must remember that. So, I sit for a while, right on the edge of the sofa, in my pyjamas, not knowing what to say back.

TOM: Anyway, starting again soon, see you Monday :)

CHAPTER
TWENTY-SEVEN

FIONA

I'm not being dramatic, but I am never leaving the house ever again and that is all there is to it. You really don't need to leave the house in this day and age, anyway. Restaurants deliver meals, supermarkets deliver groceries, TV exists, the world thinks I'm an idiot. I simply have no reason to go outside. And, do you know what? That's *fine*. It is genuinely very fine. I am more than happy to sit on my parents' sofa in my threadbare jogging bottoms and wait for death. Thrilled, in fact. Because I don't even have to cook. Mum does that.

'Love, you know you can't just sit there forever, right?' Mum asks the morning after the most embarrassing thing that's ever happened to me. 'What about work?'

'What about my ankle? I can't stand up all day.'

I'll drag out being injured for as long as possible and hope that over time my parents will forget that I used to be an independent woman with my own life. If everything goes according to plan, they will start to think of me as some kind of human-shaped cushion that just happens to live on the sofa and doesn't need to do anything with her life, or go anywhere ever, because inanimate objects don't do things or go places. And outside the house I'll become some kind of myth. People will tell each other about the woman who tried to shoot a group of runners and then fell off a stage. But over time they'll forget that it was me, because I'll fade from everybody's memories. Because nobody except my parents will ever see me again. It's a bloody good plan, if I do say so myself.

NATALIE

I wait for Tom outside the office on Monday so I can pump him for information about Fiona's celebrity appearance.

'Did she get hurt?'

'I don't know.'

'Did she seem upset?'

'I don't know. I guess she was probably embarrassed.'

'Did she seem—'

'I'm going to stop you there because, remember, I don't actually know her, so I don't know how she'd look if she "seemed" anything.'

'Right. Yeah, sorry.'

Tom holds the door for me, and I walk through. I press the button for the lift.

'Do you mind if I make a suggestion?' Tom says as we wait for the doors to open.

'Carry on.'

'Why don't you just *talk* to her?'

'I can't.'

The lift doors open and we step inside. Tom pushes the button and we wait for the doors to close.

'I know you had this whole argument or whatever, but you clearly miss her. I've known you for, what? Maybe a month at this point? And we've already had multiple conversations about her.'

'Yeah, but . . .'

Someone else gets in the lift. He nods at Tom, and then at me. Tom nods back, and so do I, but it puts an end to the conversation.

I do text Fiona in the end, because I am weak.

NATALIE: Hey, heard about what happened, are you OK?

I see her see my message. For one split second I think I see her typing, but it goes away too fast to be sure. I get nothing back. I check again, and again, until I've picked my phone up and put it down again so many times it's actually embarrassing. Nothing. And do you know what? Fine. I put myself out there to contact her. I made the first move. Even though I was not the one in the wrong in the first place. I did the thing. I did it *anyway*. And if she doesn't want to know? Well, that's not my fault, is it?

After having one last check (I did say I'm weak) I turn off my screen and put my phone face down on my desk. And then I feel another wave of anger. She wants to ignore me in her time of crisis? Fine. She wants to be a bitch about it? I can't help her.

I block her number. And put her out of my mind. Or, at least, I pretend to. If anybody asks, I'll tell them I have. Screw her.

FIONA

I know I should reply to Natalie's message. It might be the only olive branch I get. And maybe I'm ready for one? I don't know. The real problem is that I can never see or speak to anybody ever again without combusting from embarrassment. So, I wallow in my disgrace instead. This is my life now.

It takes a couple of days before I start to have any misgivings. Because . . . Well. Maybe I was too hasty? Maybe I *was* the one in the wrong when we argued? Maybe I didn't have any right to be upset when she went for brunch with Sophie instead of me? Maybe I should have just let the whole video thing die down like Natalie wanted it to, as opposed to bringing it all up again on literal television?

And once those thoughts start creeping into my brain, they're hard to stop. I try to ignore them, to stay strong. But they keep coming, no longer creeping but storming, and suddenly there are too many doubts, and my stomach seems to drop into the floor with the weight of them.

Oh my god. *I* am the arsehole.

NATALIE

I'm watching TV and minding my own business a few days later when someone hammers on the door so loudly I nearly drop the bowl of cereal I'm holding. It's, like, eleven p.m. It is cereal shame-eating time. It's also absolutely pissing it down outside. I can't imagine who'd be out in this. The rain is hammering down. I freeze on the sofa, not sure what I'm going to do if the phantom knocker knocks again.

'Natalie!' Fiona yells. 'I know you're in there. And I know you're ignoring me. Probably. I've been messaging you anyway, and you haven't answered, so I assume that's what you're doing. But answer the door. Please.'

I obviously do not answer the door. I said I was going to stop letting her get her own way mere weeks ago, I'm not just going to fold the second she happens to show up at my front door.

She shouts again, hammering so loud the chain clatters against the frame. 'Look, can you just come to the door? I'm not going to go anywhere, so you might as well.'

I still don't move. I have told her where I stand, so she must know I'm not going to come running. She will not win this battle of wills.

Except then I hear Sheila from next door open her front door. I can't hear exactly what she's saying, it's all muffled by the door, but the general tone is . . . well, it's quite aggy. To be fair, it's eleven o'clock at night, who could blame her?

'I know,' Fiona says. 'I'm sorry to disturb you, I just need Natalie to talk to me, and then I'll be quiet.'

More muffled sounds from Sheila. I silently thank Sheila for protecting me. Not that she's doing it deliberately. I risk a look out of the peephole. She's out there in her pink dressing gown and slippers, arms crossed. Her face is distorted by the lens but the scowl is clear to see. Fiona is soaking wet. She'll catch a cold. And that is none of my business.

'No. No, I don't live here anymore. No.' I see Fiona turn to look at her properly. There's a bit more chat from Sheila. 'Yes, you did see me in the *Chronicle*. Yes, and on the telly. Yes, and someone probably did send you a video as well. I don't really think this is the time to . . .'

She turns and hammers on the door again, and I duck, even though she won't be able to see me. I crouch on the floor next to the door. What a pathetic little image I must make.

'Natalie! For crying out loud, will you just let me in, please? People are starting to get annoyed.'

FIONA

The door is suddenly yanked open, and I see Natalie's face through the three-inch gap left by the chain.

'I'm not coming out, OK? And we have nothing left to say to each other. And if people are annoyed, that's not exactly on me, is it? Leave me alone.'

NATALIE

I've barely closed the door when the banging starts again. Jesus Christ, has the woman never heard of licking your wounds? Whatever happened to suffering in silence? Not that I am *suffering*. I am *fine*. I am in the right, which automatically makes me fine. But still. Is it too much to ask for her to leave me alone on a school night?

'Natalie!' Fiona continues to shout. 'I'm just going to keep making a load of noise and pissing off all the neighbours, and the longer it takes you to open the door the more awkward it'll be next time you bump into anybody in the hallway and, like I said, I'm just going to keep talking until you open the door and let me in properly and I . . .'

I wish she'd stop. I really wish she'd stop. I'm so confused. She's making it sound like such a simple thing to open the door to her. But has she forgotten all the shit we said to each other? It's surely easier just not to bother at this stage.

'I know you probably think it's easier just not to bother,' she's saying as I tune back in to her non-stop yelling, 'but you're wrong, and deep down you know you're wrong, and I don't think . . .'

FIONA

The door opens on the chain again and Natalie peers out at me. I try to smile but, honestly, at this point I've lost some of the courage of my convictions. I just . . . I really thought this would be, like, a big gesture. Especially considering I publicly embarrassed myself so recently. To be willing to publicly embarrass myself again, all for the sake of getting Natalie to talk to me? That has to be worth something. But then Natalie closes the door again.

I stand stupidly in the hallway, dripping on the carpet from the rain. I don't really know what to do now. Do I give up? I was kind of hoping my absolute insistence on talking to her would win her around. I didn't even imagine the possibility that I'd have to admit defeat. It was a dumb thing to do to just turn up here so late, I just . . .

The door opens again. Properly, this time. I only have a second to take in Natalie standing there in her pyjamas before she steps aside to let me in.

'Stay on the mat,' she orders. 'And close the door.'

I do as I'm told. 'Listen, I know you hate me but . . .'

But when I turn around again she's nowhere to be seen. Is this a test? Am I allowed off the mat? Is this some kind of trap where she asks me to stay in one spot and then she just goes and sits in another room and ignores me? I lift one foot up.

'Did I not say to stay on the mat?' Natalie barks as she reappears from the direction of her room. 'I don't want you dripping everywhere.'

'No, I met a man who was obsessed with damp once who told me that was bad.' I hope Natalie will crack a smile at the memory of her bad viewing, but no such luck.

She hands me a towel and a bundle of clothes.

'Wait.' I put most of the bundle on the floor and stretch out the sweatshirt she's handed me for a better look. 'Hey, this is mine!'

'It's bloody well not. I've had it for years.'

'*I've* had it for years. I was wondering where it went.'

'Oh great, so you're telling me you've been stealing my clothes for years on top of everything else? Anyway, you're welcome. Shout when you're decent.'

'I . . .' I want to argue that this is definitely my sweatshirt. I'm sure it is. There are pictures of me wearing it. I think there are pictures of me wearing it in other countries. But she turns around and disappears before I can say anything else, giving me the room to change in. Which is probably for the best, since I did not come here tonight to bicker about a sweatshirt that is one hundred and fifty per cent almost definitely mine. I get changed as quick as I can and leave my wet clothes in a pile by the door.

NATALIE

While I'm giving Fiona some privacy to get changed I try to think through what the hell I want to say to her. No. Not say to her. Hear *from* her. I'm done helping her. She's on her own. I have to remember that. I clench my fists until I feel my nails cut into my palms. I'm not ready for this. But I'm as ready as I'll ever be.

When she tentatively calls out that she's done, I open my bedroom door and walk back into the living room. To give her credit, I'm pleasantly surprised to find she hasn't just gone ahead and made herself at home again. She's standing by the window, fiddling with the cuff of my sweatshirt.

For a second, we just look at each other. I don't exactly look amazing in my PJs having done all my skincare for the evening, but she's in borrowed clothes with her wet hair in shining rat's tails. I desperately want to break the silence, but I keep reminding myself to have some pride.

FIONA

Natalie isn't making it easy for me, and in a weird way I feel proud. Pleased? I don't know. I very badly do not want to sound patronising, but . . . if she's really been avoiding conflict for an easy life this whole time, it's nice that she's changed. And I deserve it. When I stormed out of her house after the argument I thought she was being harsh. How could she even begin to suggest that I only thought about myself? But the more thought I gave it (and, yes, I suppose that does mean I was thinking about myself even more) the more I realised she was right. I knew that, I just didn't want to admit it, especially in the heat of the moment.

'Nat,' I say now. She looks at me. Raises one eyebrow. Still doesn't speak. 'I – listen. You were right, OK? Everything that you said I was doing. Well, I was doing it. I was. And I hate that.'

She sits on the sofa. I think the cold look in her eye softens a tiny bit, but I can't be sure. I just keep talking. It's all I can do.

'I went on TV when they asked me because . . . I guess I've just been really insecure. I used to be really confident in myself, you know? When Matt and I went travelling, I felt like we'd done this amazing thing, and it was amazing, and I will never regret it. And then when we moved back, it was shit having to work at Scoopz again, but I did what I had to do for him, and I got to live with you, and that was amazing. Easily as great as Ayers Rock.'

Natalie presses her lips together. I hope that's a good thing.

'The truth is, he wanted to move in together as soon as we got back, and I wasn't ready. But I didn't want to tell you I wasn't ready, so I spun you this lie about needing to save up first. I just . . . I didn't want to go straight from my parents' house to another really grown-up thing. He's such a grown-up. And I knew we'd have fun. And we did. I loved living with you.'

I take a shaky breath and pick at the loose hem on my sweatshirt.

'Anyway. That's not even the point. I just wanted you to know. The point is I got really freaked out for a second once I'd moved in with Matt. I found this ring, and it wasn't what I thought it was, but you can guess what I thought it was, and I bet you can guess how well I reacted too, and I suddenly just . . . realised I wasn't ready. I work in an ice cream shop, and what? I was just going to go from that to getting married to having kids, and I was never going to feel like . . . Well, like you. I look at you and I think you're so independent and, especially now, I wonder what it must feel like every day to go somewhere and just really, really love what you do. I've never had that. You're sold the idea of doing a degree so that you can get a job you love, and I did everything I was supposed to do, and to this day it's never happened. I don't know if I'll ever get to have that. And I know it's a privilege but, I mean, people get that. I just wonder why it can never be me.'

I dash a tear I hadn't noticed before off my cheek. Natalie's chewing her lip now. She won't look at me.

'I'm getting off track again. I should have written this down.' I laugh nervously, and I'm sure Natalie's mouth quirks up at the corners the tiniest little bit. 'I just really enjoyed doing the interview with the paper, and when they invited me on TV I felt special. I felt flattered. And you were right, I probably would have done it whatever you'd said, because I was just in a bad place. And that's not an excuse. If anything, it's another thing I need to apologise for.'

Natalie nods.

'And I also . . . I have to apologise to you for going off travelling. I think I was in it for the wrong reasons. I was so, I don't know, disillusioned? After university. I just wanted to get out for a while, however I could. And when Matt turned out to be the quickest route I just went with him. If I'd said we should wait for you to come too I think he would have done it, you know? We could have all gone together.'

'Oh, what, so his mum could hate me too?' Natalie says. I can't help but laugh. It feels good.

I drop onto the other end of the sofa and shake my head. 'I'm really sorry.'

Natalie just looks at me, lips pressed together again. Then her chin wobbles.

'I'm sorry too. I said some bad things. And I shouldn't have, you know, let them build up until . . .' She mimes an explosion.

I nod. 'No, I really wish you'd told me I was being a dick more often.'

She giggles. 'I promise I will.'

'Well, I promise I won't be one.'

'Maybe you shouldn't run before you can walk.'

NATALIE

Fiona groans and throws her hands over her eyes. 'Oh god, please can we never talk about running ever again?'

'But you're so involved in the running community now.' I cock an eyebrow and press my lips together. She makes a noise of despair, which is muffled by her palms.

'Nat, it was so bad, I could have *killed* someone.' She squirms and covers her face with her hands again.

'You know' – I shift myself into a more comfortable position, crossing my legs under me – 'I actually did some research about starting pistols. You're so unlikely to kill someone with one unless it's been doctored. And Reverend Roger wouldn't do that. He's not interesting enough. You didn't nearly kill anyone.'

279

She sinks onto her side and curls into a ball. 'Fine, I killed my pride, then. Which is worse. I didn't have much left by that point.'

She looks so ridiculous with her face pressed into the sofa that a giggle escapes without me really meaning it to. Fiona looks up at me, pouting. Her hair is everywhere, her face is blotchy, she looks so indignant that the giggle I'm trying to stifle becomes a full-blown laugh and I can't stop it from bubbling over, and it's not long before I can't even breathe. I blink away my tears and see Fiona laughing too, which just makes me crease up again.

'Oh, but it's not funny, though,' Fiona groans, wiping away tears and sitting up properly. 'I can never leave the house again. I'm so embarrassed. I screwed everything up. So much.'

'Honestly, it's not that bad,' I say. She narrows her eyes at me. 'It's not! And you know how easily embarrassed I am. The only people who saw it were a bunch of runners and nobody wants to listen to them anyway.'

Fiona gives a rueful laugh and then looks at me. Her expression changes and she presses her lips together. 'You know that's not the only thing I screwed up.'

I give her a small smile and nod.

FIONA

'To reiterate,' I say, 'I am really, really sorry.'

'And to reiterate, I'm sorry too,' Natalie says.

'OK, yeah, but I just want it on record that I'm more sorry. I am the most sorry.'

'OK, but—'

I hold up a hand to stop her. 'OK, I love you, but how about we don't have this competition right now?'

Natalie shuffles closer to me. She puts both of her arms around me and pulls me into a hug.

'Fiona?' Her voice is muffled by my shoulder.

'Yeah?'

'I love you too.'

NATALIE

'Nat,' Fiona says when we break apart. She keeps her voice casual. 'You still need a roommate, right?'

I hit her with a cushion.

'Hey!' she protests.

'Are you kidding me?'

'Why would I be kidding?'

'Absolutely not! Get changed. We're going to talk to Matt.'

CHAPTER TWENTY-EIGHT

Two Years Later

FIONA

The crowd falls silent when Natalie taps her fork on the side of her glass. As she puts it down, I give her a thumbs up. She shoots me back a smile and an exaggerated look of relief. She was more nervous about tapping the glass with the fork than she was about giving us the rings, making a speech, literally anything.

'What if I do it too hard and just smash it to bits?' she kept saying. 'What if one of the bits goes in someone's dessert? What if they don't see? What if they *eat one of the bits*?'

We would spend whole evenings making backup plans in case I tripped over my dress in front of a full congregation or Natalie showered everyone with broken glass. Most of the backup plans involved going into hiding back at Natalie's until we could escape to whatever fancy place she had to go next for work. We could arguably have planned to rough it a little bit, but why would you, if there's generally a free trip to a five-star hotel available? Take what you can get, I reckon.

Anyway, we're, like, five hours into this thing now (not even counting hair, make-up, brunch, getting ready photoshoot, first look) and no disasters have happened. Natalie not showering the top table with shards of glass is the final tick in the 'panic over nothing' column. I feel my shoulders relax. After this, I get to dance with my best friend for a couple of hours, smoosh some cake in my husband's (?!?!?) face, and then head off on the backpacking honeymoon I've spent months painstakingly planning. Everything from here on out is the good stuff.

'Thank you,' Natalie says. 'And just a reminder, if any of you film this and the video ends up on the internet, you will be hearing from my lawyers.'

A laugh ripples around the room and Matt squeezes my hand, stroking my palm with his thumb. I smile back. Very smiley today. I don't suppose anybody could blame me.

'So today,' Natalie says, 'I don't just want to tell you about Fiona and Matt. I want to tell you about the time that Fiona and I broke up.'

Whispers chase each other around the room and I laugh. Natalie catches my eye and I raise my glass a tiny bit. She blinks her acknowledgement.

As she launches into the story, I think about how much I love being in this room, right in this moment. Natalie over there, with everybody eating out of the palm of her hand. Matt's hand in mine. A tiny bit clammy, but better clammy than not there at all. Don't get me wrong, my strapless bra is digging into my ribs something chronic, and my hair's pulled back so tight it's giving me a head-ache. But still. There was a moment back there where I thought I might have ruined everything.

It took Matt a while to decide to forgive me, and I think that's fair enough. Natalie marched me over to the flat to talk to him the night we made up. He wasn't quite so receptive.

'I just . . . I can't talk about this right now, OK? I don't . . . I don't know if I can be with someone who would act like you have, to be honest. I'm not ready to think about it.'

I collapsed into Natalie's arms when he closed the door on me and cried until I had actual hiccups. But she stood in the rain with me, let a second outfit get wet, and didn't let me go.

'He'll come around,' she kept whispering into my hair.

'You don't know that,' I kept replying.

'I do. One hundred per cent.'

And what do you know? She was right.

'You can't do any of that again,' Matt said to me on, like, the fourth time I went round to the flat. I walked an awkward line between giving him space and being a total stalker. But, in my defence, my stuff was there. And yes, I could have moved that out, but then I wouldn't have had a cast-iron excuse to keep popping round in amazing outfits.

'I won't.' I shook my head. 'I will never, ever do that again, Matt. I promise.'

He opened his mouth but I got there first.

'And I know I promised before, and I know my promises haven't meant very much lately, and I'm sorry for that as well. I was freaking out. You know that, but it's worth saying it again. I was feeling torn between this world where I get to drink prosecco with my friends and act like idiots, and this other world where we have people round for dinner and talk about AAT and stuff, and we hide rings in our drawers, apparently.'

'That wasn't—'

'I know. It's fine. But I felt like I was outgrowing option A, and I wasn't ready for option B, and I was just, like, stuck somewhere in the middle. And I was insecure, and stupid. And I hurt you. And I hurt Natalie. And I never want to do that again. And I want you to know that I'm option B now. Fully option B. If you'll have me.'

I stood in the living room for a second, waiting for Matt's reaction. He didn't move, and then the arms he'd kept crossed in front of him the entire time I'd been talking relaxed slightly.

'You know, I don't know how happy I am to be "option B" in all this.' He frowned.

I waved that away. 'It's just a working title – we can brainstorm something else.'

I risked a step towards him. He didn't move, so I took another. 'Matt. I'm so sorry.'

He nodded and took the tiniest step towards me, too. So, I took the biggest risk yet, closed the gap, and kissed him.

And I am fully aware of how wanky it sounds but I think I had to lose everything. I had to realise that none of it was boring, or basic, or suffocating after all. I *want* a life that has Matt in it forever. We can be a dull married couple and still have adventures, anyway. Hence the wild backpacking honeymoon. You would not *believe* the discount you get when you work for a travel agency, too. Natalie recommended me via a hotel that she works with that also works with the agency, and, my *god*, she was smug when I got it.

'What?' she protested over champagne (actual champagne) in the Miner's Arms. 'I'm just happy for you.'

I narrowed my eyes at her. 'No, you're happy you were right.'

'Is it really so terrible to be both?' she said as everybody toasted to my success over the table. She downed her half glass. 'Anyway. I have to go. I have to be at the airport at insane o'clock in the morning.'

I clinked my glass against her now-empty one again. 'Tell Mexico I say hi.'

Sometimes I think about what might have happened if the two most important people in my life *hadn't* forgiven me. And I immediately hate it and have to stop. There's no question that things with Natalie have changed since, well, everything. But I think they needed to. I'm not about to become an 'everything happens for a reason' person, but maybe that all did.

'It was really hard to spend even a couple of weeks without my best friend,' Natalie is saying as I tune back in. 'If you see me over the next month while she and Matt are off god knows where, please know that I will be very emotionally unstable. But, to reiterate, if anyone films me and puts it on the internet, I will sue.'

A laugh rolls around the room again. I'm glad she's learned to make fun of herself. She's going down a storm using the infamous video as material.

'And now the time has come to give away my friend to the only man in the world who's even half good enough for her, and who's been in my life just as long as she has, and who I love like a weird brother. But no judgement, Fi. Ladies and gentlemen, please raise your glasses to Fiona and Matt.'

NATALIE

People around me stand up, repeating 'Fiona and Matt'. I sit down when the rest of them do, relieved that my part is finally over. I've had a feeling for a while that if I was ever going to end up going viral again it would be today. I would have bet good money that I'd go arse over tit on my heels down the aisle, or I'd overturn a table somehow as I stood up to make my speech.

I catch Fiona's eye and she gives me a watery smile. I blink hard, because I will *not* have her ruin my eye make-up today of all days. She paid a lot of money for me to look this good. I mean, as well she *should*, she makes enough now. Amy catches my eye too. She looks gorgeous in her bridesmaid's dress. She raises her glass a tiny bit and I nod in response.

I look out over the rest of the guests. Jasmine is about ready to pop. She was very worried about giving birth on the dance floor, but so far so good. Alice giggles with her girlfriend, who might be the funniest person I've ever met. They're all digging into chocolates and chatting to one another. Not a single one of them is looking at me anymore, which is just how I like it. The only thing left is for Sophie and the rest of the evening guests to arrive and we're on the home straight. I glance over at Fiona again. She is *glowing*. We made it.

I sigh with relief and shake my head. I waft the floaty tendrils of hair that are meant to frame my face out of position. Tom reaches over and puts them lightly back into place, brushing my cheek before he moves his hand away. I smile, and so does he. And then I get down to the serious business of catching up with everyone who's been drinking champagne all afternoon. I didn't trust myself when I still had duties to attend to.

I haven't even had a chance to put the glass back down when I notice Tom's eyeline shift to somewhere just above my head. He grins, and then I feel hands on my shoulders and a chin in my neck.

'Are you ready? I demanded that they play the "Cha Cha Slide" first thing. It's your time to shine.'

'Go on.' Tom nods. 'I'll see you out there.'

I let Fiona grab my hand and pull me out of my seat. On the way over to the dance floor she accosts a waiter and takes two glasses of fizz. I move to take one off her.

'No, you don't.' She laughs. 'You can get your own.'

So, I follow her lead, taking a glass in each hand. We stand in the middle of the dance floor, look at one another, and burst out laughing.

ACKNOWLEDGEMENTS

I'm not saying I have no chill, I'm just saying that writing acknowledgements haunts me because I live in fear of missing anyone out. So, the stakes are high.

First of all, Victoria Oundjian and Celine Kelly were amazing at helping me to get to the heart of this story and make it ten times better than it was when I started. It's always a joy to work with you both, thank you.

Thank you, as always, to my agent, Sara O'Keeffe. I've learned a huge amount from you in the past couple of years, and long may it continue. Thanks also to everyone at ACM UK.

Thank you to Jill Sawyer for her super-thorough copyediting, and to Ian Critchley for his equally thorough proofreading. Thanks as well to the rest of the team at Lake Union who've been involved with *Ready For It*.

All I ever wanted a few years ago were some writer friends and I have them now, so huge thanks to Kerry Harden, Rebecca Hilton, Susie Lovelock, Todd Minchinton, Linda O'Sullivan, Zoe Rankin, Rosie Whitaker, and Helen Yarnall for keeping me sane just by being there. It's so inspiring seeing everybody's journeys and looking back at how far we've all come.

Since this is primarily a book about friendship, I feel like I should mention some of my oldest friends. We might not always be amazing at keeping in touch when things get busy (I am as guilty as anyone else, arguably more so), but there's no doubting the impact you've had on me over the years. So, thank you to Jenni Clutten, Jessica Stewart, Hannah Jones, Danielle Le Cuirot-Dobson, Emma Colls, Emily Keep, Alice Lucas, and Mel Leung. For the avoidance of awkward questions, this list is in rough chronological order. And yes, this is a test to see who's actually reading.

This book mentions potato waffles cooked on the barbecue and it would be remiss of me not to acknowledge that I learned this from Laura Campbell. It's a thing. You should try it.

Thanks as ever to my family, especially Mum, Dad, and Lisa.

And finally, this book was brought to you by Tangfastics. Lots and lots of Tangfastics. Millions of Tangfastics. Haribo, call me.

ABOUT THE AUTHOR

Photo © 2021 Claire Wilson

Nicola Masters grew up on the outskirts of London and studied English and drama at Goldsmiths. She had several jobs before becoming a novelist, including as a receptionist, an HR adviser and an admin assistant. She now lives on the north coast of Cornwall, where she enjoys swimming in the sea and spending time at the beach. Her first novel, *Happy Happy Happy*, was published in 2021.

Follow the Author on Amazon

If you enjoyed this book, follow Nicola Masters on Amazon to be notified when the author releases a new book!

To do this, please follow these instructions:

Desktop:

1) Search for the author's name on Amazon or in the Amazon App.
2) Click on the author's name to arrive on their Amazon page.
3) Click the 'Follow' button.

Mobile and Tablet:

1) Search for the author's name on Amazon or in the Amazon App.
2) Click on one of the author's books.
3) Click on the author's name to arrive on their Amazon page.
4) Click the 'Follow' button.

Kindle eReader and Kindle App:

If you enjoyed this book on a Kindle eReader or in the Kindle App, you will find the author 'Follow' button after the last page.